HOLD ME FOREVER

LAYLA HAGEN

COPYRIGHT

Copyright © 2022 by Layla Hagen

All rights reserved.

No part of this book may be reproduced in any form or by any electronic or mechanical means, including information storage and retrieval systems, without written permission from the author, except for the use of brief quotations in a book review.

CHAPTER ONE
TYLER

I was screwed. I couldn't take my eyes off her. Her hair fell to the middle of her back in dark waves that sparked my imagination.

Focus, Tyler. You're here for the kids, nothing more.

Yep, I was here to meet the kids I was going to coach for a couple of months until my team allowed me to play again —*long story*. But I looked forward to it.

What I hadn't counted on was the program coordinator, Kendra Douglas, being such a distraction. A smoking *hot* distraction.

"I'm so happy that you're going to spend time with the kids this season. Believe it or not, we've never actually had a hockey player before," Kendra said.

"Really?"

"Yeah. I think that's going to be super exciting for them."

"How long have you been working as a volunteer coordinator?" I asked her.

"Four years. I honestly love it."

I could see that from the way her green eyes lit up. *Damn, she's beautiful.* She was curvy and tall, but at six foot two, I still towered over her.

"I love pairing up volunteers with the right program for them. My boss says I have a knack with people."

"You certainly found the perfect activity for me."

Her smile widened at my comment.

Volunteering had always been part of my job as a goalie with the NHL's hottest hockey team, the Chicago Blades. And I'd enjoyed doing it, but I didn't like it one bit that the team's management had put volunteering as a condition for rehabilitating my image after the scandal and letting me back on the ice. I was benched because of a video that went viral. I also had a shoulder injury to deal with, so the extra time to heal wasn't such a bad thing.

So here I was, at the Chicago Sports Center. Every year, they offered kids from low-income families an opportunity to meet and play with some of the sports stars of the area, which was a really cool thing. I had no idea why it was the first time I'd heard of it.

"Do all your volunteers work with kids?" I asked Kendra.

"No. It's all wildly different, to be honest."

"You don't actually work at the Chicago Sports Center, right? I got confused reading the email from management."

Kendra laughed. "Sorry for the confusion. No, I'm employed by The Illinois Volunteer Society. My job is to find placements for people who want to do volunteer activities. We often collaborate with the Chicago Sports Center. I've brought a few professional athletes here to the center, and it always makes the kids so happy. Most of them don't come from well-off families, so it's a treat for them, and I also think a bit inspiring."

She was obviously proud of her job and probably doing it because she wanted to. I'd been around plenty of people doing all sorts of volunteer stuff for public relations, but Kendra was genuine. I liked that about her.

"Anyway, the circumstances might not be ideal for you, but I'm still happy that you're here," she continued. "I hope I can make this more enjoyable for you."

It was on the tip of my tongue to tell her exactly how much more enjoyable she could make it, but I caught myself in time.

Damn, Tyler, what's wrong with you?

"It won't be a hardship," I said instead. "I like working with kids. I'm good with them."

Her eyes widened, and I went on to explain. "I have a niece. She's ten years old, so I have some experience. It's different than this, but I think I've got a few tricks up my sleeve that the kids will enjoy." I finished with a wink.

"I'm looking forward to seeing that," she said with a challenge in her tone.

I flashed her a grin. "I look forward to proving myself to you."

She looked away quickly, but I caught her smile.

Ahh, so she isn't immune to me.

"Maybe I should ask your niece for references too, just in case."

I laughed at her snarky comment. "Feel free to do that. You can ask my whole family. I'm sure they'll sing my praises."

My family was very close. I'd gotten into this clusterfuck of a problem because of a family issue. My cousin Reese had an altercation with her ex-fiancé, Malcolm, and I stepped in. I wasn't happy with the outcome, but I sure as hell didn't mind punching that moron. He'd hurt Reese so deeply that I wasn't sure my cousin would ever trust anyone who wasn't part of the family again. He cheated on her with her best friend, and Reese had discovered it shortly before they were supposed to get married. I had no clue how someone could come back from that.

Even though that moron filmed our fight and posted it on YouTube, I didn't regret standing up for Reese. My family always stuck together. We had each other's back no matter what. I had five brothers and two cousins, Reese and Kimberly. There wasn't much I wouldn't do for my family.

"Okay, are you ready to meet the kids?" Kendra asked, sounding anxious. It was just so damn cute.

"Sure. I didn't know I was going to meet them today, but yeah, that works."

"It's only a meet and greet. It'll be very short because they're about to start their tae kwon do class, but it'll give them something to look forward to."

She led me into a small room with mattresses on the floor. The second I stepped inside, the crowd of kids seemed to erupt in cheers. They were all wearing uniforms.

"Oh my God, Tyler Maxwell is here. I can't believe it. Can I get your autograph? You're the best, best, best goalie ever," one of them exclaimed.

I looked at the kids, grinning widely. They were a group of boys around twelve years old.

"If you give me pen and paper, I can sign autographs for all of you. I've got time." I looked at Kendra, whose smile widened. "But Kendra here has some good news for you, so you might want to listen to that first."

"Thanks, Tyler. Kids, can you be silent for a few minutes?"

"Yes," all of them chorused.

The room went quiet a few seconds later. "So, I promised I'd get someone to train you to play hockey this season. And I'm proud to say that Tyler here will do the job."

"Holy shit," a kid exclaimed.

Kendra glared at him. "Tim, what did we say about swearing?"

"Sorry, Kendra." He turned my way. "You're going to be our coach? That's so awesome." Tim was taller than the rest by at least a head, with dark blond hair sticking out in all directions.

"Yeah, I will, buddy. So, I can sign any autographs you want today, but we'll be seeing each other twice a week, I think. Right, Kendra?"

She smiled. "Exactly, twice a week."

I turned back to the kids. "So I'll have plenty of time to sign whatever you want."

"Can you also sign my T-shirt?" another boy asked.

I nodded.

"Do you have pics to sign?" a third chimed in.

"Not on hand, but I can bring some," I assured them.

Kendra laughed nervously. Did she think this was an imposition on me? Because it wasn't. I hadn't lied when I told her I liked being around kids. Granted, my limited experience was with my niece, but I couldn't see how spending time with a bunch of kids who shared my passion for hockey could be anything but fun. I liked new challenges and opportunities, and while it was bittersweet that I only had time to coach because I was injured and my team had benched me, I chose to focus on the positive. I could share all I knew—both technique and passion—with their young minds and maybe even play a small part in helping shape the next generation of hockey players.

The kids threw question after question at me, but I didn't mind. Most of them were about when I would play again, and more than a few looked surprised when I said I didn't know.

"Yeah, I know, it's shocking to me too," I said, unable to keep the gloom out of my voice, but why hide how I felt about it? Hockey was my life. Obviously I wasn't pleased with this development.

Kendra clapped her hands. "Okay, guys, I think we've had enough of Tyler's time today."

"Can we train now?" Tim asked, standing tall and looking straight at me.

"You don't have hockey today," Kendra said gently. "It's on Monday, remember?"

I saw the disappointment immediately take over their faces and quickly added, "I'll be here on Monday, buddy."

Tim pursed his lower lip, the way my niece used to do when she was four.

"Hey, I'll make you all a deal. Everyone who wants autographs can get one today, but that's only on paper, okay? And we can do stuff like sign pictures or shirts during our sessions."

"Awesome! I knew you would be cool," Tim said, making me smile as the other kids laughed and cheered.

For the next five minutes, I just signed random slips of paper, laughing when the kids carefully folded theirs like it was a prized possession. Kendra watched me silently, jutting out her hip. That woman was just too sexy. The way she was standing made her curves stand out even more, and I liked them far too much.

Once I was done signing, I ordered an Uber. Kendra walked outside with me, and I had to make a concerted effort not to check her out. For the foreseeable future, I would focus on one thing only: getting back on the ice. I couldn't allow myself any distractions, not even one as tempting as Kendra Douglas.

CHAPTER TWO
KENDRA

"That went great," Tyler said as we walked out of the building.

"You were a hit. I don't know anyone else who's been so well received."

"Singing my praises. I like it." He winked.

The man was sex on a stick, no question, but I'd heard rumors about him that he was not a one-woman man.

I looked at him with narrowed eyes. "You have a reputation for being cocky and self-confident."

Totally unfazed, he said, "You can add stubborn to that list. Doesn't always get me what I want, but I can't change who I am."

Something told me Tyler Maxwell didn't like to pretend to be anyone else other than who he was, and that was the part I thought was refreshing. But judging by his reply, the rumors were true. He *was* a tad full of himself.

Since I started this job, I'd met many people who were guests at the Chicago Sports Center volunteering for various reasons, and most did it for PR purposes, not because they cared about what they were doing. And to be completely honest, I'd expected the same from Tyler. I knew he came from a wealthy family. The Maxwells were a fixture in Chicago, and they'd owned the Maxwell Bookstores chain years ago before selling the business. I wasn't sure what the rest of his family was doing, only that one brother was involved in the wine business. Maxwell Wines were my favorite.

Tyler was the hockey world's darling, so I sort of jumped to conclusions about his intentions. Besides, the exact words of his team's management were "He needs to clean up his image for the sponsors."

But he'd been so open and fun with the kids. It was unexpected and made his hotness score skyrocket in my book, which was problematic for me. His smile was a little *too* sexy, and let's not even talk about that body. It was so sinful and perfect that it was hard to look away.

Thank heavens he was cocky, because that was a turn-off for me.

Whew. I'm safe.

"Okay, then, so what's the schedule?" he asked while we approached the Uber he'd ordered a few minutes ago. I tried not to focus on how sexy his ass was. The rest of him was just as delicious. He was really tall, and his muscles were so defined that I could see the contours through his shirt. The jacket he put on only highlighted how broad his shoulders were.

Oh, Kendra, get yourself together.

"They have hockey training twice a week in the afternoon. Are you sure you're going to be able to do it for the whole season?" I asked warily.

His face darkened, and he looked away. "I'm not sure. It all depends on when I'm allowed back on the team. But I do want to be prepared if that happens. I want us to have a plan so I don't leave the kids high and dry, okay? During the season, the training program is pretty much full time, so once I'm back on the team, we either have to move training to the mornings—"

I shook my head. I loved that he was trying to accommodate the kids, but mornings wouldn't work. "That's not possible. They have school."

"I thought you might say that. Anyway, we're going to need a plan for that at some point."

"Sure, that's no problem. Let me think about what might work and talk with the center's staff."

"I'm going to make this clear to them next time, so they're prepared and aren't disappointed further down the road."

Aaaaand that's my heart sighing. He could not possibly be sinfully hot *and* have a decent personality. He might have been a bit cocky—though in his line of work, it was probably a necessary evil—but to be sexy and caring? It should have been illegal to be both. "Thanks for coming here today."

"Will you be here at every training?" he asked, fixating his molten brown eyes on me as he opened the car door.

"No, but I'll be here next time just to make sure everything is going smoothly."

"I can't wait."

AFTER HE LEFT, I went to my office. The headquarters of The Illinois Volunteer Society was in Bucktown. I was currently in the Ashburn neighborhood, so I got on a bus, planning to use the long ride to write some emails on my phone. My job mainly consisted of looking at each of our volunteers and finding an activity that would interest them, then, of course, setting up everything.

I was pleased that I'd been right in Tyler's case. He looked genuinely thrilled after today's meet and greet.

The office was empty when I arrived, but that was normal

since most of us were out in the field most of the time. I knew my sister, Emma, was here somewhere, though. She'd promised to wait until I was done so we could grab dinner together. Our boss, Henrik, said we were two peas in a pod, and as soon as my sister joined the company, he put her in my small office for us to share.

I headed straight to my chair and sat down. Our office consisted of two long glass desks, leather chairs, and a small shelf for extra paperwork. Emma had hung a brightly colored painting on her wall. I just had a calendar. It seemed practical, though I could admit it was a bit boring.

My mind immediately flew to Tyler, and I started fanning myself, wondering how exactly I was going to handle working with him.

I had met my fair share of celebrities, but he was the only one who made this kind of an impact on me.

Emma burst into the room the next second, giving me a start. My sister looked nothing like me. She took after Mom, with long blonde hair and green eyes. She was also creative, like Mom used to be. I didn't remember much about Daddy, but Mom always said he had a practical side, so I guess I took after him.

I loved my sister to bits. She was my best friend, though she often said I took my big sister role too seriously. I had to constantly remind myself that we were both adults now. She didn't need me helping her anymore.

"Tell me everything. Is Tyler Maxwell even hotter in person? He seems like a bad boy."

"I've never seen him on TV. You know I don't watch hockey."

She waved her hand, tapping her foot impatiently before leaning against the edge of my desk. "We're getting off the point. Is he hot?"

"Very."

"Whew. You noticed. I was afraid you were going to just let that slide, as usual."

I grinned. "I'm not letting things slide. I usually don't notice, but... well, Tyler Maxwell is in a league of his own. I couldn't *help* but notice. And besides, he's very funny and seems to genuinely like kids."

Emma blinked. "Hmm. Clearly he's made an impression. So, what are you going to do about it?"

I frowned. "What do you mean?"

"Well, you know." She wiggled her eyebrows.

I chuckled. "I'm going to do absolutely nothing. He's going to coach the kids, and that's it. Besides, he's a bit cocky."

"Oh, I know how you feel about that. But... you're not even a teeny, tiny bit tempted by him?"

"He would tempt any red-blooded woman. The man is practically walking temptation. But I know better."

"Yes, yes. But where's the fun in knowing better?"

"I agree," I said, "but it's not like I even have time to think about stuff like that."

She rolled her eyes. "You can find time if you want to."

That was probably true, but I really had my hands full. I loved my job, but the schedule was quite intensive. When I wasn't searching for volunteer placements, I was busy introducing our volunteers and setting up a plan and whatnot. And most of my free time was dedicated to finishing my house. I'd bought a small bungalow just outside the city, a two-bedroom house that a couple started building last year. They both got jobs in Arizona, though, so they had to relocate and sold the house before they could finish it.

I got the keys already but couldn't move in. I still had to get the floors and the bathrooms done. So far, I hadn't had much time to search for construction crews. Truthfully, I wasn't sure how I'd handle it financially. I was still renting my apartment, and I'd already started paying the mortgage. Those two charges ate up most of my paycheck, so I'd probably try to do some of the stuff myself.

I couldn't believe I was a homeowner at twenty-nine! Ever since I was a kid, I used to daydream about the house I'd own one day. I was sure my parents were smiling from somewhere above us, feeling proud.

"So, you're definitely not interested in Tyler?" Emma asked, snapping me out of my thoughts.

"Nope." Besides, even if he wanted to go out, I was sure he had plenty of puck bunnies to keep him occupied.

"Hmm. Okay. Do you mind if I ask him out?"

My eyes widened with shock. "You'd do that? Just outright ask him?" I didn't think anyone could say I was shy, but I had to admit I wouldn't just up and ask someone I barely knew on a date.

"I don't know. He certainly looks hot."

"No, I don't mind," I said. But I felt a funny twist in my stomach as I spoke.

"Ha." She pointed at me, smiling triumphantly.

"What?"

"You look like a sad puppy. You totally would mind."

"No, I just think it's... Okay, fine. I would. I don't know why, but I would."

She grinned from ear to ear. "I guess that answers my question."

"Which was?"

"I'm going to leave you guessing for now. Come on, let's grab something to eat."

I shook my head, laughing as I stood from my chair. Tyler Maxwell was a superstar. I was 100 percent sure he'd perfected that charm by using it *very* often. I wouldn't fall for that smile. But that smoldering look? That might be a bit harder to resist, but I was going to do my best.

CHAPTER THREE
TYLER

I was the third youngest in my family at thirty-one. Sometimes I described myself as the fourth oldest, depending on what the situation required. Sometimes I had no idea which suited me best, like right now. We were all gathered at my brother Tate's house, enjoying breakfast on Saturday. Half my family was here.

"You don't have to babysit me," I reminded them. Ever since I was benched, they made it their mission to leave me alone as little as possible. Even though I teased them about it, I enjoyed their support. I usually only had time in the summer to spend with my family, between hockey seasons. But by now, at the beginning of October, I was usually in the trenches with my teammates, training eight hours a day. The first game of the regular season was approaching. I hadn't been to any of the preseason games.

"We're not babysitting you," Reese said. "We're keeping you company."

"Exactly," my oldest brother, Declan, added. As a lawyer, he was always the most serious out of all of us, or maybe he became a lawyer *because* he was serious.

"We can all watch the first game together from my living room," Tate suggested.

Okay, I appreciated that they looked out for me, but this was too much coddling for my taste.

My brother Travis winced. Apparently he picked up on the vibe too. The only ones missing were our brothers Luke and Sam. Sam had been here to celebrate when Travis sold his online startup and stayed after my accident, but he left yesterday to resume his stint abroad with Doctors Without Borders.

Luke was the second oldest, right after Declan, but he couldn't be more different. He'd been the chief troublemaking officer growing up. Luke had all kinds of crazier-than-shit ideas and talked us into almost all of them.

Travis, Sam, and I were a bit of both: sometimes the serious ones, sometimes the troublemakers. It depended heavily on what the situation required.

"I appreciate your concerns, but I want to go watch it from the stands."

"I can come with you and give you moral support," Reese said.

I wondered if there was more to her offer. Her shitty ex-fiancé was finally completely out of her life, but that didn't mean she could forget everything that happened. I suspected she blamed herself because I was benched, and I wouldn't have any of it. I'd decided to go after him, and I'd fight for her honor any day. Sure, he provoked me, but I retaliated, and I took full responsibility for it.

Reese smiled, batting her eyelashes, clearly waiting for a reply.

"Way to make me feel ball-less, Reese."

Gran groaned. "Language, young man."

I cleared my throat. "Sorry, Gran."

She gave me a knowing look.

Declan frowned. "Why do you want to go watch it from the stands? That's going to be uncomfortable for you."

"I'm not banned from actually going there, and I want to show support to my teammates." Oddly, Coach Benjamin didn't want me to suit up on the bench with the guys like most players did when they were on the injured list. I asked him about it, and he didn't give me much of an answer. He said some shit about how I needed to think things through before I got that privilege.

Whatever. Hockey was my life. At my age, I was practically ancient , but I was also the best damn goalie in the league. I still had one season left, maybe two.

"That's commendable," Tate said. "But I think it would suck for you. Especially since they didn't want you dressed and there with the team while you're recovering."

Groaning, I looked at Gran as she frowned and tsked.

"You boys are a bunch of misbehaving misfits today."

"Aren't we always?" I wondered out loud.

Gran tsked again. "Some days, you're better than others, and I tell myself what a fine job I've done raising you. Other days, like today, I think I'm just fooling myself."

She spent a lot of time with us as kids—almost as much as my parents. We owed our somewhat good manners to her. Dad swore every chance he got even now.

Travis came next to me, patting my good shoulder. "You know what? I'll come with you to the game. I'm so attractive that everyone else will pay attention to me instead of you."

I burst out laughing. That was a very Travis thing to say. He didn't take anything seriously, except perhaps his startup. But since he sold it just a month ago, he had a lot of time on his hands and had no clue what to do with it.

My brother's fiancé, Lexi, walked into the kitchen. She'd

been in the backyard with my niece. It only took her a minute before she asked me, "Let me guess, everyone's on your case?"

"One of the things I love most about you, future sister-in-law, is that you can read our family so well."

"How did they figure it out about Kendra already? Did Tate spill the beans?"

I groaned. She and Tate drove me to my meeting with Kendra the other day because I didn't want to bother with another Uber, but they only stayed for a couple minutes.

Tate laughed. "No, sweetheart. You just did."

"Wait, what? Who's Kendra?" Reese asked.

Declan and Travis looked at me with interest.

"The coordinator of the organization that management signed me up with," I explained. "I just met her, and I have no idea what Lexi is going on about."

"Right. You looked at her like you were smitten," Lexi informed everyone.

"She's hot. I just had an appropriate reaction to a very sexy woman," I said with a lazy smile.

Declan frowned. "You know you've got to focus on your recovery, right?"

"Yes I do. Fucking chill, Declan."

I wasn't interested in dating. Just before the fight, I had started seeing Blair, and we hit it off well. After the team announced they were benching me for the foreseeable future, she couldn't bolt fast enough. I wasn't interesting once I wasn't the team's goalie anymore. Ever since, I'd been on a self-imposed hiatus from dating. I had much more important things to focus on. Getting back on the ice was crucial.

"Young man!" Gran exclaimed. "Your brothers and Reese just want the best for you."

"You know what? I'm going to check on my niece while you

all decide among yourselves what *the best* is," I said, making Tate laugh.

This was typical of my family, but as I said before, I didn't mind. I liked knowing they had my back. We always enjoyed helping each other out when possible, and when it wasn't possible, we were there for moral support. I was pretty sure their rallying around me like this was setting a new record in my family, though. I was proud of us. Mom and Dad raised us to stick together, and we were doing just that.

They were right, however. Attending the game wouldn't be easy, but I wanted to be there. Hockey was my life. It wasn't all about making money. It had never been about that. We grew up with all the comforts money could buy. Grandma and Grandpa founded the Maxwell Bookstores chain in their youth. My parents and my uncle ran it with Grandma after Grandpa passed away. They sold it for a shit-ton when I was still in school, and they set up trust funds for each of us. I never touched mine. I didn't need it—it was all about hockey for me, and fortunately the sport paid very well.

In fact, none of us lived off our trust funds. Luke was a sought-after architect, and Tate had built an immensely successful wine business. I'd gotten the hockey bug early on, and Mom and Dad supported me through it all.

When I was drafted, most of my teammates thought the Chicago Blades just took me on because of my last name. I'd worked hard to prove I deserved my spot. I never even had to play on the Blades' farm team either, and that was because they needed a goalie on the roster ASAP. I made my family proud when I was positioned as first pick, the player all the sportscasters thought would deliver the goods. And I did.

I headed out the back door that led to the yard. My brother's enormous house was in the Lincoln Park neighborhood—a quiet area with larger homes and nice spacious yards. I lived in a condo in the West Loop. I liked feeling the pulse of the city: sirens, the hustle and bustle and all that goes with it.

My niece, Paisley, was in the swing I'd tied up last week from the sturdy oak tree at the side of the property.

"Having fun?" I asked her as she swung back and forth.

"Yes, Uncle Tyler. Thank you so much for building this for me."

"You're welcome."

She'd hinted that she wanted one and even showed me a few pictures on an app, so I surprised her with it on her birthday. Paisley had Mom's green eyes and the trademark Maxwell dark brown hair. She didn't look anything like Tate's ex-wife.

"Can you push me? I want to go really high."

I weighed the risks, but I was right here, ready to catch her if she lost her balance. Thanks to my years on the ice, I had quick reflexes.

"Sure thing." I planted my feet wide apart, pushing the swing with one hand and keeping my eyes trained on Paisley.

She laughed, shrieking every time she went higher. A few minutes later, her enthusiasm lessened.

"I'm getting a bit queasy," she piped up, and I didn't push her again.

"Don't move your legs anymore, and it'll slow down. If I stop it abruptly, you'll be sick for sure."

"Okay, Uncle Tyler."

It took a few more minutes for the swing to slow down, and then finally Paisley put one foot down, leaning her head on the rope she was holding.

Her grin was huge. "This is fun. What are you doing out here?"

"What do you mean? Can't I spend time with my niece?"

She narrowed her eyes. "Well, yeah... but you look like

you're running away from something. Are they teasing you? If you don't tell me, I'll just ask *them*."

I stared at her. She was ten years old. How did she already show signs of the Maxwell teasing genes?

"Fine, they're on my case about something."

She laughed, clapping her hands. "Ha! I knew it. And are they right about it? Wait, don't tell me. I want to figure it out by myself."

"Why?"

"How else will I hone my skills?"

I laughed, unconsciously massaging my injured shoulder. I liked giving Declan shit, but he was right. I needed to focus on my recovery—both in the physical sense and my reputation. And yet I couldn't take my mind off Kendra. She was sexy as hell, yes, but something else made me straighten up and pay attention. Her honesty and sense of humor were refreshing. Was she always that fun and unassuming?

Fortunately, I'd have plenty of opportunities to find out.

CHAPTER FOUR
KENDRA

On Tuesday, I arrived half an hour early in Ashburn and parked at the back of the sports center directly next to the entrance of the ice rink. I took out my iPad and pulled up my email account. I was on a private mission, so I felt a bit guilty using my professional email and connections, but *only* just a little.

Tim's birthday was last week, and he'd shared with me that he'd wanted so badly to go to a water park with his friends and play on the slides, but his parents couldn't afford it.

I was trying to surprise him by taking him and his hockey friends to an indoor one. There were a lot of free pools in Chicago, but none had water parks that were actually entertaining. I wouldn't get my next paycheck until after his birthday, so I couldn't simply buy eleven tickets.

Pinching pennies reminded me of the most stressful time in my family's life, after Dad passed away. Mom had to take on three jobs to make ends meet. She didn't even have time to mourn Dad. Emma and I were alone a lot, and the neighbors reported us to social services. It was terrible, and we both believed they should have minded their own business. Mom was doing the best she could. Because of them, we lived for years with constant check-ups and threats to send us to foster care. It was difficult, and it took a toll on Mom, who got sick when Emma was in college.

I shook my head, dispelling those sad thoughts and focusing on the present. I had a solution for my cash-strapped situation. I just didn't like it. Up until last year, I waitressed for a hole-in-the-wall diner at the end of the world on weekends, so I could earn a few extra bucks. I left after a customer grabbed my ass while I took his order. My boss, Jared, had witnessed it and done absolutely nothing. He still owed me two full months of paychecks, and I'd never asked him for it because I was too proud. But now it was time to set my pride aside and be practical.

I sent him an email before I could talk myself out of it.

Then I bit into my donut while racking my brain on how I could make this happen for Tim. I needed the afternoon pick-me-up badly.

My phone chimed in the meantime.

Tyler: I'll be there in a few minutes.

I replied right away.

Kendra: I'm in a red Ford five feet from the entrance.
Tyler: I'll look for you.

My stomach somersaulted. *No, no, no. This won't do.* I was determined not to notice his dazzling smile, let alone the rest of him. I wasn't staying long today, just enough time to ensure he and the kids were on the right track with their first session. I wasn't planning to stay for the rest.

A few seconds later, there was a knock at my window. I startled and accidentally dropped my donut on the floor in front of the passenger seat. There was powdered sugar everywhere. Thank God I had leather seats.

Tyler immediately opened the door.

"Fuck," he exclaimed. "Do you have napkins?"

"Yeah, yeah, I have some."

I had wet wipes in my purse, and I'd grabbed a few napkins when I bought the donut. I vigorously cleaned up the seat with the wet wipes, and Tyler used the napkins to dry them. His hand accidentally brushed mine during our ministrations, and I was completely unprepared for the jolt of heat coursing through me. I raised my eyes to his—big mistake. I was looking straight at his lips. I moved my gaze farther up, right into those dazzling brown eyes.

My sister's words came to mind. *Yeah, "hot" doesn't do him justice, not even a little.*

I thought I could ignore that smile, huh? Well, maybe I could, but there was no way I could forget his eyes. They were dark and sinful.

"Way to make an entrance," I teased, glancing at the duffel bag he was carrying, which probably contained his skates.

"I did say I was coming in a few minutes."

"Yeah, I know, but then I got lost in my research for a pool for Tim, and now my donut—"

I stopped, watching in horror as he took the donut off the floor and threw it in the nearby bin. *Why did he do that? He just wasted a perfectly good donut.* I was just going to blow off the dust, which I knew did nothing for germs, but who cared?

I tried to smile at him when he returned, but it probably looked a bit manic because he raised a brow.

"I'm dangerous in the afternoon without a snack."

"Clearly," he said with a dazzling smile. Amusement played in his eyes.

Oh, he's making fun of me, is he? Well, to be honest, I was completely ridiculous without my sugar fix.

"Come on. We still have time. I'll buy you another donut."

My heart thundered in my chest. I hesitated for a bit.

He sat in the clean passenger seat, tilting closer to me. "Come on. You don't want to be dangerous for the rest of the afternoon, do you? Who knows what else might happen?"

I chuckled, running a hand through my hair. "You got me there. Okay, come on. The donut stand is just around the corner."

I grabbed my bag and iPad, and we walked side by side. My stomach was grumbling. "This was my lunch."

"Your lunch?" he asked, stricken.

"It has eggs and milk. So it's food."

He chuckled as we arrived in front of the food cart. Fortunately there was no line. It was impossible to stand next to Tyler and not be hyperaware of his presence. He seemed to have this field of energy around him. My stomach rumbled again. *Way to make an impression.*

"One donut enough or two? Just to be on the safe side," he said.

"One is fine."

I chuckled again, unable to look away from him. How was it possible that he trapped me with his gaze every time we made eye contact?

We received the order quickly and then walked toward the ice rink. I devoured half the donut before we even arrived at the front door.

"The door is locked. The administrator will open it ten minutes before training starts. We can wait out here or in the car, if you prefer?" I offered.

"Here's fine."

I took another bite of donut. "This was a great idea. I can feel my blood sugar leveling out."

He chuckled. "Good to know. What was that about a pool for Tim?"

"Oh," I said, gripping my iPad tighter under my arm. "His birthday was last week, and he's never been to a water park. You know, the type with slides and all sorts of fun things for kids. I wanted to surprise him, but I can't afford the whole thing."

"That's part of your job?"

"Well, no... so it's not exactly okay, but I've asked some previous clients who know Tim if they would help out. So far, no answers, but I did *just* email. I usually don't do this, at all, but it's for a good cause, and I'd love to see the smile on Tim's face. So many of these kids have had a tough life, and I'd love to be able to help them all if I could."

"You're dedicated," he said in surprise. "What exactly do you have in mind?"

I couldn't believe he was interested in this. "Nothing special, just taking him and his hockey friends to a water park and watching over them while they have fun on the slides."

He ran a hand through his dark brown hair, narrowing his eyes. "A friend of mine owns a spa. It's got two pools, and I'm sure one of them has slides. He mentioned something about entertaining his guests' kids. I can convince him to let the kids have fun in there for a couple hours."

My mouth hung open. "Oh my God. I wasn't telling you this to pitch it to you."

"You said you asked previous clients, so why not me?"

"Well, because I've known them longer and have established a relationship with them."

"You don't trust me, Kendra?" He tilted his head playfully.

"I meant it the other way around. *You* don't know *me*, so I wouldn't ask for a favor."

"I'm offering."

I tried to contain my happiness, but I really couldn't. I felt my face split into a smile so huge that my cheeks were hurting.

"You'd do that? Oh, Tim will be so happy. His family is lovely, but they can't afford too much."

"You can count on me. I'll talk to the guy before training begins."

"Wow. That's amazing. Thank you so much, Tyler."

I couldn't believe he was doing this.

"This seems almost personal to you," he said quietly.

I blinked quickly, trying to hide my shock. How could he tell that?

"Well, growing up, my sister, Emma, and I relied on a lot of these programs. Mom worked herself to the bone, but there wasn't much left after everything was paid for. I know how Tim and his friends feel."

"Kendra, you're—" Tyler was interrupted by the sound of the door unlocking. Jane, the administrator, welcomed us inside.

"Want to go in?" I asked.

"Yeah. Let's go."

The ice rink was simple and modest, nothing like what I assumed the Chicago Blades' arena looked like, but it made the kids happy anyway. Tyler glanced around appraisingly, leaning against a handrail.

"This is a great place to train."

"Glad you like it. So... how about you?" I asked, eager to know more about him. "How did you get yourself in this mess?"

I instantly knew it was the wrong thing to ask. His eyes darkened for the first time. His smile faltered. "You didn't see the video?"

"I did, but I think there's more to it, right? I mean, you couldn't exactly tell the context from just seeing it. It just seemed like that guy was looking for a fight, and he got it."

"Yeah. The bloody context." He laughed, but it wasn't filled with humor.

"Bloody?" I asked in a teasing tone.

"'Fucking' is my choice of swear word when things are moderately annoying. 'Bloody' is next level."

"Interesting choice. Forget I asked. It's bothering you, so you don't have to talk about it." I leaned against the railing on the opposite side, watching him closely.

"That's fine. I think you're the first person who actually asked about what happened."

"What do you mean? Didn't your management want to know the details?"

"No, management was too pissed off because the sponsors weren't happy with me." After a brief pause, he added, "That guy was my cousin's ex-fiancé."

"Ouch. I already hate him."

That brought the real smile back. "I like you, Kendra."

"Thanks." *Is that my stomach cartwheeling just because he said he liked me? Yes, yes, it is. Oh, for goodness' sake!*

"It's not my place to say why they broke up. But they were supposed to go into business together to open a spa in a building that belonged to my grandmother. Anyway, he wanted to get on with the business after hurting my cousin, even knowing my gran didn't want him anywhere near her building. So my whole family fought against it. He showed up there thinking... Honestly, I don't even know what he was after. But the way he spoke to my cousin... I just couldn't stand by and watch without doing anything. It was the wrong way to react, but I take full responsibility for that."

His whole demeanor changed. Even his voice sounded determined and protective, and it affected me on a visceral level. He cared a lot about his cousin and his grandmother.

And so, I couldn't help myself. I moved from the railing, stepping up beside him, leaning slightly in, like I was sharing something in confidence. "I'll let you in on a secret, Tyler. I like you too."

He laughed, throwing his head back. "You're my kind of person, Kendra. You're the first one who has had this reaction when they hear the full story."

"I can't believe that. Management—"

"Was pissed, and I'm pissed in return. I love hockey more than anything in this life, but dealing with management is a pain in my ass."

A very fine ass, my brain supplied helpfully. I pressed my lips together before the words slipped out.

"What's that?" Tyler asked. "You look like you wanted to add something."

I shook my head. "No, no. Nothing."

He cocked a brow, keeping his gaze trained on me. "Kendra…"

I cleared my throat, trying to ignore the sizzle in my body. "Don't change the subject. We were talking about you. This must be hard for you. The season starts soon. The first game is next week, right?"

"Yeah."

"Are you going to watch it?"

He nodded. "I'm going to sit in the stands."

I grimaced. "Wow. That's going to be a tough evening."

"We'll see."

I had the distinct impression that he didn't want to talk about this anymore, so I didn't prod.

The front door of the rink opened, and five kids ran toward us. Well, toward Tyler, to be honest.

"Tyler, my mom wouldn't believe it when I told her you were training us," Tim said as soon as he was in front of Tyler. "Can you take a picture with me so I can show her later? You could email it to Kendra, and Kendra can send it to Mom."

"Sure, buddy. You're Tim, right?"

"Yes. Ohmigosh, you remember my name."

"It's a cool name." Tyler pulled out his phone without any hesitation, hugging the kid with one arm and smiling at the screen. Tim grinned brilliantly, and my heart sighed even more than it had last time. I didn't know why, but I found this incredibly attractive.

Tyler's honest, welcoming actions were a bigger deal for the kids than he may ever know.

After Tyler took the pic, Tim ran straight to his friends. I bet he was bragging. Out of the corner of my eye, I noticed Tyler talking on the phone. It didn't last long, though. He pocketed his cell as soon as Tim and the rest went into the locker room.

"I spoke to my friend. He says it's all good. The kids can come on Thursday. Is that okay?"

"Yes, and wow, that was fast."

"I'm good at using emotional blackmail for a good cause."

I'm not melting. I'm not melting. Who am I kidding? I'm melting.

How was this sexy-as-hell, super successful star hockey player so amazing? So real? Boy, I had him pegged wrong.

"I'll tell my boss about it. I have to clock in every activity I organize. I'll probably have to come too. It states in my job profile that I have to be there for any new activity that wasn't pre-approved."

Tyler's entire face lit up. His gaze turned even more intense than before.

"That's an unexpected perk."

"What is?" I was thoroughly confused.

He stood taller, and somehow the muscles of his arms seemed even more defined.

Eyes on his face, Kendra. On. His. Face.

"Your presence."

Oh wow. My body fired up in an instant. I opened my mouth, unsure how to reply, then shut it firmly before saying what was really on my mind. My pulse quickened. I had to fight the urge to press my palm over my heart; it felt like it might break through my rib cage any second now. *Calm down, heart.* It was one thing to acknowledge his hotness—it was impossible not to, since it kept smacking me in the face—but no heart flutters.

His smile matched his gaze, full of intent. I couldn't exactly say what kind of intent, though my body seemed to have ideas.

I cleared my throat, hoping my voice would be even. "I'm going to check with my boss and let you know the details."

"Good. I look forward to hearing from you, Kendra."

Was his voice even sexier, or was I already lost somewhere between Lustville and Sexy Town?

"I'm going to go to the locker room, put on my skates, and give the kids a pep talk," he added. "Are you going to be here when I return?"

"No, all the kids are here now, so I'm gonna go." They'd been filtering in as we'd been talking, and a few were already down on the ice.

He winked at me before turning around and going into the locker room.

The door was ajar when I made my way out, but I didn't risk a glance back inside. The last thing I needed on my mind was the image of Tyler Maxwell giving the kids a pep talk. It might just cause heart flutters—again.

CHAPTER FIVE
KENDRA

Later that day, once I arrived at the office and checked my calendar, I dialed my boss. Henrik almost always worked from home. I put him on speakerphone. My sister wasn't here, so I wasn't concerned with bothering her.

After I told him about Tyler's offer, Henrik scoffed. "The guy must *really* want to get back in management's good graces."

I frowned, not liking the implication. "That's not why he's doing it. He seems like a generous person."

"I've met guys like him. Everything they do is planned."

"He hasn't asked me to report this to his management or anything. It doesn't matter anyway, right?"

"No it doesn't. You have the green light from me, but can you fit it into your schedule?"

I grimaced. "I'll find the time for it."

"Okay, I see you're on top of everything."

"Yes, yes I am. I'll put everything in motion."

After hanging up, I immediately texted Tyler.

Kendra: Hey, superstar goalie. I spoke to my boss, and he says no problem. When can the kids come on Thursday?

Tyler: You tell me. I'm flexible.

Hmmmm, just how flexible are you, Mr. Goalie?
Oh my God, I have to get these thoughts out of my system.

I tapped my pen against the table, trying to figure out what the best way was. Usually I'd talk my sister's ear off, but she'd left early to practice her favorite sport: shopping. I'd never gotten the shopping bug since we'd been so utterly broke growing up, even pinching pennies for food. But Emma learned to make the best of thrift stores when she was twelve. She had a gift for that sort of thing.

I texted her on the off chance she might see it.

Kendra: Can I call you? I need to SPILL IT.

That was our code whenever we needed girl talk.

Emma: I'm on the train with bad reception.

Kendra: Call me when it gets better.

Emma: Nooooooooo. I need to know now.

I chuckled at my sister's enthusiasm. She was my best friend. As kids, we only had each other, and I believed that made our bond stronger.

Kendra: I'm having all sorts of sexy thoughts about Tyler Maxwell, and I have no clue how to get them out of my system.

Tyler: I have some ideas.

Of course, Emma would have—

I did a double take when I noticed the sender's name. A knot locked in my throat. I felt a bit light-headed. Had I accidentally texted him? Obviously, yes. My thumb was shaky as I pressed the Back button so I could review all conversations.

No, damn it. The texts with Emma were right there. I must have accidentally tapped his name.

Tyler: Shall I share them?

I laughed nervously, sitting lower in my chair.

This can't be happening.

Kendra: Sorry... I meant to send that to my sister.

Tyler: But you sent it to me.

Tyler: Maybe you should share your thoughts with me, so I have a clear picture.

I prided myself in always finding a sassy comeback, but my mind was blank right now. Well, no, it was full of embarrassment. I was completely out of my depth.

And just when I thought nothing could be worse, Tyler's name popped up on the screen. He was calling.

I bit the inside of my cheek, considering what on earth to do. I couldn't ignore the call, that was for sure.

Come on, Kendra. Pull up your big girl panties. You got in this mess all by yourself. Now get out of it.

Taking a deep breath, I answered.

"Kendra!"

"Tyler... hi. Umm, look, I'm sorry about the message. It was meant for my sister."

"So you said. Lucky me that it landed in my inbox."

"Lucky?" I asked, feeling totally out of my comfort zone. All I knew was that my pulse sped up again, not because I was nervous but because I was talking to *him*.

"I'm attracted to you, Kendra. Very attracted. Your message just fueled my imagination."

I licked my lips, toeing off my shoes and curling my legs under me as I resituated myself in the chair.

I laughed nervously. "I'm feeling super embarrassed right now."

"Why?"

"This never happens to me." And it was really unprofessional. Even though my work and office were informal at best, I still held myself to certain standards.

"I'm honored to be the first."

I laughed again, feeling maybe 10 percent less nervous. I wasn't sure if he was trying to put me at ease or flirting, or both.

Of course, there was no way women hadn't come on to him before—he was a professional hockey player! A celebrity! Something I needed to remember.

"There's no chance to get you to share those sexy thoughts, huh?" Tyler asked.

"Nope," I confirmed, feeling a bit of my trusted sass coming back to me. Thank God. I thought I'd lost it for good.

"I can bide my time."

He spoke in a lower tone, one that sent chills across my skin. I still didn't have my wits about me, so it was best to end this conversation. It was awkward, and if it lasted any longer, it would just get *more* uncomfortable.

"Umm... as soon as I put everything together for the pool excursion, I'll text you. But I'd like to hang up now."

"No problem. I didn't want to put you on the spot."

Hmm, I wonder what the purpose of the call was, then? But I didn't ask.

"And, Kendra? If you change your mind about sharing those thoughts, you can always text me."

I let out a sound somewhere between a yelp and a giggle. God help me, I wasn't myself when it came to this man.

I was still on edge, though feeling oddly giddy.

Tyler Maxwell was the hottest man in Chicago. The most successful goalie in the national hockey league. He had the world at his feet.

And he was attracted to *me*.

Was this a good thing or a bad thing? He probably had a trail of broken hearts behind him, and I didn't want to be one of them. I wasn't going to get to the bottom of my conundrum today, so instead, I chose to bask in this giddiness that was filling me. I turned on my favorite playlist on Spotify and tapped my feet to the rhythm of the music while I got to work.

Once I had a tentative schedule, I sucked in a breath and messaged Tyler.

Kendra: Thursday at three work for you?
Tyler: Yes it does.

A few seconds later, he sent another text.

Tyler: I can't wait to see you in a bikini.

I blushed instantly. He liked to play dirty, huh? Ha, the joke was on him. I wasn't going to wear a bikini. But I had an inkling I'd find out exactly how dirty Tyler liked to play on Thursday anyway.

I focused on work after that, trying not to think about him *too* much.

IN THE AFTERNOON, Emma and I went to a hardware store to look at tiles. I wasn't buying anything today, but I just wanted to get an idea of what was on the market and within my budget.

"Damn, I'm dreaming of a day when I'm not broke," I said, looking longingly at some amazing tiles with a Portuguese design on them. They were three times the price of most of the others.

"Hey, that day will come. I have it on my vision board," Emma said. She had future plans on this thing. It was really working for her.

We were walking at a slow pace. The shop was super crowded, but that was okay. We weren't in a hurry. We just stopped whenever we saw something interesting, took pictures, and moved on.

"Hey these tiles remind me of the ones we had in the apartment we moved in after Dad died." She pointed to blue tiles. I could see the resemblance.

"You're right. They look similar.

"You were such an awesome sister. You spoiled me rotten

even though we had nothing. Remember those amazing lemonades?"

I smiled. "Hey, it was all in the honey. You loved it because it was sweet."

"Yeah, obviously, but you were so good at helping me with homework and even super inventive to keep me from freaking out about the visits from Miss Spooky."

I stared at my sister. Miss Spooky was what I'd dubbed the social worker who came to our place, mostly on surprise visits when Mom was working. The neighbors alerted her that we were unsupervised, and I used to hide with my sister when she knocked at the door. Sometimes she left after knocking a few times, but we couldn't fool her every time.

"What do you mean?"

"You know, when you asked me to play under the table and not make any noise. Remember that one time when you said we were having a contest of who could keep still for longer, and at the end of it, the winner would get a chocolate chip cookie?"

I was stunned. I'd hoped my sister wouldn't pick up on the fact that I was basically making her hide, but it seemed I'd failed.

"Okay. Wow. I'm sorry. I honestly hoped you wouldn't notice why we were doing that."

She shook her head. "Don't beat yourself up about it. It was a tough time, and you did your best."

We made a round of the whole store, and I noted the name and barcode of the tiles that were within my price range on my phone.

"I think I'm going to have to stick with basic ones," I said, pointing to boring white tiles. "But why not? I could make them seem interesting with all sorts of accessories."

"They remind me a bit of those public pools. And speaking

of the pool, are you looking forward to seeing Tyler naked?" She wiggled her eyebrows.

I almost choked on my inhale.

"Hey, almost naked," I replied when I'd recovered. "Almost being the operative and very, very important point."

"Right, okay, almost naked," Emma said with a grin. "Still looking forward to it?"

I sighed, shrugging. I couldn't lie to my sister. "Well, who wouldn't? I bet the man's a work of art."

"Yes, I bet that too."

"But he's super good at flirting, so clearly he has lots of experience with women, and honestly, I don't want to get into all that."

Emma pointed at me. "But you said this thing he's doing for the kids is swoonworthy, right? That's your kryptonite."

"Hey, can you not remind me of that, please?"

She smirked. "Why? Does it make you change your mind? Want to flirt back?"

"Oh, I already went there with my message."

"No, that was involuntary. I don't know if it counts."

I rolled my eyes. "Trust me, in Tyler's book, it does count."

"Ha! Then your little pool trip will be even more awesome than I'm imagining it. I'm requesting a full report, obviously."

I chuckled. "Yes, ma'am."

∽

ON THURSDAY, I arrived at the spa a bit later than everyone else. It was in the Gold Coast, the most upscale neighborhood in Chicago, in my opinion, and it was pretty intimidating. The walls in the reception area were draped with dark blue silk curtains, creating the illusion of small recesses everywhere. The lighting fixtures were silver, casting a diffused light. The friendly receptionist gave me precise instructions to reach the pool, but I got lost twice in the narrow corridors lined by bamboo rods.

In the changing rooms, I only took off my shoes and put on flip-flops. They looked a bit ridiculous with my crisp white office dress, but it was forbidden to walk with street shoes in the pool area.

I was extra jumpy, and I knew it was because a certain hot hockey player was nearby. I couldn't believe he'd invited the kids here. Tyler Maxwell was in a league of his own when it came to generosity and just being an overall decent human being. I wished more people were like him.

Pulling my hair up in a tight bun because it would curl from the humidity in the pool room, I held my chin high as I walked out of the locker room.

The pool was great, and there were a gazillion slides around it. The kids were already having fun. There were no other guests here. I glanced around carefully, looking for Tyler. My body seemed to be aware before I finally spotted him and his lips curved into a smile.

This day was starting great. I was still embarrassed about my mishap with the message, but since there was no hiding, I had to own up to it. I smiled wildly as he swam to the edge of the pool closest to me.

"Kendra, I thought you might not make it."

"I have to be here, remember? Besides, I couldn't miss a chance to see Tim and his friends have fun."

"Damn, and I thought you couldn't miss a chance to see me."

I felt that molten gaze travel through my whole body.

"Did you now?" I teased.

He pushed himself out of the water, and I blinked rapidly, taking a step back.

Is this guy real? Holy hell, who even has this many muscles?

"Aren't you joining us in the pool?" he asked.

"No. I'm not supposed to engage, just observe."

"Damn. I assumed you would. I was already imagining you in a bikini." His voice was a low, deliciously sensual whisper. His eyes were playful and hot at the same time.

I fidgeted in my spot, and my flip-flops squeaked against the tiles.

"I'm going to corrupt you into joining us," he declared in a serious voice.

Fighting a smile, I folded my arms against my chest. "I don't have a bathing suit."

"There's a shop upstairs. And skinny-dipping is always an option. But only after I evacuate every single person."

I swallowed hard. "There are cameras."

"So if there weren't any, you'd agree? I'll file that information right here." He tapped his temple.

My goodness, I'd walked right into his trap. I laughed, bringing a hand to my ear out of reflex, intending to push a strand of hair behind it, but it was up in a bun. I patted my head as if I was checking if there were any hair bumps or strays. *Way to be awkward.*

"Tyler... there are kids around," I whispered.

He looked at me intently. "Right. We're supposed to be role models."

"Exactly."

He came closer—close enough that I could smell the spicy notes in his cologne. "I have a hunch you're going to be that role model, Kendra, because I won't. I intend to look a lot, and I will make no secret of it," he said right before diving into the pool.

All right. My panties aren't combusting or anything.

I sat down on one of the lounge chairs, wishing I could get in the pool and feel the cold water against my skin.

I looked around, grabbing some pics with my phone. The kids were so giddy that it made me laugh too.

A few feet away, I saw Tyler showing Tim how to do some back strokes after he came down one of the slides. This was too good of an opportunity to pass up, so I took a good look at those washboard abs before focusing on the pics again. *Don't be greedy, Kendra. You can look more later.*

I only managed a few minutes before I gave in to temptation, risking another glance at Tyler. This time I admired his biceps. The one downside about hockey was that you couldn't see the player's body underneath all those pads and that bulky jersey they wore, especially the goalies. But you could assume they were super muscular.

Tyler was sinfully sexy even in the bulky uniform.

Him wearing nothing but swimming trunks was simply *delectable.*

He caught me looking that time, and my entire face flushed as I quickly glanced away, trying to mind my own business. I'd snapped enough photos, so I opened the email app on my phone and started answering the most pressing ones.

"Trying to hide in plain sight?" a teasing voice said from next to me a few minutes later.

"Holy shit," I exclaimed, jumping a bit. I hadn't realized he'd come up beside me.

"You don't have to hide. You can admire me to your heart's desire."

I laughed even though my cheeks heated up.

"Do you enjoy putting me on the spot? It's not very gentlemanly."

"I know, but I like the way you blush for me."

And that just made my cheeks feel hotter as he sat next to me.

"You're different today than last time."

"You mean even cockier? I was holding back before."

I burst out laughing. "Were you?"

"Oh yeah."

"Well, I wouldn't say cocky. You're confident." I came to that realization sometime between him offering to bring the kids here and seeing him in the pool. "That's different. But you're... *daring*."

He smirked. "And I'm *still* holding back when it comes to that."

I laughed, and he added, "You're having fun, aren't you?"

"Yeah, it's a great day, and look at them. They're just so happy, which makes me happy."

He glanced at me with an intense gaze, but it was different than before. "The program you benefited from as a kid was this same one?"

"No, but it was very similar. I started working here right after college, and my sister too."

"I didn't know you worked together."

I nodded. "We even share an office. It's a lot of fun."

"Your parents must be proud of you."

I sighed. "They both passed away, but I think they would be."

He dipped his head. "I'm sorry for your loss."

"Daddy passed away when I was six. He was working for the railroad and had an accident. My mom was so devastated. She didn't even have time to mourn him properly."

"Why?"

"Because we started having financial problems right away. The bank took our house because Mom couldn't afford the mortgage. We moved into a tiny, run-down apartment in a shady neighborhood, and she had to take on a second and third job. She always felt so guilty for not being home. We had to make up stories so the neighbors wouldn't call child services."

He frowned. "Why would they even consider doing that?"

"Because we were home alone a lot. A couple times, they did contact them, and I convinced my sister we were playing hide-and-seek and had to stay hidden in the apartment and not answer the door. But eventually they did find out, and after that, they constantly checked on us, even threatened to take us away from Mom."

Tyler looked stunned.

"Um, sorry. Too much information. I miss my parents a lot, so once I start talking about them, it's hard to stop." He didn't need to hear about all that.

"You don't have to stop. I'm interested in you, Kendra."

Whoa...

"Yes I do, because you've got to go back to the kids. I don't know what makes Tim more excited, that you brought them to a pool or that you're here with them." I looked at the kids, then back to Tyler. "Go on, go back to them. Tim's been looking at you this whole time. They'll treasure this forever. When I was part of the program, they took us to watch *Cinderella* once. It was so magical. I still remember the whole day."

"You're the most fascinating person I've ever met."

"I don't believe that," I said playfully.

"Actually, you are, and I'm more than happy to prove it to you. In fact, I'm eager to. You're real, Kendra. I miss that in people. It's a quality I only see in my family and the team these days."

I blinked, at a loss for what to say, but Tim saved me from having to reply.

"Tyyyyyyyyyyyler, come back in the pool, please."

I chuckled, pointing to him. "Told you he's been looking at you the whole time. You've only got about ten more minutes before we have to leave."

Tyler was still looking at me intently as he stood up, and I melted into my seat.

Lowering my eyes to my phone, I quickly drafted an email where I summed up today's events. I was also required to keep a spreadsheet where I noted what I did in chunks of twenty minutes. Some coworkers considered it a chore, but I didn't mind. I liked being efficient, and it was rewarding to look back on my day and see all I'd accomplished.

Just as I was wrapping up my notes, Tyler startled me again. "Kendra, all good?"

I nodded, looking up from my phone. We were alone.

"Everyone's gone?" I asked. My heart rate quickened.

"Yes. Their parents picked them up in front of the building."

How hadn't I noticed?

I got up, putting my phone in my purse and then slinging it on my shoulder. The air between us shifted. I was far too close to him, and he had nothing but swimming trunks on.

"Okay, then, I'll go too."

We walked side by side at the edge of the pool. I took a side-step, needing some distance, and nearly went into the shower that was mounted just next to the pool entrance. Fortunately, I didn't walk into it. Unfortunately, the shower had a motion sensor, and it turned on instantly. I shrieked, instinctively lifting my arms to keep my purse dry.

I could, of course, have stepped out from under the spray, but my brain was running its own show right now. *Today shall always be known as Kendra's Awkward Day.*

Tyler relieved me of my bag around the same time I got my wits together and moved out of the way. The water stopped as abruptly as it started. I was shivering.

Tyler was laughing so wholeheartedly that I couldn't help but chuckle too.

"Come on. There are towels in the locker rooms," he said.

I followed him without a word, eager to get out of my wet clothes. The second we got into the changing rooms, he put my bag on a bench, then handed me two towels. Our hands touched briefly, and I gasped, his hot fingertips on my cold fingers sending a sizzle through me. Tyler's eyes zeroed in on my chest, and I immediately realized why. I was wearing a white bra without cups underneath my dress—and my nipples were visible.

"Kendra..." He moved forward, and I said nothing because all I wanted was for him to come even closer. "I want to kiss you so damn bad. I want to taste you."

I nodded, sucking in a breath. He brought a hand to my face, touching my lower lip with his thumb before circling my mouth. I shuddered, feeling that touch as if he'd pressed his fingers between my thighs. I looked him in the eyes for a brief second, and then he kissed me.

Oh my God, how he kissed me. My entire body felt alive and pulsing. He touched my right shoulder and cupped the left side of my jaw and cheek with the other hand, kissing me deeper and deeper, entwining our tongues.

He moved even closer, and I felt the metal door of the locker behind me. I dropped the towels I was holding as he pressed his chest flat against mine, and the shudder in my body intensified. The door was cold, his body was hot, and his kiss was smoldering.

I touched the side of his body, desperate for more of his skin, wanting to explore him, tracing his back muscles up, then down his spine. He groaned right in my mouth, pushing his pelvis into me. I could feel that he was rock-hard. Desire pooled between my thighs. I was so close to losing control that I almost forgot where we were. I'd never been kissed like this; the passion from his mouth and his grip on me nearly brought me to my knees.

With a groan, he pulled away, taking a step back. I blinked through a haze of lust.

"Oh my God, the cameras," I murmured, looking around wildly.

Tyler lifted one corner of his mouth in a half smile. "That's your first thought?"

"Isn't that why you stopped?"

"No, Kendra. There are no cameras in the changing room. I stopped because I was close to losing my mind. When it comes to you, it's inevitable, but it's not going to happen in the showers of a locker room."

His words went straight through me. My thoughts snapped back, and I composed myself just in time because we heard the patter of feet. Then, somewhere in the locker room, a door opened.

"Oh, here they are," one of the boys, Rupert, said. As he grabbed a pair of small trunks from one of the benches. He looked up and noticed us. "Tyler, you're still here. Miss Kendra, why are you in the men's locker room?"

"Oh... I didn't notice," I said truthfully.

"What happened to you?"

"A mishap with the shower. I'll dry myself off, and then I'll try to dry the clothes with a hairdryer or something." It would probably take forever, but I didn't have a better plan.

"Tyler, we have to go, then. Miss Kendra needs privacy."

I gave a nervous laugh. Tyler cleared his throat.

"Rupert's right," I said.

Tyler stepped back, looking straight at me. His gaze was so smoking hot that I was surprised my clothes didn't instantaneously dry up.

"Are you sure?"

"Oh yeah. Very sure."

"Okay. Then let's you and I be gentlemen, Rupert, and leave Miss Kendra alone."

Holy smokes. Even after I was alone, my skin was still simmering.

I went to the women's changing room and took off my clothes, putting the towels around me. Tyler's friend had graciously kept the pool private for us for a few hours, but I didn't have too much time until it would be open to all guests again. I found the hairdryers quickly and held one in each hand over my dress.

Today had been so unexpected that I didn't even know what to make of it.

And that kiss. My God, that kiss.

I committed every detail to memory, knowing I probably wasn't going to see Tyler again. I only had to be present when a volunteer started or when a new activity was added. My heart gave a sad sigh. Maybe it was better, though. After all, what could this crazy attraction possibly lead to?

More smoking-hot kisses, a wicked voice said at the back of my mind.

I usually didn't act on impulse. I'd learned to be careful about everything growing up. I learned to be thrifty and to stay healthy because we couldn't afford to be sick. I thought twice about every decision, just in case it could backfire in the future because there was no safety net.

But boy, oh boy, guess who had a smile the size of Texas right now? Yep, this girl. Because that kiss had been amazing. What was a red-blooded woman to do but swoon just remembering it?

CHAPTER SIX
TYLER

Friday started with a call from Gran while I was drinking my morning coffee. I instantly went on alert because she liked to meet up, but she only called in emergencies.

"Gran, what's wrong? I can be at your place in fifteen minutes." Technically twenty, but I was known for driving over the speed limit when the situation required it.

"I'm fine, young man. I was calling to double-check that you're still going to watch the game tonight."

I laughed, pressing two fingers to the bridge of my nose. I wasn't used to having everyone worry about me constantly *at the same time*.

"Yes, ma'am."

"Oh, don't call me that. You know I don't like it, and it makes me feel old."

"Yes, Gran."

"Hmmm... well, if you change your mind, you can always take this bag of bones out for dinner instead."

"Gran! Are you guilting me into taking you to dinner? Last time I asked, you said only people who still have all their teeth should go to a restaurant," I said, stunned. In August each year, around the anniversary of Grandad's death, she was always down. I thought going to a restaurant would cheer her up, but instead, I got scolded.

"No, no. We can do something else."

"Gran, I appreciate your concern, but—"

"It's a grandmother's prerogative to worry about her grandchildren."

For some reason, that made me feel ten years old.

"Well, you don't have to worry about this one."

"If you say so."

I knew that voice. It was her *you-know-nothing* tone, and it usually meant she had some insider info I didn't. I waited for her to go on, but she just wished me a good morning.

After hanging up, I finished my coffee, looking out the window. The view of the busy street energized me.

I was rinsing out my coffee mug when my phone rang again. This time it was Reese. I immediately answered.

"Hey, superstar goalie," she greeted.

"Right now, I'm the benched and suspended black sheep."

"Uh, sorry. I always put my foot in my mouth this early in the morning. Umm... how are you?"

I laughed. "What did Gran do, put you on my case?"

"No, we're doing it of our own initiative."

"We? Who else will call me today?"

She snorted. "I'm not at liberty to say that."

"Okay, let's hear it." I went into my living room, sitting in the armchair overlooking the panoramic floor-to-ceiling windows.

"There's nothing more to it. I'm just checking on you."

"Malcolm isn't giving you trouble, is he?" Although we'd taught her ex a lesson, you just never knew if the moron would be coming back for more.

"No, not at all. I'm just... lonely lately. Kimberly is in Paris, and my best friend turned out to be a snake, so..."

I swallowed hard, shifting to the edge of the armchair. Everyone was focused on me, but they should have been rallying around Reese instead, the way we did right after she canceled the wedding six months ago. She hadn't gotten over it yet; that was something that took time.

"You do have all of us," I pointed out.

She chuckled. "I know. It's just... hard."

Alarm bells went on. I was going to put Luke on the case. He was the closest to Reese and Kimberly, and he had a knack for these things.

He always rallied us to get into trouble as kids, but here was the thing: he'd honed the skill of assembling us all together into an art.

"I'm sorry to hear that," I said sincerely.

"Hey, don't let me get you down. Call me if you need anything, okay?"

"Sure. Thanks."

I went to shoot Luke a quick message after the call ended,

Tyler: Hey bro. Can you check on Reese? She seems a bit off.

Luke: Will do. How about the game?

I frowned, scrolling back. That's when I realized I already had a message from him, plus another one from Travis and one from Declan. At least they were more subtle than Gran and Reese.

I appeased everyone with messages before heading to my physical therapy session.

The only reason they were concerned was because they knew what hockey meant to me. I wondered how life must be if you didn't have a huge family, but honestly, I couldn't imagine it.

I immediately thought about Kendra. She'd seemed so damn fragile talking about hiding with her sister from social services. She'd had a rough upbringing, and yet she radiated happiness. It was addictive. Every time I was around her, I was more surprised by what I discovered.

THE CHICAGO BLADES' arena was one of the biggest in the country. It was located close to the Brookfield Zoo, and it was my home away from home.

I went straight to the stands. I didn't want to go inside the locker room before the boys went out on the ice. We'd start talking again about my ban, and that usually derailed every conversation. I was here to support them, not distract them.

Five minutes after sitting in the stands, I realized my family was 100 percent right. This was going to be a very awkward experience.

Excitement coursed through me when each of my teammates was called onto the ice, except when the goalie's name came up and it wasn't mine. Jett McLeod was a rookie, and I was happy he got this opportunity. Still, I couldn't say I didn't wish I was there instead of him.

I sat back down, happy that the fans were giving me my space. I'd signed some autographs before the game started and promised to take pictures with them afterward. I just asked them to let me watch the game, and they obliged. I loved the fans. Seeing their passion for the game was the best part of being on the bench. It eased the fact that I wasn't on the ice, but only a bit. I was craving to get back out there, defending the net.

Once all twelve players were on the ice, the game began. Adrenaline pumped through my veins while I watched Jett and the rest of my teammates. Everyone was in top shape, and the game was fucking beautiful. That itch to be back on the ice was stronger than ever.

Almost three hours later, the Chicago Blades scored their first victory of the season, and I was damn proud.

All my teammates went to the locker room, and I went down to talk to them.

"Congratulations, man," I told Jett. "You played an excellent game." I meant every word. Yes, I was pissed that I wasn't out there on the ice, but that didn't mean I wasn't happy for him.

He nodded. "Thanks, man. That's a lot coming from you, but I'm sure you'll be back in no time."

"I'm not so sure about that, but while I'm gone, make sure you kick ass. We have to take the Stanley Cup this year too."

"I'm on it," he said. His smile was more confident now.

I turned to my team captain, Steve. "Great job, all of you."

"Next time, come in the locker room before we go out to play."

"I didn't want to mess up the team's concentration."

He frowned. "Yeah, I guess you're right. Come with us to celebrate?"

"I have to go back to the stands. I promised the fans I'd sign everything they have for me if they let me watch the game without bothering me. I arrived too late, and I didn't get to sign too many before the game."

He looked over my shoulder. "Dude, you're going to be there for an hour."

I liked signing autographs. Our captain was a tactical genius and an excellent player on the ice, but he wasn't one to smile for the cameras or the fans.

"I don't mind," I assured him.

After the team went to the showers, I went back to the stadium seats where I told everyone to meet me.

"Okay, who's got something for me to sign?" I asked with a wide smile.

I wasn't doing this to please management. I wasn't exactly a people-pleaser. I did it for the fans. I signed a T-shirt, caps, more caps, pictures, a scrap of paper, and then a blonde approached me, rolling her shoulders. I cocked a brow.

She drew her hand across her chest. "Can you please sign it here?"

"I don't sign body parts," I said.

"Oh, come on, please? Just for me? Just this once? No one will know."

"Everyone will know. The stands are full."

She smiled, coming closer.

I shook my head. "Do you have a paper or a cap or something?"

Her smile faltered. She scoffed, turning around and walking away instead. That worked for me too. That was one thing I didn't like about fans—they could be intrusive.

Once I finished signing everything, I went outside to my car, texting Steve to ask where they were. There were several bars in the area, and I wasn't sure where they'd ended up.

Steve: We're at the Star Jazz.

That was only a few blocks away.

I checked the other messages I had while I revved the engine of my Audi. Both Travis and Declan were asking me to go out for drinks with them. I reassured them all was good and that I was going out with my teammates.

I also had a message from Kendra.

Kendra: Hey, congrats. Go Chicago Blades. The game was amazing. How are you doing?

Even though I'd reassured my family all was well, I told Kendra the truth.

Tyler: It sucks, but it was the right thing to do. How is your evening?

She first sent me a peace sign and then a message.

Kendra: It sucks too.

Tyler: Why?

Kendra: I almost got mugged.

Fuck.

Tyler: Are you okay?

She didn't reply, so I called her right away. "Kendra, where are you? Are you okay?"

"Yes, I'm home now. I'll take a long shower and eat some comfort food."

She sounded like she was trying to convince herself more than me.

"Kendra, are you hurt?"

"No, not at all. It was just a scare. I'll order pasta alfredo, my *favorite* comfort food, and relax."

Her voice was uneven. I didn't like that one bit. Kendra was strong and confident, and I had a burning need to make sure she was okay.

"Where do you live?" I asked, making a split-second decision.

"Why?"

"Because I can have a bottle of wine from Maxwell Wineries delivered to your door if you're into that kind of thing."

"If I'm into that kind of thing? Who isn't? Wine, hello? Yes. But wait, back up. What do you mean, you want to have it delivered to my door? How?"

"And you said you like pasta alfredo?" I asked without answering her question.

"That's another hell yes. But seriously, I can order that online. Oh look, I just did."

"You can't order the wine online, though. I can have it delivered to you. I can also deliver it in person."

She sucked in a breath. "Why would you do that?"

"I doubt pasta and wine are enough to make the evening better. You need me in person too. I'm *very* good at entertaining you."

"Okay. I'll text you the address," she whispered.

Her voice set me on edge. I'd expected her to call me out on my cocky comment, but she didn't.

I texted Steve that I wasn't going to make it after all before backing out of the parking lot and heading to the nearest shop that sold Maxwell Wines.

I needed to make sure Kendra was okay.

CHAPTER SEVEN
KENDRA

I was restless, even after I took a shower. Honestly, I was more than nervous. I was shaken.

Dressing in shorts and a tank top, I put my hair up in a ponytail, and tried to get the evening's events out of my mind. My slimy ex-boss, Jared, had answered my email, telling me that if I wanted the paychecks, I should come to the diner and get them myself. So tonight, I did just that, only for him to *not* be there. The bastard. He did it on purpose. I was sure of that. We hadn't parted on good terms at all. The last thing he told me before I stormed off was that I'd come back begging for the job.

As soon as I recovered from tonight's incident, I'd deal with him. I wasn't going to let that moron push me around.

I threw on a robe when the doorbell rang and went to answer it. My pasta alfredo was here. I only ordered one, but the serving size was huge, so it would be enough for Tyler and me. And just like that, I had a big smile on my face. That man sure knew how to distract me and even make me swoon. The night was looking to be a whole lot better already.

I glanced outside the window at the huge trees on the sidewalk. Most of the time, the view relaxed me, but I was too wound up tonight.

Five minutes later, my doorbell rang again.

Looking through the peephole, I nearly swallowed my tongue when I saw Tyler. He was unbelievably handsome. I opened the door, smiling widely.

"Mr. Delivery Guy, you were quick."

He leaned against the door with that muscular frame of his, flashing me a cheeky smile. Instantly, I felt my body relax.

I stared at the bottle of wine he was holding, trying not to look at those perfect biceps or his impossibly strong shoulders. My willpower completely disappeared when I caught him staring at my lips.

I pointed at him, looking him straight in the eyes, so he knew I meant every word. "We're not bringing up what happened yesterday."

That cheeky smile was even more pronounced.

"Let's open the wine bottle, Kendra," he said.

Okay, so clearly he didn't agree with me, and I didn't insist because I suspected that, far from agreeing with me, he'd make me agree with him. Maybe he'd even kiss me again.

Hmm... that wouldn't be so bad.

Oh Jesus. Who am I kidding? Of course it would be bad.

Shake yourself out of it, Kendra. Don't be greedy. One smoking-hot kiss was more than enough.

Leading him to the kitchen, I pointed at the boxes of food and said, "We can eat at the kitchen counter."

"Sure."

I took out plates, dishing out the food; it smelled delicious. He was looking at me intently, making me conscious of every move I made.

"Kendra, do you want to talk about tonight?"

"Honestly, it was just a bit rougher than I expected." I hoped I sounded convincing.

He stepped closer. "What are you not telling me?"

Okay, so I'd been transparent. I turned around slowly, training my eyes somewhere on his chest. I knew if I made eye contact, I wouldn't be able to act as if nothing happened.

But the next second, he put a hand on my chin, tilting my head slightly up, and his brown eyes looked straight into my soul. "Kendra... what happened?"

"I had some business to solve at my old workplace. I waitressed at a diner on weekends until last year. Anyway, it's not in the best part of town. Tonight, after I left the diner, a few guys followed me. I parked a few blocks away. They asked me to give them my wallet and all my belongings." My voice was shaking. I'd been so scared and operating on adrenaline the whole time. "I broke into a run and went into a store and stayed there for a while. And then I ran to my car."

I didn't want to tell him I'd gone to get my paychecks. For some reason, I felt too proud for him to know I was in financial troubles.

"Kendra, fuck, why didn't you call someone? Why didn't you call me?"

"Why would I call you?" I asked, totally bewildered.

"Because I would have come and picked you up."

My insides went completely soft, and it wasn't just because he was stroking my cheek with his thumb. I couldn't believe he would have come across town to help me.

I realized I was shivering. He touched my arm with his hand, rubbing my shoulder lightly.

"Thanks."

"Next time you're in a messy situation, call me, Kendra. Tell me, and I'll come get you. No matter when or where it is."

"But why—"

"Just agree with me, woman."

"Okay," I whispered. "I'll call you. Thanks for the offer."

I didn't remember how it felt to be looked after, protected in this way, treasured. It made me feel important.

He tilted closer, looking at my lips again, curling his fingers into my sides. Then I realized he was barely restraining himself from coming even closer.

Clearing my throat, I pointed to the plates. "Let's eat this before it gets cold. It's best warm."

"Afraid to be too close to me?" he teased.

"Hell yes. My body is still burning up from that kiss at the pool. I don't think I can handle any more heat, Mr. Goalie. I'm particularly susceptible tonight." My voice was playful, but I kind of meant it.

"Good to know," he answered in a low voice but took a step back.

We headed to my small table, which somehow looked even smaller with Tyler sitting at it. The man was huge.

"So, your evening sucked too, huh?" I asked.

"Mine was unpleasant. There's a difference."

"Yeah, but I don't want to talk about mine anymore. How about yours?"

"I probably should have listened to my family and not gone there. Or taken them up on the offer to join me."

"They offered that?"

"Yeah. We're very supportive of each other. Want me to open the bottle of wine?"

I nodded. "Yes, please. The bottle opener is in the middle drawer."

He immediately found it and uncorked the bottle. This was something I loved about Maxwell wines: they were all corked, no matter the price. It made me feel fancy whenever I uncorked a bottle as opposed to just opening a twist cap.

I took out wineglasses, and we both sat down at the table again. Having him here was nerve-racking *and* reassuring at the same time. I had no idea how that was possible.

"Which brother owns Maxwell Wineries? Is it Travis? I remember reading an article about your family, but I got the names mixed up."

"No, Tate."

"Travis, Tyler, Tate. Your family must like the letter T, huh?"

He grinned. "Yeah. We bug Mom and Dad about it pretty often."

"Does everyone's name start with T?"

"No, the others are Declan, Sam, and Luke."

"What do they do?"

"Declan's a lawyer. Sam is a doctor. He's on a stint abroad with Doctors Without Borders. And Luke has an architecture company."

"And Travis?" I liked hearing him talk about his brothers. It relaxed me. If I was honest, his mere presence was comforting.

"Travis is the one who just sold his company. He's partying like never before." He frowned.

"What's wrong?" I asked.

"Nothing. Just wondering if Declan has a point when he says Travis is partying too much." He rolled his eyes. "Oh, for fuck's sake, I'm turning into Declan."

I couldn't help but laugh. "Why is that so bad?"

"Guy's a lawyer, has a permanent stick up his ass." Thankfully, I hadn't taken a sip of wine, because I would have spit it out over the table. Tyler had a way with words.

"I think that comes with the territory for some reason. Lawyers are serious."

"I wouldn't know. I'm just the one who shakes things up."

I laughed between forkfuls of pasta alfredo. The sauce was rich and creamy, and it was just divine.

After we both finished eating, I put the plates in the dishwasher. I felt Tyler's eyes on me the whole time. Turning around, I double-checked, and I was right. He was serious again.

"Kendra, all jokes aside, I meant what I said earlier. Tell me when you're in trouble."

I rolled my shoulders. "Trouble happens. It's not like I'm helpless or a damsel in distress."

He groaned. "Stubborn woman. If you have someone to watch your back, it doesn't mean you're a damsel in distress. It means you're taking precautions. "

"I usually have pepper spray with me, but I also have one of those small devices that looks like a car key, but when you press on it, it sounds like a police siren. It scares everyone off, trust me."

His eyes bulged. "That's your defense mechanism?"

"Yes. It's not like I can physically fight someone off. Look at the size of me." I was five foot eight, but I wasn't exactly agile or strong. I wasn't one for gyms and workouts.

"Why are you so stubborn?"

"I'm not. I'm just explaining that I'm not helpless."

"I know that. Still, if you're in trouble, call me. Promise you'll tell me."

"What if you're gone?" I asked.

"I'll find a solution."

I sighed. "Are you always like this, so determined to get your way?"

"Only when I think I'm right."

His eyes were trained on me, hot and relentless. The tension between us thickened. I stepped backward and felt the fridge door against my back.

At the same time, the belt on my robe loosened and came

undone. Tyler dropped his gaze. He was looking at my perky nipples, peeking straight through my pink T-shirt.

Crap. How did I get in this situation again?

Tyler growled, and when he snapped his gaze back up to me, I noticed his pupils had dilated. His mouth was on mine the next second. It was even more desperate than our first kiss. More passionate, more everything. He cupped my face with both hands, planting his feet on the outside of mine, trapping me with his body. I felt his arms against my chest, and his pelvis was pressing into my waist.

We kissed, and kissed, and kissed until I forgot everything except him: the taste of him, the way his muscles felt under my palms. All the fears and uncertainty I had tonight just melted away. I felt alive, and safe, and wanted.

He groaned against my mouth, and it reverberated through my whole body. It turned me on to no end.

"Kendra," he whispered, pulling his mouth away from mine.

He took in a few deep breaths, stepping back, leaning his backside on the edge of the counter. His gorgeous eyes were just as hot and intense as ever. Taking my hand, he pulled me flush against him.

"Tyler..." I tugged my lower lip between my teeth, unsure what to say.

He pressed his thumb on the spot just a bit, zeroing in on my mouth.

"Your taste is addictive."

I shivered, and he didn't miss it. He rested his eyes on my shoulder, where the robe slipped a bit, and then on my neck. I waited with bated breath for his next move. To my astonishment, he *closed* my robe, fastening the belt. He lingered with two fingers on the knot as if it was all he could do not to undo it again.

Clearing my throat, I tried again. "Tyler, what are we doing?"

As soon as I said the words, my heart shriveled to the size of a pea.

He didn't miss one beat. "Discovering each other. Exploring. And you're fascinating."

"You keep saying that...," I murmured, unable to voice the rest of my fears and doubts. What could I say, anyway, without sounding ridiculous?

"Because it's true. You're fierce and strong, and you care so damn much. I've never met anyone like you."

I licked my lower lip. He groaned.

"Don't do that, or I'll kiss you again."

Heat lit up my nerve endings. "Why not do it? Since we're on this slippery slope already."

"Because you've had a rough evening, and you're still processing it. I don't want to take advantage of that."

I blinked, seeing him in a whole new light.

"So, you came here tonight to..."

"Check on you. The kiss was a blip in my self-control."

My heart rate sped up. I couldn't think straight, looking in those molten eyes. But... maybe I didn't need to. I had this sexy and totally surprising guy here in my kitchen. For once, I could stop playing safe and simply enjoy the moment. I wanted to.

"Your hand is on my shoulder. Are you about to have another blip in your self-control? Because I fully approve."

He flashed me a half smile, cupping the side of my face. "Kendra, don't tempt me. Not tonight. But starting tomorrow, you can tempt me all you want."

"Shucks, I can't fit that into my schedule," I teased. "I'm flying to Seattle tomorrow evening for work. I'm attending a seminar."

He groaned. "Cancel it."

I burst out laughing because he didn't only sound serious but also domineering.

"No, I won't. Besides, I don't even know how to do that."

"What?"

"Tempt you."

His smile widened. It was confident and sexy and made me weak in the knees. "In that case, I'm more than happy to tempt *you*."

"Oooh... should I brace myself?"

"Fuck yes."

CHAPTER EIGHT
TYLER

"Dude, you're in better shape every day," Donnie, the newest transfer to the Chicago Blades, said on Tuesday.

We were in our team's gym. Hanging out with the guys was hands down the one thing keeping me sane. I felt I was part of the team just because we were working out together. The guys had lost the first away game, and morale was low. Jett was avoiding conversation.

"I feel great, and my physical therapist says my shoulder is healing." During the session, I was also lifting arm weights, but I was under strict instructions not to do them on my own so I wouldn't accidentally reinjure anything. Here with the guys, I only did cardio, weight training for my legs, and core muscle building. We had a team trainer, but my PT was a control freak, and until I was good as new, I didn't mind following the program.

I wasn't one to follow the rules, but I'd do anything to get back on the ice.

"How is your volunteering going?"

"I like it. Working with kids reminds me why I started playing and loving hockey in the first place: because I liked the game. Winning is just the icing on the cake." I increased the speed on the treadmill again, thinking about Kendra. Every time I remembered how she grew up, it had felt like a punch to my stomach. I'd always had my whole family backing me up no matter what. I honestly couldn't imagine how it must feel to take the world on by yourself. I had immense respect for Kendra and her sister.

Last night, it had taken every ounce of my self-control to leave Kendra's apartment. All I'd wanted was to stay. I wanted *her*. But even though she'd tried to put on a brave face, she'd been shaken, and I wasn't an asshole. I wasn't going to take advantage of her.

I had a great plan. I was going to lay the groundwork while she was away, and once she was back, all bets were off.

"Dude, we need to bring the Stanley Cup home this year too," Steve said. He was on the rowing machine. Damn thing was practically a full-body workout.

"I second that," Bob said. He was closest to us, lifting weights and eavesdropping. Bob was on the first line, left wing —and nosy.

"Hey, why don't you all stop gossiping and focus?" Steve called out.

"Yes, Captain," Bob replied.

Once I finished training, I went to our lounge area, where we relaxed after workouts. We also had a huge screen and comfortable couches here. We used the room mostly to watch games and analyze plays, both of other teams and ours.

To my surprise, our manager joined us. He rarely came here. John Daniels was fifty-five and was known as the most business-oriented manager in the league. He had gray hair cropped short, and always wore a suit. I respected him for his ability to bring in the best players. But he saw this as a business only, and I didn't like it.

"Boys, don't let me keep you from whatever you're doing," he said as Steve pressed Play on the last game. "I only want to talk to Tyler."

We stepped outside the room.

"How is your shoulder?"

"Didn't you get the report from the physical therapist?"

He nodded. "I did, but I want your take on it. There's a lot of medical jargon in there. I want to know how you feel about it."

"It's solid. In about two more weeks, I'll probably be able to start training with the team again and shortly after ready for play."

He looked at me, nodding and frowning. "Good. Keep up with the physical therapy and the weight training. And the volunteering, how is that going?"

"I'm enjoying it. The coordinator the center assigned me is great to work with. Kendra's very involved in what she does and one of the best people I've met."

Daniels cocked a brow. "I trust you're keeping things professional?"

I frowned. "Meaning?"

"Exactly what I said."

"My personal life is no one's business."

"You're on thin ice, Maxwell. Don't fuck things up."

With that, he walked away, leaving me even more pissed at him than I already was. Daniels was way out of line. He had no business telling me what to do in my personal life as long as it didn't affect my performance. No one dictated what I could or couldn't do. *No one.*

. . .

I WAS STILL FUMING LATER that afternoon, but I had a skate session with the kids, and I for sure was not going to miss that.

"Tyler, what am I doing wrong?" Rupert asked, skating and stopping right in front of me. He'd missed *again*. Poor kid.

"Buddy, your hold on the stick is still not a hundred percent where it should be."

He slumped his shoulders. "I'm the worst on the team."

He had the most trouble, no question, so I gave him a pep talk.

"Practice the way I told you, and you'll eventually get the hang of it. But it'll take a while. Just don't give up."

"But everyone else can already do it," he argued.

"I know that's frustrating, but there's no way around this. You just have to keep trying. Practice even when you're not on the ice. You'll get the hang of your stick, and it'll become second nature."

"You're always so good at everything."

I shook my head. "I didn't start like that, buddy. I started like all of you, playing at school, doing my best. It takes commitment, true dedication. Just set your mind on it, and you'll eventually get it done."

"Really? You were like us?"

"Yeah. I was a kid too." I grinned. "Come on, go back to your teammates and show them what you can do."

"I'm ruining the game."

"No, don't say that. Be confident, okay? I can already tell you're getting better," I assured him.

I enjoyed training these kids even more than I thought I would. They had enthusiasm and innocence, and they had a competitive streak too, but not in the do-or-die mentality that was the battle for the Stanley Cup. I'd always assumed I would coach a professional team after retiring, but it was unexpectedly rewarding to work with kids. As a bonus, there was no fucking management to answer to.

The skate session ended twenty minutes later, and while the rest of the kids changed, I showed Rupert some tricks and how to hold the stick. The guy had determination, and in my experience, if you wanted something bad enough and you were willing to put in the effort and sweat, it would eventually work out.

Half an hour later, everyone was ready to go. There was a supervisor in the stands too, as usual. I'd found out that the club picked the kids up with a bus, but they needed a teacher present. Mr. Dawson was their biology teacher.

"Kids, I have some bad news for you," he said while we all went out. "The fundraiser didn't work out. There's not enough money for the field trip, so the principal decided the funds will be used to buy new school books."

There was a collective groan from the group.

"But we did so much research about the Apple River Canyon State Park," Tim said, sounding disappointed. He was the group's spokesman of sorts. "How can we complete the assignment if we don't see it?"

"We'll watch videos," Mr. Dawson said, trying to appease the kids.

The boys didn't look happy at all. I didn't blame them. If someone got me excited for a trip and then canceled it, I'd react the same way.

"What happened?" I asked the teacher as I nudged him over to the side of the walkway.

"I wanted to organize an outing for the boys, but even I knew it was a long shot. I shouldn't have gotten the kids' hopes up."

"When was it supposed to be?"

"In two weekends."

"Is The Illinois Volunteer Society involved with this?"

"No, no. The fundraiser was something the school organized."

We chatted about it a bit more, and I started thinking about the possibilities. We said our goodbyes, and I headed to my car.

I mulled it over in my mind on the ride home, ideas forming in my head. As soon as I stepped inside my condo, I called Kendra, but she didn't pick up. It was six thirty. Her workshop should have been over by now.

Tyler: Call me back when you can. I want to talk to you about something.

Kendra: We're having drinks tonight, but let me find a quiet spot.

She called me a few minutes later.

"Hi," she answered, almost out of breath.

"Hey, you. Were you running?"

"Yeah, sort of. The group is trying to decide where to have dinner, and I wanted to call you before we leave."

Fuck, she was cute.

"Couldn't wait to talk to me, huh?"

"Ooohhh, your cocky side is strong tonight. In that case, I didn't."

I liked that she changed from shy to sassy in a split second —that she went toe to toe with me every time. Our dynamic was definitely changing, becoming more comfortable, and I liked it.

"So... what did you want to talk about?"

"The kids told me that the school was trying to do a fundraiser so they could go to the Apple River Canyon State Park. It didn't work out, so I want to pay for it."

"Oh my God. Why?"

"Because they looked disappointed, and because I can do it."

She let out a sound that nearly made me think my ear was going to explode. I moved the phone a little farther away from my ear.

"I can't believe you want to do this. First you took them to the pool, and now this? You're spoiling them."

"Someone should. They're good kids, Kendra, and they were so excited to go. You should have seen how deflated they were when their teacher told them the news."

"No, I get that. I hate for this to have happened to them too. This is obviously out of the scope of your volunteering, but I can run it by my boss and the school. The school principal knows me because The Illinois Volunteer Society has brought some speakers for their Career Days."

Career Days? Jesus, the kids are only twelve.

"I think it's better if I speak with them rather than you contacting them directly. I can help them understand the importance of this to the kids, okay?" she went on.

"Yeah, sure. Whatever gets them to agree is fine with me. I totally trust you," I responded. And really, I trusted her more than she'd ever know. The sincerity and kindness I'd found in this woman was a magnet for me. I then asked her, "Since this isn't a preapproved activity, does that mean you'll join us?"

"Oh, so that's the real reason you're doing it." I could tell she was teasing me, but I didn't want to give her the wrong idea either way.

"No, the kids matter to me, you know that. But I want you there. It's a win-win. The kids get their trip, and I get you. I have big plans for the day."

"Should I be afraid?"

"No, just prepared."

"You know, you talk a big game, Tyler, but I only got two kisses out of it all."

"That's because I want you to trust me first, implicitly. And we're not there yet."

She gasped. "Why would you say that? I mean... did I do anything that made you think that?"

"No, it's a guess. Am I wrong?"

"I do trust you. More than any guy, but I'm... careful. I've always been like this."

I understood. Her life hadn't been easy, and she always needed to fend for herself. I didn't want to move too fast. I wanted us together on her terms.

"I thought so."

After a brief pause, she added, "I love that you want to do this for them."

"I love that you'll be there."

"With a bunch of others."

"We're going to sneak in some alone time. You should expect a lot of flirting," I said.

"And you should expect the same in return. A word of warning. You might not be able to handle it."

I grinned at the thought. "Game on."

CHAPTER NINE
TYLER

"This place is like a time capsule," I said. I was at The Happy Place, Gran's bookstore, ready to pick up my cousins, Kimberly and Reese. We would meet my brothers at the bar on top of their building, where they all had offices, except for Sam and me, obviously. We were the odd ducks in the family who chose not to go into our own businesses.

"I know, right. I'm happy Gran preserves it this way," Reese said. When my family sold the bookstore business, Gran insisted on keeping this one because it was the first one she opened with our grandfather.

"Okay, you ladies ready to go?" I asked.

"Yes we are."

"How is the jet lag, Kimberly?"

"Not too bad. I'm just generally tired because we've had a few intense months."

"You could take it easier," I suggested. "You don't have to prove anything to anyone, you know."

She worked in Paris for a travel agency and literally traveled everywhere to scout out the best spots for her clients. She worked hard and barely had time to visit us. I asked her once about it, and she said she didn't want to live off her trust fund. She wanted to *do* something.

"Look who's talking," she said with a wink. "Mr. Superstar Goalie, remind me, who was training overtime as soon as you started on the team? Just to prove to your teammates that the Blades didn't take you just because you're a Maxwell?"

I scoffed. "I didn't do it just because of that. I like being at the top of my game."

"You know what I mean."

"Yes I do," I admitted. We all had that need inside us to prove to ourselves that we were more than heirs to the Maxwell fortune. Kimberly even took it a step further and moved to France, where no one knew us. She could have gone to London, where we had a billion cousins from Mom's side, but she chose Paris instead.

"Anyway, I don't want to be a travel agent forever, but I like it for now. Besides, it gives me a chance to pop over to London to meet our dearest cousins... and Dad."

Reese smiled sadly. "How is Dad?"

The two of them never had a very close relationship to my uncle—Dad's brother. After their mom passed away when they were kids, he spiraled out, burying himself in work. Kimberly and Reese were at our house most of the time.

"Oh, you know. Just... Dad. He's happy when I visit, though."

"How long are you here for?" I asked Kimberly.

"Just a week, and then it's back on the other side of the pond for me."

"You do like it there, huh?"

"Yeah, it's a different experience, and I love it."

Reese winked. "I can tell. You're starting to dress French."

I had no idea what Reese was talking about.

"Awww, thanks, sis. I do miss all of you, though."

"Oh good, I was waiting for you to say that," I said, feigning being wounded.

She grinned, taking my arm and leading me out of the shop.

"I have a feeling that Operation Cheer Up Tyler isn't necessary anymore," Kimberly said.

Reese tilted her head, narrowing her eyes. "Yeah, I think he's got the worst behind him. Seems back to his old self."

"And so are you—sort of." Kimberly was looking at her sister. "You can always come to stay with me for a while, and we'll find you a Frenchman. Or two."

Reese burst out laughing. "Oh, Kimberly. I'm tempted to take you up on it, but I promised Gran I'd look after The Happy Place. The manager is going on maternity leave soon, so I can't take off."

TWENTY MINUTES LATER, we stepped inside the office building on LaSalle Street. We took the elevators directly to the top floor and headed straight to the bar.

Travis, Declan, and Luke were already sitting at one of the tables. No one had drinks.

"This feels so surreal," I said, "being able to hang out with you guys spontaneously during the season."

Reese laughed. "The perks of being benched."

"Ouch, that still hurts."

"Yep. Sorry. No more joking about that."

But this did give me a view of how my life would look once I was done with the ice. Most hockey players retired when they reached thirty. I knew I had one or two seasons left before retiring, but I sure as hell wasn't ready to say goodbye right now.

I took advantage of the fact that Luke was next to me and

Reese was out of earshot to check how things were going with our cousin.

"Did she tell you anything about why she's feeling off?" I asked. On the way here, she kept asking about Travis and me, avoiding talking about herself.

"It's been a few days. I need more time. I'm not a miracle worker."

I cocked a brow. "What are you talking about? No one was subtle with me when you all intervened."

He patted my shoulder twice. "Brother, you need the balls-to-the-wall approach. Reese needs subtlety."

That sounded like bullshit, but what did I know? He was the people whisperer of the family.

"Okay, good, you're all here," Travis said when I sat down. "I was just waiting for everyone to arrive. I'm having a party, and you're all invited."

I whistled appreciatively. "You're on a roll, man. Count me in."

Declan cocked a brow. "You're kind of starting to like parties." He was using his older brother serious tone.

Travis shrugged. "I never had a wild phase in college. I have some catching up to do."

"That's exactly my concern," Declan said.

Travis turned to me. "He needs that stick out of his ass. You're excellent at that. Can you take over from here?"

I brought my hand to my temple in a mock military salute. "Yes, sir. You can count on me. I'm going to make sure that one doesn't sulk at your party. When is it?"

"On Saturday."

"This Saturday?" I questioned.

"Yeah."

"Then no can do, man. I'm going on a trip from Friday to Sunday." I felt all eyes on me.

"What trip? You didn't say anything," Reese asked.

"I have an overnight trip with the kids I'm coaching. We're going to the Apple River Canyon State Park."

Reese smiled at me. "Oh, that's so nice of you."

"Yeah. I'm looking forward to it. And Kendra—" I was about to say more and thought better of it.

"Oh, Kendra is going?" Kimberly asked. "I'm starting to put two and two together."

"How do you even know about her?" I asked, knowing one of the family blabbed.

"Hello? I have a phone, and we have a WhatsApp group, and I like to be on top of my gossip, even if I'm far away from the action."

"Of course you do," Declan said. "So Kendra's coming too?" he asked me.

"Yeah. She's the program coordinator."

"Yeah, obviously," Reese said in a mocking voice. She was barely holding back laughter.

Travis grinned. Even Declan was laughing.

"Gran called it," Declan exclaimed.

I raised a brow. "Called what?"

Travis leaned down a bit toward me. "Said you looked whipped when you talked about Kendra."

I jerked my head back. "Gran doesn't say *whipped*."

"No, my bad. I was paraphrasing. She said starry-eyed." He looked at the table. "Right?" He got a few nods of confirmation, and he looked back at me. "Is that better?"

"Not one bit."

∼

Kendra

I LOVED SEMINARS. I liked learning new skills and gathering information based on the latest practices. The only thing I wasn't totally on board with was that it set me back at work.

After lunch on Wednesday, I waited with my fellow workshop attendees to be let back into the conference room. To give me something to do, I took out my phone. Tyler had texted me!

Tyler: Can you talk?

Kendra: Lunch break is over, and we're going into the conference room.

Tyler: When do you get a break?

Kendra: Why?

Tyler: For flirting.

Kendra: We need a flirting break? I can pay attention to both things at once.

Tyler: No, I want all your attention.

I giggled, checking the line in front of me.

Kendra: Okay, I think we might still have a few minutes until we go inside the room. We can talk.

He called me right away. "Hey, Kendra."

My God, that voice was so sexy! It was almost husky. *Is he having dirty thoughts?* Maybe I was overanalyzing.

"Hey, you."

"How's your day so far?" he asked.

"Oh, it's good. I like it. It's informative. What are you doing?"

"I just finished laps in the pool."

"How often do you swim?"

"Three times a week. It's part of the physical therapy."

"Oh yeah. Swimming is probably good for your shoulder."

"Yes. It's a risk-free way to strengthen the area. I can't stop thinking about you in that wet white dress."

Ha! No overanalyzing here. He *did* have sexy things on his mind.

77

I looked around and took a few steps away from the group. Hopefully no one heard him.

"Tyler," I admonished, "I'm in public."

"That doesn't mean I can't tell you all the things I wanted to do that day."

My breath caught. "Like what?" I whispered.

"I wanted to peel it off you and then do the same thing with your bra and panties."

Usually when I blushed, I felt it creeping slowly. My face would warm up gradually, but now I suddenly felt on fire, like I was emanating heat. I rolled my shoulders, pulling myself taller, which was a bit ridiculous. It wasn't as if he was here to see me, but this was my *extra-confident* pose.

"And I fantasized about tracing all those muscles with my fingers and possibly with my tongue."

A guttural sound came through the phone, filling me with pride. "Jesus, woman!"

"Hey, you started it with the sexy talk. This is not a one-way street, you know." I heard footsteps heading my way and looked up. "Wait, a colleague is coming. Don't say anything," I warned as my friend Sylvie came up to me.

"Kendra, are you okay?" she asked, frowning.

"Yeah, why?"

"You're so red in the face. I thought maybe you have high blood pressure or ate some hot chilies or something."

Oh my God. I laughed nervously. "I'm fine. It happens to me sometimes."

"Are you sure you're okay?"

"Yeah, I'm perfectly fine." *I just have a sinfully hot hockey player whispering naughty things in my ear in broad daylight.*

"Okay. I'll leave you to your conversation. This line isn't budging anyway. They've yet to open the door."

I focused on my call again as she stepped back in line. Tyler was laughing, and not just decent laughter but with guffaws.

"See what you do?" I tried to admonish him, but I was grinning from ear to ear.

"This is hilarious. What I wouldn't give to see your blush now."

"Okay, that's it. New rule: no sexy talk on the phone."

"Is that a whole day rule, or does it just apply to daytime or seminar time?"

He was incorrigible!

"Why don't you just pencil in a phone call tonight, so you can make sure no one will bother you?" he continued.

"My sister warned me about you, and she was right."

"What did she say?"

"That you're a bad boy."

"That's not how I'd describe myself."

"How would you, then?"

"A gentleman with a *very* dirty mouth."

Holy shit. And now I was fantasizing about that dirty mouth, because clearly he was holding back.

"Okay, let's move on from this dangerous topic. What else are you doing today?" I asked.

"I'm on family duty."

"How so?"

"Travis is planning a party, and Gran wants to hang out, which could be code for anything. Either she wants to cheer me up or she needs me to cheer her up. I'll see."

"Busy day, mister. No time for flirting breaks, then, huh?"

"I can always make time for flirting," he said seriously.

"The line is moving. We're going back into the conference room. I have to go." I told him as we shuffled along.

"Wait, before I forget why I called—"

"Oh, you mean besides making me blush furiously?"

"Yes, though that was a primary reason."

"Obviously."

"My cousin Kimberly is going to send you some pictures of a cabin she found in the canyon area that look good."

"But the school already has cabins lined up."

He snorted. "Yeah, I saw pictures. It looked like someplace where you send kids when you want to punish them and scar them for life."

I burst out laughing. Sometimes I forgot Tyler was a Maxwell. Those cabins had been modest indeed, but they weren't that bad. It was certainly better than the apartment we moved into after Dad passed away.

"Oh, Tyler!"

"You'll like this one, trust me."

I was sure I would, and so would the kids.

"Okay, I've got to hang up. Everyone's going in, and I want a good spot."

"Have fun, Kendra."

I sighed as I hung up.

Sylvie was still looking at me intently as we approached the room. "Hey, all good?"

"Yes, thanks."

"You look back to normal now. I just thought maybe, I don't know, you got bad news on the phone or something."

I cleared my throat, pressing my lips together before saying assuredly, "Oh no. Not at all."

As soon as we sat down, I put my phone on mute, but I noticed an email. It was indeed from Kimberly. My eyes bulged when I looked at the pictures of the cabin. It was huge and luxurious, with eleven bedrooms. At closer inspection, I realized it was actually a B&B. Kimberly wrote that the owners were able to rent the whole place out to us. It even had a jacuzzi. It was a glorious space, and I couldn't believe Tyler wanted it for the kids. This man was simply something else.

I sighed, running a hand through my hair. I'd always been careful. But with Tyler, all I wanted was to let go. Was it smart, though? I didn't even know him that well. What if he was a heartbreaker? What if I regretted this later?

He was a hockey star, and I was sure a million women wanted him. Did I want to involve myself in all that?

Slow your roll, Kendra. It's not like you're going to marry the guy.

I had a gazillion flutters in my belly, and I knew it wasn't because of his flirting skills. Even though they were something to write home—or to my sister—about.

CHAPTER TEN
KENDRA

My workshop ended on Friday morning, and I made arrangements to travel directly to the state park from the airport. I didn't have time to go home, so Emma met me at Arrivals to give me an extra bag with warmer clothing. We also used the time until my train left to have another spill-it session. We drank pumpkin spice lattes at the coffee shop in the airport. I loved November and the whole spooky season because I could find pumpkin lattes and pies everywhere.

"What do you think will happen on the trip?" she asked after she finished telling me about her latest dating fiasco. My sister was a brave one.

I sipped my latte, considering my next words. "I'm not sure."

She wiggled her eyebrows. "What do you *want* to happen?"

I grinned, taking yet another sip to buy myself time. "Lots and lots of naughty things. But not during the trip. And anyway, I'm not sure that's the smart thing to do."

"You deserve good things in your life, Kendra. Live a little."

"I know."

"Do you? Sometimes I'm not sure about that," Emma pushed.

"What do you mean?"

"That you're used to having shitty luck."

I shrugged, realizing that might be true. I was overly cautious. "Hey, luck is always changing. I mean, I did buy the house of my dreams."

"I can't wait to see it. Did you find a construction crew?"

"None I can afford. I'm going to figure out how to do some of the stuff myself."

Her eyes bulged. "But you're terrible at it. And I'm worse. But I'll help you in any way I can."

"Thanks."

"Did you manage to get ahold of Jared? There has to be a way to legally force him to deposit your paychecks in your bank account."

"I'm looking into getting a lawyer to send him a letter. That asshole thinks he can push me around."

"Or I could loan you some money until—"

"That's a firm no." Emma was always there for me, as I was for her, but this was my problem to deal with.

"You only took the job at Jared's to help me with my college loans. So it's only fair—"

"You don't owe me anything, Emma. You're my little sister, and I wanted to help out any way I could. Let's change the subject."

"Okay. Tyler. Tell me about him." She grinned.

"He's sexy and amazing, and I haven't met anyone who can melt my defenses faster than him. And that's so scary."

"Good scary, right?"

"I think so. I hope so." I finished the last sip of my latte, pondering my next words. "I know so little about him."

But despite knowing so little, he made me feel *so* much.

When he showed up at my apartment after I was almost mugged, he genuinely wanted to be there for me. His sincerity and protectiveness were something I'd longed for... probably most of my life. But I cautioned myself to be careful. This was probably just a fleeting moment with a wonderful man, and then it would be over. Could I handle that?

Emma pointed at me. "Awww, sis. Whether you want to admit it or not, you're smitten. Or at the very least on your merry way to being smitten with Tyler Maxwell."

"Shush. Don't say that out loud. You're putting all sorts of ideas in my mind."

"What are little sisters for?"

I laughed, stealing her cup of coffee from the table and taking a sip.

"Hey, why did you do that?" she protested.

"You snooze, you lose."

We bickered about the coffee for about ten more minutes before it was time for me to leave.

After bidding her goodbye, I took a train directly to the state park. I was traveling separately from the group because they'd already arrived a few hours earlier. From the train station, I took a prebooked transfer to our cabin, looking out curiously on the way.

I sighed when I got out of the car in front of the *huge* B&B. My God, it looked so gorgeous, even better than in pictures. I walked up the front porch, inspecting my surroundings. The A-frame was made from wood logs that had darkened already. There were two swings on the porch with folded gray blankets on them and a swinging armchair. Laughter and the occasional shriek filled the air. I couldn't see the kids, but I suspected they were in the backyard; the property was narrow in the front, but I remembered seeing a huge yard in the back in photos.

The front door swung open when I arrived in front of it. Tyler stood before me, tall and impossibly handsome.

"Hey. How did you know I was here?"

"One of the kids saw the cab pull up. Welcome."

Stepping closer, he brought his mouth to my cheek. My whole body tightened up when I felt his hot breath on my skin. And when his lips touched my cheek, every nerve ending was on edge. Tyler was exuding even more sexy vibes than usual. I felt them in every fiber of my body, as if he was feathering his lips all over me.

Stepping back, he pointed to my suitcase. "I'll take that."

I stepped to one side so he could pick it up. Yummm, that bicep flexed deliciously while he brought my bag into the house.

"This looks amazing," I said. "You went all out."

"I told you I was going to get the best for them."

I'd only just arrived, and he was already waking up the butterflies in my stomach. I could feel my defenses melting away now that we were 150 miles away from Chicago.

I focused on my surroundings again, taking it all in. The cabin was so cozy, yet luxurious at the same time. Like the exterior, the interior was also all wood logs. It had hardwood floors and an old-style open fireplace.

How much did he spend on this place?

Five of the kids were storming about the living room, jumping on the couches and running up and down the staircase leading to the upper levels. One of the boys tried to climb the railing at the top, presumably to slide down, but Mr. Dawson stopped him just in time.

Thank God Mr. Dawson had come with us. While I could handle kids for about half an hour at a time, I wasn't qualified to keep this many safe at once—especially for two days.

"Kendra," Tim said loudly, coming up to me. "Mr. Dawson

says he found a cool place where we can eat and look at all sorts of stuffed animals."

Stuffed animals? He must have been referring to mounted animals from a taxidermist. Regardless, that sounded like a nightmare to me.

"Okay," I said cautiously, wanting to be more enthusiastic, but honestly, that just gave me the creeps.

"I made reservations at six o'clock. It's called The Bear," Mr. Dawson said.

"I have a phone call at five thirty that will probably last an hour, but I can join you all afterward."

Taking out my phone, I searched for The Bear and then opened it in Google Maps, zooming in. "Okay. As long as I don't get lost on the way. How can the route be so complicated?"

It wasn't far away, just twenty minutes on foot, but the directions were super twisty, turning this way and that.

Tyler stepped closer to me, and my entire body tightened with his presence.

"I'll stay behind and wait for you. We'll go together," he offered.

I craned my head up, looking straight at him. "Why would you do that?"

"I'm good with maps." There was a dangerous twinkle in his eyes and an edge to his smile that made all my lady parts dance with joy. "We wouldn't want you to get lost, would we, Kendra?"

"Then that's settled," Mr. Dawson said, fortunately missing the exchange between Tyler and me.

"I'll show you to your room, Kendra," Tyler added.

I nodded, walking side by side with him.

"Our rooms are up in the attic. Everyone else is spread out on the floors below."

Wait a second. Tyler and I have rooms near one another?

I licked my lips, narrowing my eyes at him. "Did you have anything to do with that arrangement?"

Tyler flashed a devastatingly sexy smile. "Not at all. Mr. Dawson decided. I *might* have suggested that it would be safer to have the kids on the same floor with him. *Might*."

"Of course you did." My heart was beating insanely fast. "Tyler... there will be no sexy times during this trip. I mean it."

"We have to be role models," he said seriously.

"Exactly."

"Sexy time was not what I had in mind, Kendra. But glad to know you did."

Wait, what?

As we went farther up the staircase, I felt his presence beside me so strongly it was as if we were touching the whole time. *Sweet heavens.*

Two minutes later, we arrived in front of my room. He brought a hand to my lower back, and that little bit of contact singed me.

"This is one of the rooms. Take a look at mine too. We can switch if you prefer. I didn't unpack in case you wanted it."

Such a gentleman.

He opened the door to the only other room up here. They looked identical. Only the view out the window was different. There was a huge fir tree in front of this one, whereas you could see a good distance from the other one.

"I'll keep the other one," I said.

He took the bag back into the first room, putting it up on a luggage rack so I could unpack. He flexed those biceps again. *Yumm...*

When he turned around, I schooled my features but immediately felt the heat of my skin exposing my true feelings.

"I'll be next door," he said. "Just knock when you're ready."

I nodded, pushing a strand of hair behind my ear. "I will. Thanks for staying behind with me."

"My pleasure." His voice sounded huskier than before, and it sent tendrils of heat between my thighs.

"And thanks for doing all this. It's amazing, and I'm sure the kids will treasure it forever."

"It's easy to make them happy." He stepped closer until I had to crane my neck to make eye contact. "What will it take to make you happy, Kendra?"

I swallowed hard. "Ummm... not sure. I've never thought about it."

No one's ever asked me.

He gently caressed my cheek with the backs of his fingers. The touch electrified me.

"Think about it. And tell me."

"How are you even real?" I murmured. "Who says stuff like that?"

"Someone who means what they say and wants to know you intimately, Kendra."

I instinctively knew he wasn't only talking sexually. He wanted to know *me,* and this was a first for me. I had no idea what to say.

He stepped back, moving toward the door like he hadn't made me swoon and heat up at the same time. "It's almost five thirty. I'll leave you to your call."

"Okay. Thanks."

The second he closed the door, I hurriedly took out my laptop from my bag and sat on the chair in front of the small vanity table.

I didn't have time to process everything Tyler had said to me. I was hyperaware of him as if he was right behind me and not next door. Even through the closed window, I heard the yelps of joy of the kids playing outside. I put on my headphones and typed in the Wi-Fi password that was written on a sticky note. I shut out the rest of the world as I joined the Zoom meeting. This was a pitch for a new project, and I was excited. I liked sharing my ideas and finding the right people for them. In this case, I was trying to arrange for volunteers from the ice skating world to meet up with kids.

"Kendra, this sounds like something our skaters would love to do. After all, it's important to interest young people in sports. I'll talk to them, okay?" Dorian, the manager of the skating club said.

"Sure. Text me or email me if they need more details or if you have any questions at all."

"Yeah, sure. Thanks!"

The call disconnected, and I took off my noise-canceling headphones. For a few seconds, I felt that maybe my ears weren't working properly because it was so quiet. I couldn't hear any voices or noises at all, but then I realized it was already past six o'clock. Everyone was at the restaurant—everyone except Tyler, who was waiting for me.

I jumped from my chair, suddenly feeling butterflies in my belly. I pressed a palm against that spot. Smiling to myself, I put on a super thick sweater and jeans. I was about to take my trusted Ugg boots from my luggage when I heard a knock at my door. "Come in."

I sucked in a breath when Tyler stepped inside. He was wearing a Henley shirt that covered far too much but somehow still looked incredibly sexy, probably because it was so tight that it showed off every muscle. *Yum. There should be a rule: only tight shirts on Tyler.*

The air instantly changed in the room.

"I just finished a few minutes ago and was changing."

"I thought so when I didn't hear your voice anymore. Are you ready to go?"

"Yes. Yeah, we can go."

He looked at me intently. "We don't have to."

"You want to skip dinner with the group?" I didn't know what to make of that. What would everyone think?

"Fuck yes." He stepped closer, looking me in the eyes. "I just want to spend this evening with you."

"Wow. Way to be straightforward."

"I told you I would be."

"I wasn't sure you were serious." The thought of an evening with Tyler was ohhh so tempting...

"Oh, I'm always serious when it comes to going after what I want."

I felt his gaze like a physical caress. And when he touched my face with the back of his fingers, I knew I was a goner. The intensity in his eyes and the barely restrained passion in his touch were almost too much.

I blew out a breath, then took a step back. I planted my foot the wrong way, losing my balance and almost fell on my ass.

"Wow. That was close," I whispered as I righted myself in his arms.

"It was, but you're okay. Does your ankle hurt?"

"No, I'm okay." Clearing my throat, I took a step back. "Tyler, we said no sexy time, remember? Or, well, I said it. You agreed."

"You make me lose my mind." Swallowing hard, he pointed to the door. "After you."

Was it my imagination, or were the muscles of his arms extra bulgy? Or maybe I was more sensitive to his insane sex appeal? Whatever the reason, I couldn't stop the huge smile from forming on my face.

Mr. Perceptive didn't miss it. "What's with that look?" he asked.

"I was just admiring you. Can't I do that?"

The corners of his lips twitched. "Let's go before I change my mind."

"Oh, and you assume I'd change mine too?"

"Yes."

I laughed, shaking my head as we left my room, taking out my phone to look at the map.

It was cold outside, and I hugged my jacket tight around me as we walked through the twisty streets. I pulled my beanie down to cover as much of my ears as possible and crossed my arms over my chest to keep myself a bit warmer.

Tyler put an arm around me. "You're cold?" he asked.

"This is better. Now I'm extra warm from your body heat." It was the beginning of November and the chill was settling in.

"Really? You feel my body heat through three layers of clothes?"

"Oh, I think I could feel it through a wall. It just pours off you, like the sexiness. It's irresistible."

He kissed my cheek, making me melt.

"You're something else," he murmured. "You're not a winter person, are you?"

"Hell no. Ever since I was a kid, all I did in winter was sit inside and read."

"I was out all the time. My brothers and I seemed to get all sorts of ideas in winter. We drove Mom mad. I mean, we did in general. It was just worse in winter. She used to run around after us with extra clothes because we forgot to put on jackets and stuff."

"How can you forget to put on jackets? It's freezing."

"Yeah. Not something we noticed. We were too busy being up to no good." He changed the subject then, asking, "What was your call about?"

"I'm trying to convince some prominent skaters to drop by

some of the schools. I want the kids to know they can dream big."

Tyler's eyes softened. "I've never met anyone like you. How are you even single?"

My mood plummeted. I sighed. "How much time have you got? It's a long story."

"I've got time, Kendra."

"How about you?"

"It's not exactly a secret that I've always been single. I've had hookups."

"Puck bunnies?" I asked, and his eyes widened. "Yeah, I know the term."

"Honestly, that lost its appeal a long time ago. Anyway, before all this madness with the video, I met this woman, Blair, who didn't even seem to know much about hockey, and I thought that was a plus. But after the scandal, she said she didn't want to be tied to someone whose career was going down the drain."

I stopped in my tracks, utterly shocked that someone could be so callous. "She told you that?"

"Yeah." His eyes darkened. "I was blind to the signs, if I'm honest. She loved posting stuff about us on social media. That's most of what she did while we were together. But I thought it was normal. So many people seem to have this dire need of posting everything they do or eat in a day. It's not my style, but I understand that other people like it, and it didn't bother me. I just didn't realize that she was doing it in the hopes of, I don't know, becoming famous or something, and once she realized I wasn't her ticket to fame, she decided I wasn't worth her time after all."

"I'm shocked. But you're *you*," I said. "Hot and... you know. Everything else."

He chuckled again, smiling, and that dead look in his eyes dissipated. "It's all fine, Kendra. It wasn't such a big deal."

But I got the feeling that he was minimizing the impact because he wanted to appear strong or something. I could only imagine how it felt when your whole career seemed to collapse around you, and then the person who was supposed to be your partner and support you bolted as well.

"You didn't tell me your story," he went on.

"It's pretty basic. I went out with Peter for a year before I brought up the idea of moving in together, and he freaked out. Broke up with me the next day."

"What the fuck!"

"Sums up my thoughts. I mean, I've never been a huge romantic or anything."

"No?"

I shook my head. "I'm... practical. I mean, my parents were very much in love. But after he passed away... Mom was in two long relationships that both ended with the guy leaving when things became tough. She worked for a car manufacturer that ended up moving production elsewhere. The guy she was dating at the time, Mateo, left her two weeks later. Then she started seeing Alex, who was around for a while... until she got sick with MS."

"I am so sorry."

"She was inconsolable after he left." It was horrible. I hated to think about those times. I felt so bad for my mom, that someone could treat her that way. I loved her so much, and I wanted everyone else to love her like I did. Some people could be so cruel.

"When did she pass away?"

"Seven years ago." And I missed her every day.

"I'm sorry for your loss."

"Thanks." I racked my brain for a way to change the topic.

"So, as I said, I'm not much of a romantic, but I do believe in soul mates. I just don't think they necessarily meet, at all."

"Soul mates?" he asked on a laugh, clearly taking my cue about changing the subject. "Can't say I'm a believer. What happened after you ended things with Peter?"

I appreciated the way he phrased it: "after *you* ended things," not "after he dumped you."

"That was two years ago. In the meantime, I've been on maybe three dates. That includes the one you're going to take me on," I said boldly. Peter was in the past, and I'd wasted enough time thinking about him and what I might have done wrong and why I hadn't been enough. I was probably lucky it was over.

"Fuck yes, I will." He stopped walking, cupping my face with both hands. "I promise I'm an excellent date."

"I'm counting on it, Mr. Goalie. I'm not sure how you can make me swoon or heat up more than you already have at this point, but—"

"I'll do my very best."

After a few minutes of walking, Tyler looked around, frowning. Then he glanced at the map on his phone.

"We got lost, didn't we?" I asked.

"Yeah."

I burst out laughing. "I thought you were good with maps."

"I am... when I'm not focused on you. I'll figure it out."

We arrived at the edge of the property where the restaurant was twenty minutes later. My face was frozen, but my body was heated up from all the walking.

Lamps lit the path leading up to the restaurant on either side, but I still felt a bit on edge while walking.

When I stepped inside The Bear a few minutes later, I gasped.

"Holy shit." There *really* were stuffed animals, as Tim called them, everywhere, but I stood corrected. They weren't creepy—they were downright scary. They looked so lifelike that it was hard to believe they weren't alive. The restaurant seemed to love bears the most because they were mounted everywhere.

Tyler and I walked side by side to the table where our group was. The kids were talking about what costumes they wore for Halloween two days ago.

"Tyler, you're here. We thought you forgot about us," Tim said.

"Of course not, buddy."

"Hmm, I don't believe you."

"Kendra here can vouch for me, right?" He turned to me. "I've been on my best behavior, haven't I?"

I felt my ears heat up. "Yes, you have been."

A behavior I was liking very much.

CHAPTER ELEVEN
TYLER

"Tyler, can we play Twister?" Tim asked as soon as we got back to the cabin.

The honest answer was no. All I wanted to do was go upstairs with Kendra. But Tim was looking at me with huge eyes. It was a tactic kids often used; I knew it from Paisley. I'd always assumed it worked on me because she was my niece, but no, it seemed to work generally, because I suddenly couldn't tell him no.

"Sure. Who else wants to play?" I asked loudly.

It turned out that everyone wanted to play. There were two sets of Twister, twenty kids, and four adults, so we took turns. I couldn't take my eyes off Kendra. The woman was beautiful inside and out. I wasn't attracted to her just because she was smoking hot. She was also a kind soul. She radiated happiness and inner strength that I admired. For some reason, she'd held back while we were in Chicago, but she'd opened up this weekend, and I wanted to use every opportunity to spend time with her.

It was midnight by the time everyone went to bed. Everyone

except me and Kendra, who was sitting on the couch, looking at her phone. I sat next to her.

"Want to stay down here longer or are you tired?" I asked.

"I am tired, but I want to stay." She turned the phone to me. "I was looking at pics of my new home. I've already packed some boxes with stuff I don't need on a day-to-day basis and will move them there as soon as possible."

"Congratulations."

"I'm so happy about it. I've wanted to be a homeowner since I was like eleven, I think."

He smiled. "Thanks for telling me that. I want to learn more about you."

"More what exactly?"

"Everything. What's your favorite food?

"Steak."

"What do you like to do in your free time?"

"In cold weather, I'm a homebody. I have my reading nook, though I've always wanted to have one of those fancy rocking chairs with a remote, where you can relax and stretch out."

I made a mental note about that.

"And in the warmer weather," she continued, "I spend a lot of time around the lake. Swimming, sunning, kayaking, just doing summer stuff. You?"

"I typically don't have a lot of free time during the fall and winter seasons. I make sure I see my family regularly, but that's about it."

"Stop making me swoon. It's unfair."

"No it's not." I leaned in, dragging the tip of my nose up the side of her neck. "And I've got all day tomorrow to do the same."

Clearing her throat, she placed her hands on my chest, pushing me away a few inches. "I'm supervising this event, so I have to pay attention to stuff."

"And you will. But in between all those walks in the canyon, I'll have plenty of time to interrogate you."

The corners of her mouth twitched, even though she was fighting to stay serious.

"I bet you will."

NEXT MORNING, we woke up early, and we were one of the first visitors in the national park. Mr. Dawson was leading the group of kids. Kendra and I were in the rear. The kids were throwing question after question at me, just like last night.

"Okay, we need brochures," the teacher said as soon as we reached the information point.

"I can get some," Kendra said.

"I'll come with you," I added, looking at her intently. She blushed. All morning, all we'd done was exchange glances, but now I wanted more. I knew the kids were going to ask about hockey during the whole trip in the park, and that was fine by me, but right now I wanted a few minutes alone with Kendra.

"Sure. Let's go," she said. "We'll be back right away."

"Okay. Come on."

We walked side by side.

"Are you afraid I wasn't going to find the way by myself?" Kendra asked in a teasing tone once the group was out of earshot.

"Yes. That, and I'd eyed those trees there ever since they came in my visual field."

She followed my gaze. "What for?"

I leaned in, right in her ear. "Kissing."

"Tyler," she whispered, but laughed as I took her hand and brought her right behind them. You had to step through three bushes to get there. That's how I knew no one would bother us.

"You are full of ideas in the morning."

"To get what I want? You bet I am."

I captured her mouth, puting my right hand on her cheek, keeping it in place so I could kiss her the way I wanted. Oh, fuck. The more I kissed her, the more I wanted. I groaned, pulling back.

She looked at me through hooded eyes, but then cleared her throat. She smiled. I was proud that the look in her eyes was dazed. "I think this will be the last kiss you'll get today, mister. The kids seem obsessed to keep you talking."

"That's possible. But Kendra, on Sunday, we'll be back in Chicago, and then all bets will be off."

CHAPTER TWELVE
TYLER

As I predicted, I didn't get to spend nearly as much time as I wanted with Kendra, but that was okay. I had a plan.

We returned to Chicago Sunday evening. We rode the bus with the kids to their school, where the parents were waiting for pickup.

"How are you getting home?" I asked Kendra when we stepped down into the parking lot.

"I'm taking a bus."

"My car is here. I can drop you off at home."

She grinned. "Thanks!"

"Tyler Maxwell! I can't believe this. Can I get an autograph, man?" a guy asked.

Ah, I should have known the parents would be hockey fans.

I leaned in to Kendra. "I'll do this quickly. Don't go, okay?"

She sucked in a breath, licking her lips. "I won't."

I signed autographs and took selfies for what felt like a million years. Then I led Kendra to the car, putting our bags in the trunk.

"You were such a hit with the parents," she said once we were in the car.

I took her hand, kissing it. "It was a great weekend. Although we didn't get as much time together as I wanted."

She giggled. "I have to say I found it hilarious that the kids wouldn't stop throwing questions at you."

"They were very curious, true. I like their passion for the game. I forgot what it's like when you're their age. You care about the competition, but more about the sport itself." I paused a moment. "Kendra, do you have plans tonight?"

"No."

That one word was enough to snap my control. The thought of having her all to myself... fuck. It was all I could think about.

I tried to make conversation on the rest of the drive, but the tension between us was messing with my concentration. When we reached her building, I took her bag out of the trunk, following her.

Once inside the apartment, she took off her coat, putting it on the hanger.

Turning around, she pushed a strand of hair behind her ear. "Want to come in? I'll hang your jacket too."

"I'll do it."

I took it off quickly, getting rid of my shoes too. She did the same. "Kendra, I want you... tonight."

"I want you too," she whispered, pressing her fingers into my biceps.

I captured her mouth the next second, pushing a hand under her sweater. She moaned, pressing herself into me. She rose on her tiptoes, wrapping her arms around my neck, pulling me down.

"Do you want this?" I asked.

"Yes. Yes, yes. God, I do. I want this. I want you," she said.

I kissed her ferociously, and she did the same in return. My hands were all over her body, taking off her clothes. She was busy undressing me too while we moved to the bedroom, throwing the clothes on our way. I was completely naked when we reached the bedroom. She still had her bra and panties on.

We were both on edge. There was no way I could step away from her, not tonight. I kissed her. *Scratch that*. I devoured her, owning that kiss, capturing every ounce of passion. I'd wanted to kiss and touch and explore her for weeks, and now I wasn't going to hold back any longer. I was going to make Kendra mine.

I pushed the strap of her bra to one side, tracing the patch of skin it had covered with my forefinger, then mapping the same spot with my mouth. She shuddered, and I knew she was going to give in to whatever I asked of her tonight.

I unclasped her bra, throwing it to the side.

"You're fucking beautiful, Kendra," I said, cupping her breast, flicking her nipple with my finger while making eye contact so my intentions were clear. Every inch of her was mine to pleasure tonight. Her breathing accelerated.

Bending at the waist, I kissed between her breasts, moving slowly under the right one, licking the underside and then kissing it back up on the side. I felt her contract the muscles of her stomach as if she was bracing herself and expected me to do more. I was going to move farther down, but I wasn't done with her breasts yet. They were so damn perfect and delicious.

"I'm going to explore every inch of you, Kendra."

"Every inch," she whispered. "That might take a long time."

"Are we in a hurry?" I asked, teasing her, knowing what she meant.

"Tyler!" Her voice shook when I moved to her left breast, giving it the same attention with my hands, but instead of flicking her nipple with my thumb, I captured it in my mouth. She gasped, rocking up and down on her toes.

I looked up at her while I moved my mouth down her stomach, slowly circling her navel. "I'll explore you. I'll find out what you like. Then I'll give you so much pleasure." Her skin pebbled with goose bumps. "You're going to scream for me tonight, Kendra. You're going to try very hard not to, but you will anyway because there will be no way to contain the pleasure I'll give you."

She exhaled sharply, digging her nails in her outer thighs. I traced that spot between her navel and the upper hem of her panties with my thumb, feeling her clench her muscles tighter still. Then I put my mouth there, laying a trail of wet kisses while moving my thumb between her legs, parting them wider.

I touched her inner thigh, barely brushing the hem of her panties with the tip of my thumb.

"Oh, Tyler, please," she whispered.

Fuck, I couldn't resist her plea. I put my tongue on the fabric covering her pussy, tracing a line over her entrance. Her legs shuddered, and then her knees buckled, but she didn't lose balance. She braced both hands on my shoulders, clasping them tightly. Then I brushed my thumb over her clit.

"Tyler!" she cried out, rolling her hips.

Fuck, this wasn't enough. I wanted to touch her skin. I wanted to see her reaction to that. It was intoxicating.

I moved the fabric to one side, blowing cold air on her pussy. She sucked in a breath. Then I pressed my thumb over her clit again, sliding in two fingers.

"Tyler!" she shouted, clenching tight.

My cock was rock hard, imagining how it would feel if she clamped around me, and my control snapped. I took my fingers out, moving back a few inches. She looked at me questioningly.

"Take off your panties, Kendra, or I'll rip them apart."

She swallowed hard, immediately obliging, pushing them down her thighs.

I clasped my cock tightly in my right hand, needing the pressure, but I knew it couldn't feel as good as she would. The second she stepped out of her panties, I pushed her down on the bed. Her legs were bent at the knee over the edge. I was too greedy to wait for her to move farther on the bed. She leaned back on her forearms, watching me, eyes wide, pupils dilated. She was just as crazy for me as I was for her.

"I want to taste you."

She widened her thighs. Her responsiveness to my words drove me insane.

I clamped my mouth over her pussy the next second, darting my tongue inside before moving up a few inches, focusing on her clit, alternating between teasing it with the tip of my tongue and brushing the flat of it against it.

She thrashed on the bed, gasping and moaning. The sounds drove me mad with the need for her. I grabbed my dick again, moving my hand up and down. When I felt the muscles in her thighs contract, I knew she was close. I slowed down, taking my time.

"Tyler!" she protested.

"You're going to come hard, baby. Trust me to give you the best orgasm you've had."

"Please, please, please," she begged, and I nearly sank inside her the next second. I wanted her to come like this, to get her ready.

I pulled her clit in my mouth, and I felt her explode. She cried out, filling the room. She stretched out her arm, probably in search of a pillow, but they were too far away for her to reach.

"Tyler," she said again.

I worked her with my mouth until I felt her calm down and her thighs were no longer clenched. Then I put on a condom, rolling it quickly, watching her. She was flushed, and her eyes were a bit watery. The smile on her face slayed me. I put it there, and I was damn proud of myself.

I kept her on the edge of the bed, lifting her legs and putting her knees over my elbows. She yelped, losing her balance for a second before propping herself on her palms.

She was so damn tight that she nearly pushed me back out. It had been a while for my girl, and the possessiveness in me liked that. I groaned, tightening my grip on her ankles, watching my cock sliding inside her, but then I looked at her face again. I wanted to see her reactions, to commit them to memory, to know everything she liked and do it again and again and again.

I only moved slowly until I was inside her to the hilt, and then my control completely disappeared. I moved faster and then even faster.

"Fuck, I can't slow down." The friction of her tight pussy was amazing! Even through the condom, the feeling was intense. We were perfect together.

"I don't want you to," she replied.

I pressed my right thumb on her clit, brushing it between every thrust. I wanted to alternate the shots of pleasure so I wouldn't overwhelm her. For now.

"You feel good. You feel so damn good."

I felt her muscles clench again, and it about undid me. Energy coiled through me as my cock pulsed, wanting release. My orgasm would hit in the next few seconds, and I wanted to make her come first.

"You're going to come first, baby, and so hard," I promised her.

I doubled down, sliding inside her at an insane pace, pressing down on her clit and then circling it with my thumb until she completely came apart. She clenched tightly around me, sending me over the edge.

I came so hard that my legs were burning. Every muscle clenched in my body.

I continued thrusting until I was spent, then pulled out and lay down next to her.

CHAPTER THIRTEEN
KENDRA

I could barely breathe properly, but I didn't let that stop me. I pushed him on his back, taking a good look at all those muscles. God, how could he be so sexy? I traced my fingers over every ridge in his six-pack, taking my time and then tracing it again with my mouth, moving up to his chest.

He grinned. "What are you doing?"

"What I've been dying to do since I saw you in that pool. Touch all this gorgeousness and kiss it too."

He chuckled, and I looked up at him. "You hid that well."

"Yeah, I was a master at self-restraint, and now I'm finally getting my reward. Unless you mind." I straddled him, so I had better access.

He bent his arms at the elbows, putting his hands behind his head. "Not at all."

I continued my exploration, also moving up to those biceps that looked extra bulky. Now that he had his hands behind his head, I was careful not to come too close to his armpits because he seemed ticklish. He lowered one hand. When I felt it move up my right ass cheek, I swatted it away. "No, no. I'm exploring now. Don't distract me."

He put his hand back under his head, watching me hungrily. Next, I focused on his chest, tracing my fingers along his clavicle, kissing around those insane pectoral muscles.

"Which shoulder is injured?" I asked.

"The right one."

I kissed it delicately so I wouldn't hurt him. "My God, you hockey players can be so sexy."

"Hockey player. Singular. *This* hockey player," he said in a surprisingly serious voice.

I looked up at him again and was startled by the intensity in his eyes. "What other hockey players do you see? No one, Mr. Jealous. Just you."

"That's right," he said. "Just me."

In a fraction of a second, the balance of power changed. He pushed himself up in a sitting position, securing one arm under my ass and lifting me off the bed. He walked with me to the nearest wall, holding me against it.

"Just me," he repeated in a strong voice before kissing me so intensely that I couldn't think straight.

I groaned when he touched my right shoulder blade, but not from pleasure. He seemed to realize it instantly.

"What's wrong?" he asked.

"I think I strained something this weekend."

"Where? Show me," he said.

He carried me back to the bed. I moved to the center of the mattress, turning with my back to him, pointing with my forefinger at a spot below my right shoulder blade. He pressed his thumb there, putting pressure on it for a few seconds.

"Oh wow, this is good. I can feel the pain sort of melting away."

"Are you sore anywhere else?"

"If I say no, will you take your hands away? I kind of like them there."

He laughed in my ear. "I won't take them away." He massaged my shoulders, descending to my shoulder blades a few times, applying pressure with his thumbs on certain spots.

"Oh wow, can you do this all night?" I asked, leaning into his ministrations.

He brought his mouth to my ear. "My pleasure, Kendra. You're so beautiful."

"I like your hands," I said.

"Before, you seemed to like my biceps too."

"Oh, those too," I said in a reassuring tone. "And your abs, your ass, your calves, your ankles—basically every part of you."

"Aren't you forgetting something?" he teased.

"Hmm, what could I be forgetting? Your cock?"

"Kendra, babe." He moved his hand up in my hair, tugging at it. "Don't turn me on."

"Why not?" I was genuinely perplexed.

"Because then I'll want to have you again."

"What's the problem with that?"

"I don't want you to be sore tomorrow."

I shimmied in the bed. "I'm a little bit sore already. But I don't mind."

"That ass of yours is perfection."

"So you're an ass man?" I asked.

"Not sure. I'm conflicted. I'm going to worship every part of you."

I turned around as he moved his hands down from my shoulder to my waist, touching the sides of my breasts on the way. "I thought you said I'd be too sore."

"I can make you come in other ways, babe."

"That you can. But remember, we left off somewhere else. I was the one exploring you."

He flashed me a slow, lazy smile. "Yeah we did, and I liked it a lot."

"See? Let's get back to that. So, how do you know this massage?"

"We learned a few techniques. It helps with muscle soreness."

"Hey, any time you need someone to take care of you, just call me and I'm your girl," I said.

"You'd do that?"

"Yes I would. But you'd have to give me precise instructions."

"I love giving instructions," he replied.

My eyes widened. "Yeah, I noticed. I like it. I didn't think I would, but I do. So... instruct away, Tyler."

He captured my mouth. This kiss was different than the ones before. It was like he wanted to own me, body and soul, and I hoped he never stopped kissing me.

I wanted this to last forever.

CHAPTER FOURTEEN
TYLER

The next afternoon, my brother Tate invited us to one of the vineyards he owned about an hour away from Chicago to try out two new wines he planned to bring on the market. We often had get-togethers like this, though usually it was scheduled in advance. It was more of a catch-up time with the family, because he didn't actually need our opinions. I drove there with Reese and Travis, as it made no sense for everyone to drive their own car.

"How was your field trip?" Reese asked.

"It was great. The kids had a lot of fun. And so did I."

Fun was an understatement. Spending time with Kendra was addictive. The more I got, the more I wanted. I drove home early in the morning, and that was only because she had to go to work today.

Reese half turned to me in the back. "Sooo... Kendra still likes you, or did she come to her senses?"

"Any particular reason you're mean today?"

She grinned. "Several."

"Dude, next time you put Luke on a mission, tell him not to

be so obvious. He was pestering Reese during the party," Travis said.

Reese rolled her eyes. "Yeah, I had a lot of fun when I wasn't running away from Luke, who was doing your dirty work."

I grimaced. "Not dirty work. But he's better at getting stuff out of you."

"Next time you want to know how I am, just ask me. I have nothing to hide. And I'm gonna tell you exactly what I told Luke. I'm not doing too well. I thought I'd gotten over... well, everything. I certainly felt better the last couple months. But then I saw some pictures of them on Facebook. They announced they're going to have a baby, and it messed me up. And with Kimberly away... Anyway, that's my life right now. Two steps forward, one step back. But I'll get there eventually."

I had no clue what to say to that. We needed Kimberly back, but she was happy in Paris, so Reese was stuck with six half-useful cousins. Though she and Lexi were quite close, so at least there was that.

We arrived last. Tate and Lexi came with Mom and Dad. Luke and Declan came together. Gran had stayed back in Chicago with Paisley.

"Ha! I knew you three would be last," Luke exclaimed when Reese, Travis, and I stepped inside the cellar. Everyone was standing around the huge wooden table in the middle of the basement. The walls were filled with bottles from floor to ceiling.

"Hey, we like to make an entrance," Reese said, theatrically throwing her hair over her shoulder.

"If you want to pick on anyone, pick on Tyler. He's the one who made us late," Travis said.

I scoffed. "Thanks for having my back, dude."

Travis held his hands up in defense. "It's true."

"Punctuality is not my forte," I admitted. "How about we all accept it as a fact instead of giving me shit every time?"

Luke winked at me. "Never. I live for the small pleasures in life, brother."

"Now, now, Luke. It's too early for you to torment your brothers." Mom looked once around the room, making eye contact with each of us. "And no surprises, okay?"

"Mom, we're adults now," Luke said reasonably.

Travis nodded. "Yeah. If we were to prank you, it would be in a more evolved way."

Luke grinned. Declan shook his head. We pranked Mom once, twelve years ago, when Tate asked us here for the first tasting. Luke put tequila in her glass instead. I'd strategically put a glass of "water" next to her, knowing she'd reach for it. It was also full of tequila. All these years later, Mom was still scarred by it all. She warned us every time that we were in for it if we ever pranked her like that again.

Dad chuckled, putting an arm around her shoulders and kissing her temple. I'd never seen my parents fight. Not once. I was sure they'd had their misunderstandings over the years, but we didn't get wind of it. They gave us the best childhood possible.

"Gather up, gang. It's officially happy hour," Tate said. "Thanks for coming up here on such short notice. My team and I only decided on Thursday to add these to the list of wines we're considering. We'll be quick, and then everyone can go ahead with their Saturday plans. I've got the first one here. My lovely fiancée already tasted it, and she said it's great."

"Hey," Travis protested. "Why did she get to before us?"

Declan shook his head. "Man, you get engaged, and suddenly we're second-class citizens."

Tate winked at Declan. "Wait until you're engaged, and then you'll see. I can't say no to her."

"He really can't," Lexi said.

"Oh, your brothers don't know what it's like to be in love," Mom said. "Don't mind them."

"I don't," Tate assured her. "Okay, everyone. We've got two bottles. Let me know what you think."

Dad and Travis uncorked the bottles of white wine. Tate poured enough in each glass for two or three swigs. I didn't have the wine bug the way Tate did—he and Dad could spend hours on the vineyard next to our house when we were kids—but I did appreciate a good glass of wine. I twirled the glass, inhaling the aroma. Then I took a sip, swishing the liquid in my mouth. It had a hint of smokiness.

"I like this one," I declared.

"It's too heavy for a white for me," Travis said, "but you know my taste is different. I'm like the adopted kid when it comes to wine."

Everyone proceeded to give their thoughts. Dad was the most opinionated, but the man knew his wines.

Travis came up next to me. Reese was right behind him. "Hey, man, they uploaded new pics from the first game, and you're in a few. You didn't look all that unhappy, especially with that blonde all over you."

I looked up from my glass at Travis. "What are you talking about? What blonde?"

"You didn't check the Facebook posts?"

"No, I've avoided social media since the fucking video," I said.

"Oh, right. I'll show you," Travis said, tapping his phone screen. Reese stepped between us, looking at the screen too.

"Oooh, is that Kendra? Is that why you didn't want us hanging out with you?" Reese asked.

I groaned. "It's not Kendra. It was a fan who wanted me to sign her skin." I took the phone, looking closer. The photo was blurred, but it looked like we were kissing or about to. "Fuck."

Had Kendra seen this at all? She was important to me, and I wouldn't want her to get the wrong impression with this stupid picture.

"What's wrong?" Reese asked.

"I don't know if Kendra saw this."

Her face lit up. "Wait, does that mean there's something going on between the two of you? What happened on the trip?" she singsonged.

"I'm going to call her," I said, stepping away from the group. There was no signal down here, so I went up the cellar steps and headed outside, pacing in front of the building as I called her. It went straight to voice mail. I tried a second time with the same result.

I went back to the group, taking my place between Travis and Reese.

Reese looked at me but didn't get a chance to ask anything because Tate spoke.

"I have the next one ready." He poured a bottle in fresh glasses. Technically you could do the tasting in the same glass, as there was minimal aftertaste, but it was clearer this way.

The bottle was three months older than the last one, and it tasted even better. The smokiness was much more intense.

"Son, this is my new favorite," Dad exclaimed.

Mom, Lexi, and Declan all weighed in with details, but my mind was on Kendra. We hadn't set any rules, obviously, but if I saw a picture of her with another dude, I'd lose my cool.

Maybe she didn't see it.

After everyone gave their opinion on the second wine, we ate bread and cheese, Reese, Travis, and I sharing a plate. Usually, Tate gave us something between tastings to clear the palate, but since we were only trying out two today, it wasn't necessary.

"What did Kendra say?" Reese asked me.

"Call went to voice mail."

"Did you try again?"

"Yeah, three times."

"Wait, you've called her several times?" Reese asked.

"Yeah."

"I'm just putting it out there, but she might be purposely not answering your calls."

Travis grimaced. "Yeah, man. Not a good sign. Not that I'm an expert."

Fuck. That was my instinct too, but I didn't want to creep her out with twenty calls.

I went closer to the steps of the cellar and sent her a message. There was enough signal for that.

Tyler: Kendra, I need to talk to you. I'm not sure if you saw the picture, but it's not what it looked like. I know it sounds cliché, but it's not. Call me when you see this.

Going back to the group, I saw the party was already breaking up. The tastings never lasted long, because typically Tate had a conference with his team once it was over, giving them our feedback. Besides, since this was a last-minute thing, most of us had plans for the rest of the day. Mine consisted of watching some old games and hopefully talking to Kendra.

"Everyone, thanks for coming," Tate said. "This was helpful. I'm going to discuss your input with the team. It'll make for great marketing copy."

Travis patted my shoulder. He'd linked an arm with Reese. "Ready to go?"

"Sure."

We all left at the same time, except Lexi and Tate—he was

doing the conference on his laptop from here, and she'd wait for him to finish—and Mom and Dad, who decided to walk around the vineyard.

I checked my phone as soon as I was in the car. Kendra had replied.

Kendra: My phone was on mute. I'm at the Local Arts and Crafts Festival. I'm going to a dinner thing for work in one hour. Anyway, it's super loud. I did see the picture.

Fuck. I needed to find her and explain everything. I didn't want her to think I was dicking around.

"Anyone know anything about the Local Arts and Crafts Festival?" I asked.

Reese perked up. "Oh yeah, they've got several bands and lots of booths selling handmade items and local crafts. It's in Millennium Park. Why?"

"Kendra's there. That's why she couldn't pick up. I'm going to go there after you drop me off at home."

They were silent for a bit, and then Travis said, "You know, it would be much faster if we just drop you off there."

"And we promise to stay in the car and not peek, or come with you unless you want us to," Reese said.

I burst out laughing. "You think I need chaperones?"

"Honestly, I'm not sure," Travis said.

"Oh fuck off," I said good-naturedly.

"So, should we go to the fair?" Reese asked, looking far too excited.

It *was* smart to go directly there. Especially since Kendra was leaving for her dinner soon.

"Hey, why not, man?" Travis asked. "We can vouch for you. You're a good guy and have a good head on those shoulders. You have good taste in women most of the time. Well, judging by Blair, actually, no."

"Travis, darling, I think you shouldn't talk at all," Reese noted.

"I have a better idea. Why don't both of you keep quiet?" I grumbled.

CHAPTER FIFTEEN
KENDRA

"We can just grow old together and buy cats," Emma said, trying on a hat from The Hat Booth.

"I do like cats," I said.

"Want to continue our 'spill-it' conversation?" she asked, looking at me from under the huge pink hat. It actually looked good on her.

I shook my head. "No. That pic took the wind out of my sails," I confessed.

This morning, I called my sister and had one of our spill-it sessions. Like a good sister, this afternoon, she texted me a picture from the game, asking me if I was sure Tyler was single. The question shocked me because, honestly, I didn't even think about asking. I didn't take a good look at the picture at first, but once I zoomed in a bit and saw how close they were, I zoomed right back out. But it was branded in my brain.

I wanted to be reasonable. It was before we even kissed. But I was really hoping she wasn't his girlfriend or something, because I absolutely didn't want to be participating in cheating in any way. My heart had already shriveled to the size of a peanut, though. I tried to cling to those happy moments during our trip and last night, but a small voice kept taunting me: *You don't really think you can be this happy, do you?*

"Do you want to talk to him?" she asked, taking a sip of her pumpkin spice latte. Every booth seemed to have at least a pumpkin on the counter. Some were plain, and some had the typical Halloween eyes and mouth carved out.

"He did text me saying he wants to explain." Which I thought was good. It meant he cared. I knew he'd dated a bit; he'd said as much. But was it dated or dating—as in present tense? I was petrified at the thought that I might have been fooling around with someone who was in a relationship.

"That's a good sign."

"But let's not talk about him anymore, okay? Let's enjoy the fair."

I loved going out with my sister. Emma talked me into coming to the festival after work. Well, in between work was more appropriate. I was having dinner with some past volunteers who wanted an update on a project we'd started together. I only had about half an hour left before I had to go to the restaurant, which was only a couple blocks away.

The fair was lively and packed, and I loved the energy. There were booths lined up all over the perimeter. The band played a number of catchy songs. They were talented, but it was too loud for my taste. Currently, we were looking at stands with trinkets, colorful jewelry, and hats. I wasn't buying anything, but I was giving my opinion to Emma.

"Those earrings would look fabulous on you," she said, pointing to a pair with dangling half-moons.

I shook my head, "No can do. After I move and stop paying rent, I'll finally be able to spoil myself a bit, but until then, I'm going to suck it up."

"I can buy them for you," she said excitedly.

"No, no, no, I won't hear of it." I appreciated the thought, but Emma didn't need to be spending her money on me.

"Oh, come on, sis. You've always bought me things. Let me do the same for you now, please? Pretty pleaaaase?"

I shook my head, dragging my sister away from the stand before she got other ideas. "No. I'm the older sister. You don't get to invite me or buy anything for me."

"One of these days, I'll change your mind on that."

"Let's change the subject. How was your date?" I asked. "You haven't said one word about the guy, so I'm assuming it didn't go well."

She scrunched her nose. "No, that was one of the worst dates I've had, and I didn't think it was possible to surpass the guy who showed up half an hour later and then shamelessly told me he was coming from a date and had one after me."

I grimaced. "Okay, I won't ask for details, then."

"Exactly. I don't think I like these online dating apps at all."

"Told you they're tricky. You can't really tell anything about a person when they're hiding behind a screen."

"Let's focus on finding a hat. I've decided I need one. They have touristy prices here, but I like supporting local artists. Give me your honest opinion."

She tried on five different hats. One looked like something out of *The Great Gatsby*, but it looked great on her. Two had a round, decent bowl, and the other two had huge ones. I didn't like the last two.

"I understand huge hats in the summer. They protect you from the sun. But when it's cold out, they're just weird."

"Yeah, you're right." Turning to the sales associate, she handed her the black one with a small rim. "I'm taking this one."

She paid quickly, and then we scoured the perimeter, deciding what to do next.

"Hey, isn't that Tyler there?" She pointed to the entrance booth.

I turned around abruptly, and my heart somersaulted.

"Oh wow."

"What's he doing here?" she asked. "Did you tell him where we are?"

"Yeah, I did. But..."

"Oh my God, then he must be here to talk to you. Oh look, I think he's spotted us."

He had indeed. I also noticed two people behind him, a man and a woman.

"I'm staying right here next to you," Emma exclaimed.

"Thanks."

Tyler walked straight to us.

"Hi, you must be Emma," he said, looking at my sister.

"Yes I am. Nice to meet you, Tyler."

"This is my brother Travis and my cousin Reese," he said, and they both waved.

"Hey, nice to meet you both," I said.

"I want to talk to you, Kendra," Tyler said without further ado, looking straight at me.

I steeled myself, rolling my shoulders. "Okay."

"Let's go somewhere quieter," he suggested. That was probably a good idea, because you could only hear someone if you were very close with all the loud music around.

"It's rather empty over there," Reese said, pointing to the right. "The stands there closed already."

We turned and headed in that direction. I walked in front of him, acutely aware of his presence just a few inches behind me. Had he told me he was coming and I didn't see the message?

When we reached the area with the closed stands, I turned around, looking straight at him.

"I'll cut to the chase, Kendra. I only saw that picture when my brother showed it to me."

My shoulders slumped. "I saw it earlier today."

"Why didn't you say something?" he asked, sounding confused.

"Like what? 'Hey, Tyler, do you have a girlfriend, and am I your dirty secret?'"

He jerked his head back. "You thought I have...? No, I don't. Damn it, Kendra, I don't. What kind of an asshole do you think I am?"

I put my hands on my hips, shifting my weight from one leg to the other. "I don't know. It was the first thing that came to my mind. And why shouldn't you have one? You're hot and a great kisser and—"

"You think I'm a great kisser?"

I sighed. "Really?"

"You brought it up," he said, then shook his head, turning serious once more. "Kendra, no, I'm not seeing anyone." He came a bit closer, looking me straight in the eyes, and I was rooted in my spot. "I kissed you. I flirted with you. I made you mine. I want to do it all over again and again. That was just a fan who wanted me to sign her chest. I shut her down. Want to know what I was thinking about?"

"What?" I whispered.

"You."

I licked my lips, pushing a strand of hair behind my ear. "But you barely know me."

"And I'm going to change that." He tilted his head, coming closer. "I want to know you. Your thoughts. Wishes. Desires. Everything." His voice was decadent now. Somehow the energy between us changed. It was more charged.

"When is your dinner?"

"In twenty minutes."

He groaned, looking around. Then he shook his head as if having a conversation with himself.

"Come on, let's get back to the group."

Hmm... this is suspicious.

He put his hand at the small of my back, and I straightened up as if a current went through me. Energy zipped through my whole body. I felt so connected to him that it was surreal.

His passionate confession of the incident was real; could I hope that Tyler was as into me as I was into him? I felt on cloud nine right now and very thankful I wasn't an unwitting cheater. I would never do that to someone knowingly.

Emma, Reese, and Travis were in front of a booth, enjoying drinks, laughing their asses off. My sister had a talent for making friends quickly, but this was a record even for her.

She glanced straight at me, and I knew what that look meant. She was silently asking: Is he an asshole, or was it a misunderstanding? I smiled to indicate that everything was fine. She instantly lit up.

She wasn't suspicious of Tyler at all anymore. And neither was I.

"You two are back already?" she teased. "After what these two told me, I was thinking you might have thrown her over your shoulder and kidnapped her."

"Crossed my mind," Tyler said seriously, pressing his fingers deeper into the small of my back, and holy shit, this time, the energy crawling through me went right between my thighs.

Ha! That was why he was checking out the area.

"What exactly did you tell her?" Tyler asked.

"Well, you said we should keep quiet around Kendra, but you didn't warn us specifically about her sister," Reese said, "so obviously we told her you're a decent guy."

"That you don't double-dip your dick," Travis added.

Tyler burst out laughing. I felt my cheeks heat up.

"This one's very outspoken," Reese explained, pointing her thumb at Travis.

"Duly noted," I murmured.

Emma zeroed in on Tyler. "You're looking a bit too territorial, Tyler."

"Emma," I admonished. Like Travis, she was very outspoken too.

"And like you might not let her get to her dinner at all."

Tyler looked at me. "Is your sister a mind reader or something?"

"You were thinking about interfering with my *work* dinner?" I asked.

He flashed me a cocky smile. "It crossed my mind."

"Yeah, we should warn you," Travis cut in. "Sometimes he sort of runs his own show."

"Most of the time, actually," Reese said, "with complete disregard for manners."

"Good to know," I whispered.

Tyler's hand moved to my waist, pulling me close to him. "You'll have plenty of opportunities to witness that, Kendra. What's your schedule like for the rest of the week?"

"Work and... that's it. Why?"

He didn't reply, just looked at me intently—like he had *plans*.

My pulse sped up as he pinned me with those determined eyes, and I just knew this sexy hockey player was going to turn my life upside down.

Excitement bubbled up inside me, even though I wasn't 100 percent sure I was ready for what was to come.

CHAPTER SIXTEEN
KENDRA

I left for my dinner a few minutes later, ordering an Uber even though it wasn't too far away. I didn't want to be late.

As soon as I got in the car, my phone lit up with a message from Tyler.

Tyler: I can't wait to see you again, sexy girl.

Kendra: Hey, don't make me blush. I'm in a car, I'll be at the restaurant in seven minutes, and I don't want to be red in the face.

Tyler: That way, everyone will know you have someone to make you blush.

Kendra: Or they'll think I ate chilies, like in Seattle.

I held my breath, waiting for his reply, shimmying a bit in my seat. A small part of me was all for some sexting, but...

Tyler: Text me when you're home, beautiful.

Oh, I planned to do just that. During the ride I also got a message from a contractor I'd asked for a quote on tiles and flooring. He didn't have time until spring. I needed someone as soon as possible, but I had to push the issue to the back of my mind for now.

. . .

THE DINNER LASTED until 10:00 p.m. I liked catching up with past clients, and it filled me with joy when they came back for more projects. But this time, I couldn't wait to get home. I debated messaging Tyler on the way, but I didn't want to start blushing in the Uber. I could wait a few more minutes until I was in my apartment; then there would be no one to witness it.

I practically jumped out of the Uber after it pulled in front of my building. There was a line in front of the elevator, so I took the stairs two at a time. My apartment was only on the third floor, so I often took the stairs; I felt like I was getting my cardio in whenever I avoided the elevator.

The second I entered my apartment I took out my phone and messaged Tyler so quickly that I nearly broke a nail.

Kendra: I'm home.

He called me the next second. I hadn't even finished taking off my shoes. Grinning, I darted straight to my bedroom, sitting on the bed, and answered him.

"Hey, Kendra," he said.

"Hey."

"How was your dinner?"

"Great. I love catching up with past volunteers. It's been an amazing evening." Except for the part where the contractor didn't have time for me. I groaned just remembering.

"But you sound a bit off."

"You're observant. You know how I told you about that house I bought? Well, I'm still waiting on contractors to quote me on tiles and flooring, and one said he doesn't have time until spring. I need someone who can do it now."

I moved to the center of the bed, propping myself against the pillows.

"I can talk to my brother, Luke. He's an architect, and he works with a lot of contractors."

"Oh my God! You think he'd be able to recommend someone to me?"

"I'm sure he can."

I smiled. "That would be great. Thanks so much. Wow, you are so thoughtful."

"I'll talk to him. When do you plan on moving?"

"As soon as it's done. I've wanted to own a house for years. It's almost like a dream that I thought might never happen." I held my breath, biting the inside of my cheek. This was an intimate part of me that I didn't often reveal.

"I'm guessing it's making you feel safe after everything you've been through."

"Yes, exactly." But the weird part was, I felt safe with him, and it wasn't a feeling I was used to.

"What are you doing tomorrow?" he asked.

"Well, I'm going to be at the office all day, going through a lot of admin stuff that I couldn't do while I was away. You?"

"Management wants to talk to me."

I sat up straighter. "Oh, why?"

"They didn't say, so it could go either way."

"I'll keep my fingers crossed, and toes, and legs." I stretched out, crossing my legs at my ankles, and leaned back into my pillows. "My God, my bed is so comfy."

"You're in your bed?" he asked.

"Yeah."

"What are you wearing?"

"Um, my clothes."

"Take them off for me."

"You're bossy on the phone too."

"Hell yes."

My nipples perked up. Hmm, I could play this game. I'd

never flirted like this on the phone, but there was a first time for everything.

"What should I start with?"

"What are you wearing?"

"The same thing I was wearing at the fair."

"You had a jacket on."

"It was open."

"Kendra, the only thing I was focused on was clarifying what happened, so you had no doubt about my interest in you."

"I don't," I assured him in a whisper. And I didn't. For him to come see me at the fair and clear my mind of any concerns was proof of his caring in itself.

Clearing my throat, I decided to turn things playful again. "I'm wearing a skirt and a sweater." I left out that I was also wearing tights because there was nothing sexy about that. But I desperately needed them starting in November or I'd freeze off some pretty intimate parts.

"Take off your sweater slowly."

I did as he asked, dragging my fingers up over my bra as I went. Goose bumps prickled along my skin. I heard his breathing on the phone. It was almost like he was here with me.

"It's gone," I whispered.

"And now your skirt."

"You're getting naughty."

"You have no clue just how naughty I want to get."

I pushed down my skirt and the silly tights, letting my fingers wander back up.

"What do you want me to do with my bra and panties?"

He groaned a guttural sound that turned me on. I was instantly soaked.

"Nothing."

I blinked rapidly. "What do you mean, nothing?"

"I can't do this and not race to your place and knock down the door."

I swallowed hard. "So why don't you do it?"

"Because first I want to take you on that date I promised you. I don't want you to think this is just physical."

I blinked. Had he really said those words? I'd been dating on and off for my whole adult life, and I was sure I'd never heard it.

"Wow," I breathed, not sure what to say back.

"I mean it, Kendra. I don't want you to feel like you're my secret or something. You're special to me, and I want you to know that."

I winced. "Is this because of what I said at the fair? I just said it because of the photo, you know?"

"I know. But I have big plans."

"Oh? Details?"

"Just one: tomorrow will be a big day," he said cryptically.

"Don't be mean. I want to know more."

"I don't know how long the meeting will take with management. It's at five."

"Okay." I debated trying to lure out more of what he had in mind, but I decided to let it go. I yawned, pushing down my soaked panties.

"What are you doing?" he asked.

"Yawning."

"There was another sound."

"Are you sure you want details? You might break down my door."

"Kendra." His voice was raspy and oh-so-deliciously commanding.

"I'm taking off my panties, okay? They're wet, and it's all your doing. You don't even have to be here and this happens to me. I'm not even sure how it's possible."

"You're driving me crazy, woman."

I bit my lip. He wanted to take me out on a date. I wanted him to come bang down my door. Even though the devil on my shoulder was egging me to continue teasing him, he was being such a gentleman that it wasn't fair.

"Okay, how about we call it a night?" I suggested.

"I'll be in touch tomorrow, beautiful. Good night."

I was giddy once we hung up, and I took off my bra. Instead of going to bed, I went to my pantry, glancing at the mountain of boxes I had there. They were full of books, summer clothes, along with all sorts of stuff like extra plates that I didn't need on a daily basis. I'd booked a moving company to take them to the house the next day, so I stayed up late and packed six more boxes.

All the time, I couldn't stop thinking about Tyler. I'd always been realistic—too realistic and focused on reality, according to Emma. Growing up, that had seemed like the only way to get through the day, and in time, it became a habit. I never let myself be silly and daydream.

But I couldn't help but daydream about my sexy hockey player.

CHAPTER SEVENTEEN
TYLER

Meetings with management were not one of my favorite things, but I put on my most amicable smile as I sat across from John Daniels, our general manager. He got up, pacing his huge-ass office, not looking at me, just talking, as if he spoke to himself. I'd been fazed the first time he did this but then got used to it.

"I'm happy to say that the board is pleased with your volunteering efforts, and our sponsors too. You're taking it seriously. Actually, from what we've heard, you're going above and beyond what was asked. That's always good."

"I like volunteering," I said honestly. "I like the kids and enjoy teaching them the game. They're quick learners."

He straightened up, looking me in the eye. It was maybe the third time he'd ever done that. The last time was when he told me I was benched for the foreseeable future.

"The board and I discussed this, and we've also consulted with your physical therapist. He said you still need a couple of weeks to get back in shape. The shoulder's good, but your skating needs some practice to get back your reflexes, though that shouldn't be a problem. After that, we'll put you back on the ice. Obviously, Jett is still going to be the main goalie until we're sure you're in top shape."

Holy shit, is he serious?

I rose to my feet. My heart slammed against my rib cage, and adrenaline pulsed through my veins. Although I was disappointed that I wasn't the main goalie, it was fair to Jett since he already had a few games behind him, and he was in better shape than I was. But it was a start. I used to be the best goalie in the league before all this, but I'd have to earn that title back.

"Tyler, it's imperative that you keep pleasing the sponsors, the press. Everyone needs to see your commitment to the team."

"I never gave anyone any reason to doubt that."

He sighed. "We've been through this before. As a public person, everything you do is being watched, scrutinized, judged."

"Let's not go through this again," I said, my voice hard.

"We're not. I was just reminding you."

"Is this a probationary thing?" I questioned, wanting him to put all the cards on the table. The man was so reserved. It pissed me off. He always minced his words, and then when you least expected it, he'd pull the rug from under you. It was his team, obviously, so he could do whatever he wanted. But to him, this was a business; to me, it was about the game.

"No it's not. I want 100 percent from you. But if things escalate again outside of the ice rink, anything is possible, even a trade."

I blinked, narrowing my eyes, "I'm your best goalie. Why would you let me go?"

"I just explained that to you."

Fuck him, I didn't want to be traded. The Chicago Blades had been my team for eight years. My family was here in Chicago. I wasn't going to go anywhere. I only had two more years on the ice max, and I planned to spend them with *my* team.

"Thanks for the warning," I said. The ball was in my court to make this happen. If I fucked up it was on me.

"And I trust you heeded my advice about Miss Kendra?"

"No. And that's 100 percent my business. If you're gonna warn me—"

"That was just advice, not a warning. Mixing business and pleasure is never a good idea."

"I've given the Blades everything I've got for eight years. My personal life is *my own*." As was every other players'—but he didn't get into *their* shit.

"Fair enough. I trust you know what you're doing. Just make sure your head is in the game, Maxwell."

"I will."

Even though I was pissed off at Daniels, I was in a good mood when I came out of the club. I felt on top of the world. I was going to get back on the ice faster than I'd expected. My shoulder was still giving me a few aches and pains, but I knew I'd bring it just where I needed it to be in a few weeks, and then the game was on.

I called my brother Travis right away. I wanted to celebrate with my family, and I knew he had the most time right now.

"Hey, man, what's up?" he said.

"They're putting me back on the ice."

"What? That's fantastic news."

"I want to take everyone out for drinks tomorrow."

"Tomorrow? Why not tonight?" Travis asked. Like I said, the man was bored.

"I've got plans already."

"So cancel them, and let's hit the town."

"I've got plans with Kendra."

He whistled. "Damn."

"So tell everyone that Operation Coddling Tyler is over."

"That was never the name of the operation."

I chuckled. "Whatever it is, it's not necessary anymore."

"Roger that. Have fun."

"I will."

I hadn't actually made plans with Kendra yet, but that was just a technicality. This was one of the best things to happen to me, and I wanted to celebrate it with her.

I texted her right away.

Tyler: Hey, what are you doing?

Kendra: Still at the office, trying to finish a schedule. Feels a bit like putting together a puzzle that's beyond my age limit, and I can't make all the pieces fit together.

I decided to surprise her.

Once I arrived at the office building, I found the front door open and went straight inside. I was expecting to find Kendra with her sister or on her own. Instead, there was a guy in there.

"Thank you so much, Alex," she said. "I'll sign everything for you, and you can take it right back."

He was carrying a backpack. He was probably a bike messenger. His eyes were fixed on Kendra while she signed some papers. He was obviously checking her out, and I didn't like it one bit.

"Kendra, I'm here," I said. She looked up at me, and the corners of her mouth instantly lifted.

"Tyler, hey!"

"Holy shit," the guy exclaimed. "You're Tyler Maxwell. Man, I'm such a fan of the Blades. I hope you get back on the ice soon. You're the best goalie they've got. How's your shoulder?"

"Healing," I said.

"Can I get your autograph? I have a pen. Damn, I don't have paper!"

"Here, I have one for you," Kendra said, taking a sheet from the printer.

"Can you autograph this for me, man? My name's Alex."

I quickly signed my name for the overecstatic Alex, eager to get him out.

"Kendra, you didn't tell me you knew this guy."

"I'm not at liberty to talk about my clients," she said.

Client. I wasn't just a fucking client, and I wanted this guy to know it. I stepped closer to Kendra, putting an arm around her waist. I felt her tense. Didn't she want us to go public? Then I tilted my head to take a closer look at her. Her eyes were wide in surprise. Okay, surprise was good.

The guy's mouth hung open when he looked at the autograph, and then his eyes rested on my arm. Yeah, I was damn possessive, but I wanted him to get the message. And he did.

"Kendra, thanks for being so quick. And thank you too, man, for the autograph. I'll be going now."

He secured his backpack, folding the sheet of paper and putting it in his pocket before leaving, closing the door behind him.

The second we were alone, Kendra looked up at me.

A smile was tugging at the corners of her mouth. "Mr. Superstar Goalie, what's with this?" She tapped the fingers I had on her waist.

"He was checking you out."

She cocked her brow. "Um, well, he's asked me out a few times."

I jerked my head back. "You went out with him?"

"No, he *asked* me. I didn't say yes."

"Woman, you want to drive me crazy?" I tightened my grip on her waist, bringing her flush against my chest.

"Me telling you a random guy asked me out like a year ago drives you crazy?"

"Fuck yes. Drove me crazy just seeing him looking at you."

Her lips parted. "Wow. How can *you* be jealous of anyone?"

I hoisted her up on her desk, parting her legs wide and standing between them. "I don't know."

I touched her face, stretching my fingers on her jaw and cheek, fixing her with my gaze. "Any time I think about a guy even looking at you, I want to make it clear to everyone that you're off-limits."

"And why is that?" she whispered.

"Because you're mine, Kendra. Your kisses are mine. Everything is mine."

"Tyler..."

"I want you so damn bad. But that's not why I came here."

Clearing her throat, she flashed me a smile, shimmying farther back on her desk. "Let it be noted that I *wouldn't* give in. I mean, I know it looked like that, but I'm tough, and I can ignore the sexiness you're exuding."

"Is that a challenge?" I wiggled my eyebrows.

Her cheeks flushed. "Why don't you tell me how it went with management?"

"They're putting me back on the ice in a few weeks."

She gasped. "That's amazing. I'm so happy for you."

"And I want to celebrate tonight with you."

Her face exploded in a huge smile. "You're looking at me like you want to devour me."

"That's exactly what I want."

"One kiss, and then we're out of here." She grinned, pulling me closer to her.

"I'm gonna try real hard to make that happen."

I kissed her hard, wanting to leave a mark of sorts on her. I needed her with an intensity that was new to me, one I'd only felt before when I was on the ice. I didn't want to fight it. I wanted to claim her in every way possible.

CHAPTER EIGHTEEN
KENDRA

"Where are you taking me?" I asked him as we walked along Columbus, stopping for a few minutes in front of the Buckingham Fountain. He'd parked nearby so I assumed the location for our date wasn't far away.

"To the best steak restaurant Chicago has to offer."

"Ooooh, I can't wait. I love steak."

"I know. You told me at the cabin. That's why I made reservations there."

I warmed up in all the places where we were touching. He still had an arm possessively around my waist as if he wanted to make sure anyone passing us knew exactly what was going on here. This was surreal. Ever since I met him, I sort of felt like I was living in a parallel universe.

A gust of wind blew around us, chilling me completely. November was here. The air was brisk and a bit foggy. Thank God for the lampposts, because it was already pitch dark.

"How was your day?" he asked.

"It was great. I started it with a visit to my house. A moving company took my boxes there. I'm keeping them in the basement."

"You're really looking forward to moving, huh?"

"Yeah. I feel like I'm almost living there because at least I brought some stuff over."

"You're cute."

We arrived at our destination a few minutes later. The restaurant was very cozy, giving off a cosmopolitan vibe with wood-paneled walls and brass chandeliers—it was an eclectic mix. Some seemed to be of oriental origin, while others were more industrial.

Tyler and I were seated at a corner table with a bench, so we sat on adjacent sides of the table. He had a particularly smug smile.

"Why are you smiling?" I asked. I didn't mind at all. I just wanted to be prepared for whatever he had in mind.

He didn't say anything because the waitress appeared, bringing us the menus. After she left, he looked at me out of the corner of his eye.

I was acutely aware of him sitting very close to me. My eyes popped when I glanced at the prices, and my stomach sank. *Holy fuck.* Steak was usually expensive, but this was completely ridiculous. How could a steak cost as much as a dress?

They didn't have too many options, so I glanced quickly to see what else I could order.

"Um, I'm not that hungry. I'll just take a Caesar salad." It was by far the cheapest thing on the menu.

Tyler's brows knitted together. "What do you mean? You like steak, right? You were excited about it."

"Yeah, but I'm not feeling too hungry." I sounded ridiculous.

"Kendra, what's wrong, baby? If you don't like it, we can go somewhere else."

"It's just so expensive," I whispered, looking around.

"Babe, this is a date. I'm taking you out. You don't have to worry about anything, and you're not paying for any of this."

I shook my head. "That's not the point. I feel guilty spending anyone's money like this."

"If I want to splurge to treat my girlfriend, I will."

Okay, wow. He just called me his girlfriend.

I looked back at the menu, biting the inside of my cheek. Splurging had never been part of my vocabulary. It couldn't. The most splurging I ever did was treat myself to popcorn *and* nachos when going to see a movie.

"Kendra, if you're feeling uncomfortable, tell me, and we'll go somewhere else. But if you want to stay here, if you're curious to try this, just let me do this for you, okay?"

"Okay," I said.

"You promise you'll enjoy it? We don't have to stay because we came here. I don't want you to be uncomfortable."

I sighed, looking up at him. "How can I not enjoy it? I'm here with the sexiest guy alive."

He smirked. "The sexiest guy alive? I don't think anyone's ever called me that."

It was my turn to cock a brow in disbelief. "Maybe not to your face. I'm—"

"Are you ready to order?" the waitress interrupted, appearing in front of us.

Tyler looked at me.

"Yes," I said, "we're ready."

We both ordered the house specialty: steak with fries, fried green beans, and salad.

"And champagne," he said.

I shimmied in my seat after the waitress left. "That's right. We have something to celebrate."

He covered my hand with his over the table, stroking my

palm with his thumb. "Ever since I got the news, I wanted to celebrate with you."

"I'm so happy for you," I said honestly. "Especially because it happened so quickly."

"I was expecting them to keep punishing me for a while. I can't wait to get back on the ice."

"Hockey is important to you."

He nodded. "It's my life, to be honest."

"How did you get into it?"

"We played after school, and I was hooked. Then I begged my parents to take me to lessons, and they did, and from there it was history. I only realized later how much of a toll it would take on them, especially Mom, to drive me to games or take me to train and then for her and Dad to spend all that time in the stands. I didn't know it at the time, but it added a lot to their already busy day. But their efforts paid off. I'm the best goalie in the league."

"I'm sure they're proud. But again, I think they would be proud no matter what."

"Yeah, I think so too. They're great people."

"Did you ever think about going into the bookstore business back when they still owned the chain?" I asked.

"Honestly, no. I got the hockey bug early on, and by the time I was in college and playing, my parents had sold the company. They even set up trust funds for all of us kids. But I left all the money in the Maxwell trust. Maybe it's going to help future generations. I don't need the money anyway."

My eyes bulged. "Wow. I can't even wrap my mind around the idea of anyone working this hard when they don't need it."

"I can't say it's hard work."

I chuckled. "You train for hours a day, and you travel all the time. It *is* hard work. Your hotness score increased."

He looked at me with genuine surprise in his eyes. "The things that are important to you fascinate me."

Our food arrived a few minutes later.

"That was quick," I said.

The steak was mouthwatering. When I tasted it, I couldn't help but close my eyes and hum in pleasure. It truly was the best I'd ever had. It said on the menu that they cooked it with the sous vide method, so it was extra tender. And the flavor was to die for. I tried to block out the price, but it was dancing behind my eyelids, mocking me.

I opened my eyes, looking straight at Tyler, determined to enjoy this without even one ounce of guilt. Easier said than done.

"And?" he asked.

"It's amazing. Thank you for bringing me here."

"I'm glad you like it."

We chatted a bit about his schedule and how training the kids would change while we ate. The fries and the beans were perfect too, of course. Honestly, I couldn't wrap my mind around the fact that food could taste like this. But I'd never been to a restaurant this fancy.

We both ate quickly. I only paused to breathe after my plate was clean, as Tyler finished his meal too.

"By the way, I asked Luke about contractors. He said he found someone, and he'll have him contact you directly in a couple days. If you don't like him, no problem."

"Oh my gosh, that's amazing. I'm sure I will, but it depends if he's in my price range. I can't wait to move in. When Emma and I were kids, we daydreamed about the house we'd live in together all the time. We wouldn't have any nosy neighbors, and we'd each have a room. This one comes pretty close in the layout. However, I've yet to talk my sister into moving in with me. We're a bit too old for that now, but I'd love it."

"You're a remarkable woman, Kendra."

"Because I bought a house?" I asked, genuinely confused.

"Because you've been through a lot, and you're such a fighter."

"It wasn't a big deal, and I got used to it pretty fast. Though it was a bit stressful to always walk on tiptoes and make sure the neighbors couldn't tell we were home alone."

"How was your relationship with your mom?"

"She was a very sweet person, always talked and reasoned with us and played a ton of games. She rarely yelled. After Dad passed away, she was mostly working. When she came home in the evening, she was too tired to do much. I used to heat up her dinner, and the three of us would sit on the couch, and she'd ask us to tell her about our day. She always listened. I miss her. I hope she's looking down on me and is proud."

He squeezed my hand. "I'm sure she is. You're a great person. I admire that about you."

"Oh yeah? What else?"

He shifted closer. "Everything. That you're hardworking and caring." He put a hand on my leg, moving it from midthigh to my knee and back up. "And so damn sexy when you follow my commands in the bedroom."

I gasped, pressing my thighs together. "That escalated quickly."

We'd only had a bit of champagne, not nearly enough to go to my head. I was just drunk on him. The fact that he brought me here and looked at me with that mix of possessiveness and admiration was more than I could have dreamed of.

"It's going to escalate a whole lot more. You're damn sexy in this skirt."

Hmm... maybe he had more to drink, and I didn't notice? Because I was still wearing my office attire: skirt and blouse.

"You're looking at me like you're already planning to take it off."

"That's exactly what I'm thinking about."

He feathered his thumb on my thigh, pinning me with those soulful eyes. "Spend the night with me, Kendra."

I sucked in a breath, leaning in slightly. "I thought you'd never ask."

"Is that so?"

"Hell yes. I appreciate you being such a gentleman. But since last night, all I can think about is you knocking down my door."

He groaned, pressing his fingers into my thigh. "You're killing me, Kendra."

CHAPTER NINETEEN
KENDRA

I never saw anyone move so fast. Within minutes, he'd already paid the bill. We ended up going to his place, a condo in a modern thirty-story building in the West Loop. The sexual tension between us was palpable, and we barely spoke during the elevator ride. The second we were inside his home, he sealed his mouth over mine.

He undressed me right there in the foyer, and I wasn't too shy either. I needed my man naked. Pronto.

When I was completely naked, he took a step back. God, the way he looked at me was like I was the most beautiful woman he'd ever seen. That was how I felt right then anyway. He first looked down, focusing on my mouth before descending to my chest, resting on my hips, and then between my legs. When he slid his gaze back up, we made eye contact, and I felt myself blushing. I was desperate for him, just because I was seeing him naked up close like this. I stepped even closer, and I could smell his shower gel.

"What do you want, Kendra?" he asked.

"You. I just want you."

We were both too lost in each other to move from where we

were. He smiled slowly. It was a wolfish expression like I'd just walked into a trap. Oh sweet Lord, I'd let this man trap me all day long and do with me whatever he wanted.

A second later, I realized that was exactly what was about to happen.

He turned me around, so I was facing the wall. I was so excited to let him take the lead, shaking with need and anticipation and a crazy desire for him. I felt him at my back, chest to my shoulders, cock pressing against my right ass cheek. Goose bumps broke out on my skin. He smelled so decadent and delicious. He skimmed his hands down my arms, clasping our fingers together, then brought his mouth to my ear. At the same time, he propped our hands at the same level with my head on the wall.

"Keep your hands here, or I'll stop," he said in a strong, no-argument-allowed tone. I didn't have to ask what he meant, because I knew exactly what he planned: to turn me on and give me pleasure. And I was absolutely in favor of that.

He kissed my right shoulder, moving down my arm. I could still feel his cock between us, pulsing. I gasped. He moved to my other shoulder, teasing me there too, before kissing down my back. The lower he went, the more aroused I became. I wanted him so much that I could barely breathe. I didn't know what to do with all this desire I had pent up in me. I couldn't even move my hands. But somehow, internalizing all this just made me more sensitive to him. I guessed that was his plan all along, and it was working.

When I felt his lips on my right ass cheek, I gasped, and then he slid one finger inside me. My vision dimmed at the corners. I didn't expect the wave of pleasure ricocheting through my body. It was almost too much. Then, just as quickly, he took his finger out. When I was about to protest, I felt a wet kiss on my left ass cheek, and he slid in two fingers. If I thought it was too much before, now I felt like I was about to explode. When he curved his fingers, I cried out, pressing my forehead against the wall. My legs weakened. My pussy was on fire. I was so overwhelmed that I didn't even know where I was or what was happening. I just knew I was hyperaware of this pleasure and *him*.

"I love seeing you like this," he said in the same rugged voice as before. Wait, no, it seemed even richer somehow, and it had an edge.

"Tyler, this is so good, so good. Can I drop my hands now?" I asked somewhat shyly.

"Why?"

"I want to touch you."

He said nothing for a few moments, and then he drew out his fingers and took away his mouth. For a split second, I thought he was carrying through with his initial promise to stop if I lowered my hands.

Then he flipped me around. I licked my lips, watching him take out a condom from his wallet and roll it on. *Oh my!* Tendrils of heat spread through my body. He moved his mouth from my pussy to my navel and then back down, putting one of my legs up on the chair by the entrance. He kissed my inner thighs slowly. I touched him, first tugging at his hair and then groping his shoulders. I loved his shoulders so much. I made a mental note to truly explore them tonight.

When he reached my pussy, I fisted his hair. There was nothing gentle about it; I wanted him so much that I was close to climbing on his face. I felt him smile against my folds before he pressed his tongue over my clit, and I pushed back against the wall, steeling myself. But the wave of pleasure was still crushing, and I cried out. The orgasm reverberated from my center throughout my whole body: my arms and legs, my throat. I blinked my eyes open, but I only saw black. I felt him kiss up my body, moving over my navel, between my breasts, and then finally up my neck.

"Fuck, you're so beautiful. I want to make you come all night and watch you."

"Mmm, I like that plan," I whispered.

He cupped my face with the hand he'd had on my thigh the whole time, drawing his forefinger and middle finger over my lips. His other hand was still between my thighs. Feeling his fingers over my mouth and between my legs at the same time was enough to bring me to the edge yet again in seconds. He knew just which buttons to press, where to kiss and touch to make me desperate for him. He knew my body even better than I did.

He looked at my mouth for a few seconds before sealing his lips over mine. At the same time, he cupped the backs of my upper thighs, brushing the tips of his fingers on my ass cheeks, lifting me. I propped my knees around his thighs.

He was still kissing me when he slid inside me, all at once, knocking the breath out of me. He was so damn huge. He stilled, not moving even an inch. I braced my palms on his shoulders, pressing my forehead against his chest and breathing hard until my inner muscles relaxed around him. The tightness I felt with him inside me wasn't uncomfortable, just filling, and I shuddered with pleasure. The wall was cold and a bit rough, scratching my skin. His chest was so damn hot. He moved his hand on my ass to make a buffer between my skin and the wall, and I rolled my hips back and forth.

"Babe, are you okay? Was I too rough?"

"No, I love it. Please don't hold back."

He groaned, a loud feral sound, then slid in and out, and I knew he'd lost control. He was so in control of himself during foreplay and while he pleasured me, but once he was inside me, something unleashed within him, and that made me immensely happy. I clung tight to his shoulders, digging my fingers into his skin. I wanted to touch him with at least one hand, but there was no way I could support myself with just one palm.

"Tyler, I want to touch you. I need it," I said in a pleading tone.

He slowed his pace, and then he stilled, looking me in the eyes. God, this man was just so sexy. He put me down, and then we went to the living room. He kept kissing my shoulder from behind with an arm around my waist. We only made it to the dining table.

I lifted myself on it, spreading my thighs wide. He looked at me with a wry smile before thrusting inside me. "You're so fucking sexy, Kendra, and you feel so damn good." Then his words turned to grunts, and instinct overpowered again.

I was overwhelmed by pleasure. Every muscle screamed for release, every cell tight with tension, ready to explode. I felt him thicken inside me, and his grunts turned feral, his thrusts desperate. And then we both gave in to pleasure.

I clamped down on him, throwing my head back and crying out loud, not even bothering to cover my mouth. I felt free with him, free to express myself. Wave after wave of my climax spread through me. It was like my orgasm had mini orgasms, and I realized it was because he was still thrusting madly inside me.

Sweat dotted his forehead, and a few drops landed on my chest.

"You didn't finish?" I said in surprise.

He slowed down, bringing me closer to him.

"I told you I want to watch you come all night. That means I only get my release at the end."

He held me to him, bringing me down from the table and swinging me around. He fondled my ass cheeks, patting them. I was sensitive from the two orgasms I'd already had, but even so, I knew he was going to make me come again. My knees buckled at the thought. He didn't slide inside me straight away. First, he skimmed his fingers up and down the side of my body. When I couldn't take the tension any longer, I pushed my ass back. One second later, he was inside me. And even though I liked his plan of focusing on me all night long, I wanted him to climax, to feel overwhelmed just like I was.

He kept a hand at my lower back, pressing me slightly into the table while he thrust inside me. My previous orgasms gave me notice, and I felt them forming in the pit of my body. But this one took me completely by surprise, and it hit me so hard that I clamped my mouth shut so tightly my teeth chattered.

But even through the haze of pleasure, I heard him cry out my name, finally lose control, and let go.

~

It took me longer to clean up than Tyler, of course. I loved his bathroom. It was huge and looked supremely elegant with black tiles and golden hangers. I used his shower gel and even applied a bit of paste on my teeth just to freshen up. After I stepped out, I wondered how the rest of the evening would go. I was so happy that he brought me here to his condo.

"Ready?" he asked, stepping in the doorway, startling me.

"Yeah."

He was waiting for me with a huge towel. I walked to him with my arms up in the air. His eyes zeroed in on my breasts. I cleared my throat, cocking a brow, and he immediately snapped his gaze up.

"Baby, you're beautiful. Of course I'm looking."

"I don't mind. I just find it funny."

He wrapped me in the towel before walking into the

bedroom. Since the bathroom was en suite, I'd seen it when we went inside, but I didn't pay much attention to it. He had a huge bed with a gray headrest and a dresser. But other than that, the room was pretty empty.

He walked behind me, arms still wrapped around my waist. A boom of thunder startled me, and I realized it was raining furiously. I hadn't noticed at all before. Tyler sure knew how to make me lose my head.

"Lie down on your belly," he said in a commanding tone, and my body immediately reacted. My thighs suddenly felt sensitive, especially on the inside. I lay down, putting my arms in front of me and my head on the backs of my hands. To my astonishment, he started massaging my calves.

"What are you doing?" I asked.

"Helping with muscle relaxation after all the sexy activity earlier."

I sucked in a breath when his hands reached my buttocks. He palmed my ass cheeks with both hands.

"Muscle relaxation is code for sexy time?" I double-checked. "I don't have anything against it, I just want to be prepared."

He laughed, and I closed my eyes, losing myself in the feeling of his hands on me as he went up to my back and then my shoulders, wondering how long I was going to have this wonderful man. My body tensed a bit at the mere idea of losing him.

"What's wrong, baby?"

Holy shit, the man can read my body.

I looked over my shoulder, playfully saying, "You're just so great at taking care of me. What are you trying to do? Make me fall for you?"

Even though my voice was teasing, I felt raw. I wasn't used to exposing myself like this. I couldn't believe I'd said that out loud, but he was so open and honest, and it made me want to reciprocate.

In a fraction of a second, Tyler lay next to me, propping himself on an elbow and turning me on my side. He drew the tip of his nose along the side of my neck.

"Tyler," I whispered.

He straightened up, looking me in the eyes.

"I'd tell you that that's the plan, but I have no idea what I'm doing. I like you, Kendra. More than I've ever liked anyone else. I want you to know that."

Oh wow. My whole body seemed to react to that statement with an inner joy that just exploded through me.

"We can just figure things out as we go. I promise I'll make every minute of that ride delicious."

Licking my lips, I put a palm on his chest, feeling the muscles under my fingers.

"And you think you have no idea what you're doing, huh? This, right here, proves the opposite."

CHAPTER TWENTY
KENDRA

The next morning, I felt as if I was floating on a cloud. Sitting on Tyler's fancy leather couch, I was drinking coffee while feeling my man up. I couldn't help myself. He was sitting next to me wearing jeans and nothing on top, and those muscles were way too tempting.

"You're feisty this morning."

"You inspire me."

He chuckled and thankfully didn't move even an inch away.

"And so does this place," I continued.

"I like my space. Bought it a few years ago. It's perfect for unwinding between games."

"What do you usually do?"

"Just hang around here, or meet up with the family. Sometimes I have them over here, but we meet at Tate's often because he's got a yard."

"Oh, that's nice."

"It is. But his house is one of those old-school mansions. You have to like it, I guess. I'm more of a modern setup guy."

I nodded. "True. So am I. This condo is the perfect mix of

modern and cozy. I like it. And I like the owner too. So sexy and talented in bed. And let's not forget swoonworthy."

He kissed my forehead, then got up from the couch. I pouted before realizing he was taking my empty cup, heading to his espresso machine.

"You look so hot in those jeans," I remarked. "But just saying, you look even hotter without them."

This didn't feel like my life, but more like a dream. I was brought back to reality pretty quickly, though, when my phone rang. My new neighbor was calling. My stomach bottomed out. I'd given her my number for emergencies. She also had a spare set of keys.

"Morning, Diane," I said. "Is anything wrong?"

"Unfortunately, yes, darling. It rained heavily last night. There's water in your basement."

"Oh no," I gasped. "How much water is there?"

"Not too much, but all the boxes you had on the floor are half soaked. I'll send you pictures."

My phone chimed with several incoming messages. My insides twisted as I looked at the photos.

Shit. How much bad luck can I have? I just took the boxes there yesterday.

Why did I think that moving them to the house so early was a good idea? I didn't plan to do any work on the basement floor, and I'd been so excited to get a start with the move. "Thanks so much. I'll come as soon as possible and do damage control." I was trying not to hyperventilate at the thought of what it would cost to drain the water.

Tyler turned around, watching me intently. The sound of the coffee machine drowned out most of my words, but judging by his expression, he'd heard enough to put two and two together.

As soon as I hung up, I rose from the couch, pacing the room.

"Kendra talk to me," Tyler said. "What happened?" He put both hands on my shoulders and looked me straight in the eyes.

"There's a lot of water in the basement of my house. I'm going to have to find a company to pump it all out."

He ran a hand through his hair, narrowing his eyes. "You know what? I'll call Luke. I bet he has some contacts to drainage companies."

Taken aback by his offer, I felt my eyes widen. "You don't have to bother him with this. I'll just look up options online."

"Trust me, I wouldn't be bothering him. And why pick some company you know nothing about when my brother can probably recommend one he's been working with? Besides, not all companies will come in on a Saturday."

"Okay," I relented. "Thank you."

Tyler immediately called his brother, and I listened to his side of the conversation.

"Okay. Thanks, man." He frowned. "I'll ask Kendra if she had anything in there." After hanging up, he said, "Here, he just forwarded me the number. He says they're great and reliable. And he's going to give them a call."

"Okay, thanks."

"Do you have anything in there?" he asked. "I heard something about boxes."

"Yeah. I took them there so I could get ahead with the move. I have to take the boxes out." I turned my phone, showing him the pics. "Sorry to bail on you today, but I need to go there and sort everything out."

He looked at me like I'd just grown a second head. "We're both going there."

"What? Why?"

"You're probably going to need help carrying the boxes, and my muscles are very good for that."

"Wow. Really? Thanks so much." He chose to spend his day like this. Who was this guy? "But is that okay with your shoulder?"

"Yeah, I'm supposed to use it a lot. I just need to make sure I control the movements. There are a lot of boxes there. And from the picture, it looks like a steep, curving staircase, so you can't put them on a handcart. We have to carry them out one by one. I'll call my brothers and see who's got time to drop by and give us a hand."

For the second time today, I was stunned. It took me a few seconds to shake myself out of my stupor. "No, wait a second, Tyler. I've got this. I'll call my sister. Oh no, wait. She isn't in town. But you don't have to call your brothers."

"Trust me. They won't have anything against it." I seriously doubted that, but Tyler called before I could protest any further. "Luke, it's me again. What are you doing today? There are like a million boxes in that basement." A few seconds later, he nodded. "Thanks, man."

"He said yes, just like that?" I asked when he lowered the phone.

"Yep, and he's going to call the rest of the clan. Whoever's got time will pop up at the house. The family motto is 'Don't outsource anything you can do well, and that can count as a family activity.'"

"I... Thanks."

I fiddled with my thumbs, hunching my shoulders. I'd never had this kind of support before, and although I was pleased, I wondered how I'd ever repay them.

"You look nervous," he said.

I shrugged, pushing a strand of hair behind my ear. "What

kind of impression will I make if the first time they meet me, it's because I'm asking them for help?"

Tyler chuckled, kissing my forehead. "Don't you worry about the first impression. I like you, so they'll like you. Come on, babe, let's go."

He interlaced our fingers, rubbing his thumb over the back of my hand as we left the condo.

Was I dreaming? I had been in a crisis mode not five minutes ago, and now everything seemed doable.

FIFTY MINUTES LATER, we arrived at the house. It was in a sleepy neighborhood on the outskirts of Chicago. The street was lined mostly with bungalow-style homes. The draining company was already there, unloading the gear from their vehicle.

I opened the basement door carefully. Oh God. I had clothes, books, and bedsheets in the boxes on the floor, and I was sure some of them would need replacing. If I didn't have Tyler with me right now, I'd probably be a basket case, but he grounded me.

The draining company came in a few minutes later, and they immediately started to work.

"My brothers are gonna be here in about an hour, and Reese too."

I seriously couldn't believe this was happening. I'd prepared myself to slog through this the whole day, but now my sexy man and his family were going to help me.

"Let's grab something to eat while they're draining the water," Tyler suggested. "No use getting in their way, okay?"

"Sure. Why not?"

We had pancakes at a small coffee shop two blocks away. When we returned to the house forty minutes later, I was surprised by how much progress had been made. The floor was a bit soggy—the previous owners had put in carpet, which I'd have to replace—but at least we could walk on it without getting water in our shoes.

"I'm going to start taking boxes out." Tyler declared, and for a few seconds, all I could do was stare at him, leaning down in all his perfection and picking up a box. His muscles flexed with each one.

Oh my, this is going to be a hugely fun day. There were perks to having this mountain of a man helping me.

"Where do you want them?"

"Huh?"

He smirked. "Kendra? Work first, ogling later."

"But why?" I asked, quickly checking the area. The guy overseeing the pump was at the other end of the room.

Tyler winked at me, nodding at the box.

"Oh, let's put them outside. I'll need to check the contents and see if I can keep everything. And some stuff will need drying. I'm going to call the company where my sister stored some stuff last year. They offer a pickup service."

I was already making a plan in my mind. I could go to a laundromat to wash and clean my clothes and bedsheets. As for the books, I didn't have an idea yet. Maybe I could put fans in the storage room. The important part was to take them out.

I called them right away, explaining the situation. The woman who answered told me to call again once we were done taking the boxes out of the basement.

After that, Tyler and I got to work. We realized we had to tape the bottom of all the boxes; otherwise, they'd just break. That took considerably longer than we thought because they were wet, and it became a challenge for the tape to stick.

Half an hour later, Reese, Travis, and two hunks joined us.

"Hey, I'm Luke," one of them said as they descended the steps.

Declan also introduced himself; he was nice but much more subdued than the others.

Luke didn't look anything like Tyler, except the fact that he was also tall and muscular. Travis and Declan were tall too, though only Declan came near to the stature of Tyler. Luke and Travis were both more slender. Travis had slightly longer hair that brushed his shoulders, and Declan looked crisp and serious, like someone you wouldn't want to cross.

"Thank you all for coming here. I seriously can't believe you're doing this," I said.

Reese smiled, covering a yawn with her hand. "Hey, emergencies suck. We're here for you."

Luke inspected the pump before joining us. "They're moving fast."

"You need to notify your insurance," Declan said.

"The rain last night wasn't strong enough to warrant this. I think the pump the previous owners installed wasn't good enough. I'm assuming the house was inspected before you bought it?" Luke asked me.

"Yes."

"And they didn't mention any issue with the pump?"

"No."

"Right. The draining company will draft a report. If it turns out the pump was faulty and the previous owners didn't disclose that, you might be able to sue them to get back the cost of the draining."

"Thanks. Good to know."

Declan immediately began explaining the steps of suing the previous owners. It sounded like it would take a while, and I didn't know if I had a case anyway. But I appreciated his advice.

"Brother, I know you're the brains of the family, and I'm the brawn," Luke said, "but move that ass and grab a few boxes."

"Yeah. Don't try to just supervise us," Travis said. He was

currently taping a box. "He did that all the time as kids, pulled the older brother card and said someone had to supervise us."

"And I did," Declan said, but now he was grinning. "Otherwise, you would have gotten in even more trouble than you did."

Tyler burst out laughing. "I seriously don't even think that's possible."

Travis wiggled his eyebrows at me. "If there was a smart way to do things and a stupid way to do things, we always chose the stupid one."

I smiled back while I was taping a box myself. "And let me guess, you were the one with the ideas, Travis?"

Travis whistled. "I'd like to take credit for that, but actually, Luke here was the one with the ideas. The rest of us just followed."

Luke nodded solemnly. "I had to use my position as second oldest to get them all to listen to me and give this one headaches." He patted Declan's shoulder.

"Okay, so I think this is going to take us a while. We need a better system," Declan said, looking at the boxes. "Most are heavy, so I don't think you're going to be able to do much lifting, are you, Kendra, Reese?"

"Between the two of us, we can do it," Reese said.

Declan looked around. "I have a better idea. Why don't you two tape up all the bottoms so we don't risk anything breaking, and we're going to carry it all out."

I perked up. "Okay. That's a good idea. I think that's going to make this go even faster."

Reese and I turned every box that looked to have a soft bottom on the side and just put as much tape as possible on it. I debated only taping the ones with books and other solid items, since I planned to take clothes and bedsheets to the laundromat, but it was easier to carry everything out in boxes.

"Thanks so much for coming," I told her. "I don't even know what to say."

I felt like a broken record.

Reese waved her hand. "Oh, come on. It would have been silly for you two to spend a whole day here, and between all of us, we'll be done in a couple hours. And anyway, I wanted to hang out with you too."

"You did?"

"Yeah. We didn't chat much at the fair, but I already like you. You make Tyler smile. After the incident, it took the combined effort of all the Maxwells to lift his mood."

I found it heartwarming that they took the well-being of the others so seriously.

"Your family's really something else. I mean, my sister and I are also super close, but I thought that was because..."

"Because?" Reese prompted.

I cleared my throat. "Never mind. I mean, we had a few rough years as kids, so I thought that was why we were so close. I didn't realize normal families could be like this too."

She smiled warmly. "Well, we are. It's something our parents and Gran instilled in us since we were kids, and honestly, I'm happy about it, because lately the only people I feel comfortable with is my family."

"Is this because of what happened with your ex?" I grimaced as we taped yet another box. "I'm sorry, it's none of my business. Tyler told me that he was involved in the fight, but he didn't give me any details as to why the two of you broke up."

Reese jerked her head back. "He didn't? Wow, so there *is* a Maxwell who respects privacy. He deserves a prize. The rest of us aren't this evolved." She chuckled. "Joking aside, yeah, it is because of my asshole of an ex. We were supposed to get married, but then I found out he was sleeping with my best friend."

"Oh my God. That's horrible."

"Yeah, it is," she said quietly, and I saw her wither a bit in front of me. That was the most appropriate word, *wither*. I searched for something to say, but I knew some wounds just needed time to heal, or at least not hurt as much, and words didn't help.

"Okay. I think we're good here. Let's move on to the next group of boxes."

We were making real progress. It was much faster than the previous system. The guys didn't have to waste any time taping, so they just carried out box after box, and one short hour later, everything was in front of the house.

"I'm going to call the storage company again," I said and pulled out my phone.

They picked up right away. A woman greeted me.

"Hi! I'm Kendra. I spoke to one of your coworkers today. I need to book one of your storage rooms, and I also need the pickup service."

"Sorry, our last room was booked half an hour ago."

I clenched my jaw. "What do you mean? I spoke to your colleague a few hours ago. My name is Kendra. I'm sure she noted it somewhere."

"We're first come, first served."

I pressed two fingers on the spot between my eyebrows, feeling a headache coming on. "This is no way to run a business. Why didn't the other person tell me that?"

"I'm sorry. There's nothing I can do."

I bit my lip, running a hand through my hair. "Okay. Thanks."

Tyler was looking at me intently when I hung up. I felt foolish. Could one thing go right today?

Travis came up to us. "What's wrong?"

"I'm just going to search real quick for some storage companies. The one I called before doesn't have space now."

Travis nodded, but then his eyes lit up. "Wait a second. Don't our parents have that huge empty shed? Mom keeps teasing Dad about it. He had it built, saying it was going to be his man cave, and it's been empty for fifteen years. They use it for storage."

"I'll call them," Tyler said.

"What? No, no, no." I was beside myself. "You all did so much for me already. I'll handle this. I'll find a spot. It's not that hard. Besides, I also have to take some of the things to a laundromat as well as dry out the books."

"Babe, my parents have a couple washing machines and dryers. And I'm sure we can come up with a way to dry your books. They won't mind."

"They truly wouldn't," Luke said, but there was something interesting in his eyes, like a twinkle of mischief. He had something in mind. "Why don't you give them a call, Travis, and tell them *Kendra*"—he emphasized my name, for some reason—"needs their shed to store her boxes. And we'd all come over, of course."

"Got it," Travis said with a wink. It was like they were having a secret conversation between the lines.

Tyler pressed his lips in a thin line. Dimples appeared in his cheeks. He was holding back laughter. *Wait a second. What's going on?*

I turned to Declan, who seemed thoroughly amused as well.

"Why don't you call Gran too while you're at it?" Declan said.

"Oh, I'm sure your mom will do it," Reese said. She was also grinning.

Wow. Okay. They were all in on the joke, and I had no idea

what it was about. I searched my brain for a way to ask Tyler without being obvious, but if I pulled him to one side, they would know something was up. I was obviously in for more surprises today. I mean, it had already been bewildering, so I decided to just go ahead with it. I wasn't used to doing things spontaneously. I liked to plan things in detail, but where had that gotten me? I'd made contingency plans for moving and for storing, and look what happened. If it wasn't for the group popping up here today, I would have had a lot more headaches.

CHAPTER TWENTY-ONE
KENDRA

Everyone was here with their car, and it took a while to put the boxes in the five trunks. It was double work because of the storage company. I was going to treat everyone to a delicious dinner tonight!

The restoration company still wasn't done by the time everything was loaded up. I shuddered to think about how much it would cost. I told them to leave the key with my neighbor and email me the invoice.

After that, we all got in our cars. The second we were inside, it hit me that I was going to meet his parents. My palms were sweaty, and I needed a distraction.

"Okay. What was that with your brothers and Reese before Travis called your parents?" I asked.

"What?" he said, but the tone of his voice clued me in that he knew exactly what I was referring to.

"You were joking about something, but I didn't get it. The way Luke told Travis to call your mom, it seemed like he meant more than he was saying out loud."

Tyler took my hand, kissing the back of it. "Mom is going to be beside herself that she's getting to meet you. I think that even if she didn't have a spare space, she'd make one so we would all show up there. And yes, Reese is right. She's instantly going to call Gran too."

"For what?"

"So Gran can meet you too. Everyone's excited."

"No pressure," I murmured.

"There really is no pressure."

"Tyler," I said seriously, "No one's done anything remotely close to what you and your family did for me today, so it is a big deal to me."

As he stopped the car at a red light, he looked me straight in the eyes. "I'm here for you, whatever you need, babe. I meant what I said before."

"I know that now."

He narrowed his eyes, pinching my thigh.

"Hey, what was that for?"

"So you didn't believe me before?" he asked as the car lurched forward once the light turned green.

"I'm not proud to own up to it, but I can't say I did. It's just that when you're used to not being able to trust people around you, you learn not to expect anything from them, not even when they promise it."

"Babe, you can always count on me," he said. His voice was soft, and when he looked at me, so were his eyes.

I was a bit on edge, and I wanted to diffuse the emotional tension.

"Thanks."

"Now, let's think of a punishment because you didn't believe me." His tone changed to playful as if he'd guessed exactly what I needed. He snapped his gaze back to the road.

"Oh?"

He peeked at me from the corner of his eye. "Undo the top button of your shirt."

I burst out laughing. "My punishment is taking my clothes off?"

"I just wanted a peek, but if you're volunteering to take everything off, I won't say no." He cleared his throat before adding, "On second thought, I am saying no."

"What changed your mind so quickly?"

"We're not alone on the street, and I don't want anyone to see you."

I pressed my lips together to keep from laughing again. "So no peek either, then?"

He groaned, looking at me sideways. "I'm weak for you, Kendra. And you're taking advantage of it."

Giggling, I brought my fingers to the top button.

We arrived at his parents' house in Forest Glen forty minutes later. At the sight of the mansion, it dawned on me that this was *the* Maxwell family. *Oh my God.* Somehow, it had been easy to forget before, when everyone had been carrying around boxes and just teasing each other like they weren't one of the richest families in Chicago. I was a bit intimidated, especially because there was a welcome committee waiting in front of the house. It was all red brick, with white windows and doors and a gray roof.

"These are my parents, and... Oh hell. What did Mom do? How is Gran already here?" Tyler asked as he parked the car in the huge driveway.

I assumed Gran was the older woman with white hair pulled back at the base of her head.

I laughed nervously. "Who's that next to Gran?" I asked.

"That's my brother Tate."

"Oh, wait. I recognize him. He brought you to the first meeting, along with the woman standing next to him."

"That's right. His fiancée, Lexi. And that's my niece, Paisley. She's Tate's daughter from his previous marriage and one of my favorite people on the planet."

Who's melting hearing this sexy hunk talking like this about his niece? Not me.

"Come on, let's get out of the car," he said.

My legs felt like spaghetti as we walked up the front porch.

"Hi, everyone," Tyler said. "This is Kendra."

"Hi," I said before pressing my lips together. My voice sounded so high-pitched, like I was a young girl.

"Hey, Kendra," Tyler's mom said. "Nice to meet you. Call me Lena."

"Emmett," his dad offered, shaking my hand. "And this is my mom, Beatrice."

"Everyone calls me Gran," Beatrice said with a warm smile.

I shook everyone's hand, including Paisley's.

"Thank you so much for doing this," I told his parents. "I hope it's okay. I'm going to check again with the storage company where my sister had her stuff before, and as soon as they have something open, I'll take my stuff there."

Lena smiled. Emmett was looking at Tyler, who put a hand around my shoulders, pulling me toward him. "Babe, relax. My parents are cool with your stuff being here until the house is ready."

I smiled sheepishly. "I'm sorry. I'm just a little bit intimidated," I said, deciding to lay out all my cards before they thought I was a weirdo. "Today was tough, and I wasn't expecting your sons and Reese to all show up and help me."

"Oh, they'd better," Emmett said in a deep voice. "That's how we raised them."

He looked toward the driveway, where four more cars pulled in, and Travis, Declan, Luke, and Reese got out.

"Dad, we're gonna need the keys to the shed," Travis said.

"It's already open," Emmett replied. "Let's get a start on the boxes. I already put some fans in there."

It took us about half an hour to lay the books out on the floor to dry. I took my clothes and bedsheets directly to the basement of the house, where they had two sets of professional washing machines and dryers.

"I think we can get all the loads done today," Lena said. "There's a quick-wash and quick-dry program."

"That's great." I smiled. "Do you have any trash bags? So I can put everything in them afterward?"

"Yes I do. Come on, let's go up."

The house was even more spectacular on the inside. The ceiling was high, and the interior was a mix of classic and modern. I'd never seen this design before—modern light fixtures, but ornate molding on the ceiling and Persian rugs. There were pumpkins everywhere.

"I like the Halloween decor," I said.

"Paisley had a party here for Halloween with her friends from school. She asked us to keep them for a while longer."

"It's so fancy but at the same time cozy," I said.

"Thanks," Lena replied. "We upgraded it a bit once the boys were older. When they were kids, we had all sort of pictures hanging up and drawings they brought home, so they could play around and touch everything."

I loved that they did that instead of just telling them to behave so they wouldn't ruin anything. Whenever I thought of the Maxwell family, I'd figured they'd be... different. And yet they were so down-to-earth, all of them.

We went into the living room, and Lena stepped behind their beautiful mahogany bar. Lexi, Paisley, Reese, and Gran were already here. The guys were still outside, it seemed. We all sat on the bar stools, except Gran, who sank into a plush armchair right next to it.

"What's everyone having?" Lena asked.

"White wine for me," Lexi replied.

"I'm with Lexi," I added.

Reese tapped her palms against the counter, saying in a singsong voice, "I'm always up for wiiiine."

"So am I," Gran exclaimed.

Lena opened a white wine by Maxwell Wineries, of course, pouring it into five glasses. Paisley got orange juice. It felt like I'd barely sipped once from my drink when the guys returned, and they were a sight for sore eyes.

"Okay. Who's hungry," Travis said, "because I'm famished. Is there any food?"

"No. Your dad and I were just going to have a light dinner," Lena said.

"I can treat everyone to takeout," I exclaimed, coming down from my bar seat. "If you like that."

"We sure do," Luke replied.

There was a chorus of yeses, and for some reason, I felt less intimidated when they started to fight over whether to order pizza or sushi.

"We can order both," I said in a slightly raised tone to make myself heard.

Luke grinned at me. "No, no. The whole fun is to get to agree on something."

"It seems like it might never happen," I replied.

Travis came up next to me. "I'm with you on this one. We never agree on food, but we always try. I don't know why. But they better hurry up, or I'll eat up everything Mom's got in the fridge. I haven't eaten anything today."

"Thanks again for coming and helping me."

"No problem. I have lots of free time anyway, so I can help out with anything my family needs." He spoke like this was a common occurrence.

"How come you have so much free time?" I asked.

"I just sold my company, and I'm in no rush to start something else. I've been working on it for years, so now I'm just catching up on everything I missed. It's a bit weird, honestly, but it did come in handy when Tyler needed company."

Gran came up next to us with her glass of wine.

"Ma'am, your grandsons are true gentlemen. And Reese is... whatever the female equivalent is."

"Oh, call me Beatrice or Gran. 'Ma'am' makes me feel like I'm a hundred years old, and I still have eighteen years to reach that milestone."

I laughed. "Okay, Beatrice."

"I'm glad to meet you, Kendra. I've heard a bit about you through the grapevine."

"Oh?" I raised a brow.

"Yes, yes. I was most curious about you."

"I've heard a lot about you too. I'm happy to meet you, though I'm feeling a bit guilty that the reason we're meeting is that I've roped the entire family into helping me."

She patted my arm. "That's what we do, child. No need to feel guilty."

"Exactly," Reese exclaimed, coming up to us with Lexi. "Girls, the three of us should plan something. I need new friends. My sister's still in Paris, and since I suck at picking both guys and friends, I don't trust anyone I'm not related to right now—or someone who my cousins didn't choose."

Tyler chose *me*.

I smiled from ear to ear, deciding not to worry about how I would pay for the catastrophe today. Instead I would just enjoy this day and this fantastic group of people.

CHAPTER TWENTY-TWO
KENDRA

I never quite understood the saying "floating on a cloud" until I met Tyler. Scratch that. Until he became a part of my life, along with the rest of the Maxwells.

In the three weeks after the basement fiasco, my sexy goalie was busy getting back in shape and training. Somehow, he still found time to make me swoon. Case in point: he seemed to have put his whole family on task.

The contractor Luke had put me in contact with gave me a quote that wasn't at all in my range, so I didn't hire him. After a feeble attempt to do some of the work at the house on my own, I realized it was truly beyond my skill level, though. Luke suggested I could pay in installments, so we were meeting today in the afternoon to discuss that. Declan was coming too. The restoration company had written up a report on the pump, and it turned out to be faulty after all. Declan insisted I could sue the previous owners for withholding information.

They'd both taken their advising me so seriously, you would have thought it was their job. Last Thursday they even asked me to join them for Thanksgiving dinner, but I politely refused.

Tyler was away with the team that day, and it felt weird to have dinner with his family on my own.

Right now, though, I was in my office, waiting for my sister. She was unusually late this morning. I sipped my coffee while tapping away at my keyboard. I was organizing a volunteer experience for a high-profile blues singer. It was obviously for PR purposes, but it didn't matter. At the end of the day, it was going to make a retirement community happy, even if it was just for a day.

I was also busy replacing Tyler as a coach to the kids. I'd had contingency plans in place from the beginning, of course, but I hadn't anticipated that he'd be back with the team so fast. But this was nothing I couldn't handle. The only downside of being so busy was that I hadn't even managed to start working on the house. At this rate, I'd never get to it.

I was smiling like a fool the whole morning as I poured myself a cup of tea and opened my laptop. I even smiled while doing a particularly boring spreadsheet.

At ten o'clock, my sister finally arrived, looking like she hadn't slept all night.

"Party girl, how are you feeling?" I asked her.

"Oh, Kendra, I'm getting too old for this. Please remind me not to accept any party invitations during the week. I feel like I can't even put a sentence together."

"I'll make a black tea. That will whip you back in shape in no time." Emma sometimes preferred tea to coffee.

She yawned while shaking her head. "I doubt anything can get me back in shape today, but you're welcome to try."

I was so jittery that I was looking for an excuse to get up from behind my desk and move around. I prepared her tea at the small appliance table we had in the corner.

"What's up with you?" she asked. "You're a bit jumpy."

Right, so she thought she couldn't string two sentences together, yet she still picked up on that? That was my sister to a T.

"I don't know. I just have this nervous energy, but in a positive way. I'm smiling for no reason."

She narrowed her eyes. "I think I know the reason. Tyler Maxwell."

I cleared my throat, fiddling with my thumbs, feeling like I was a teenager confiding in my sister about my first kiss. "Yes."

"Oh my God." Emma sprang to her feet, accidentally spilling the tea all over the table.

"Sis," I said with a grin, hurrying to bring napkins.

"Oh, forget it. I have nothing valuable—oops, except my laptop. Let me put that away."

I returned with a stack of napkins, cleaning up. She helped too, and after throwing them away, Emma sat down and massaged her temples.

"What are you doing?" I inquired.

"I'm trying to determine if I'm fit enough for a spill-it session right now, or if I should ask you to tell me everything later when I'm awake."

I barely held back a laugh. My sister didn't believe in delayed gratification. I would bet anything that she'd ask me to spill the beans right now.

Not a second later, she dropped her hands to her sides, rolling her shoulders and looking straight at me.

"Okay. I think I have enough neurons awake to listen."

"But you already know everything." I leaned against the edge of the desk.

"Yeah, but I've been missing something."

"Are we going to get any work done today?" I asked.

"No, I'm declaring this Sisters Day. I don't think I can be of any use anyway, and by the look of your smile, neither are you. You're falling for him, aren't you?"

Sighing, I pressed a palm against my chest. Somewhere between spoiling the kids and spoiling *me*, he got under my skin.

I nodded.

"Wow, wow, wow," my sister exclaimed. "You've been holding out on me."

"It wasn't intentional," I said truthfully. "I think I just realized it. And I'm basking in all its glory."

She flashed me a smile. "As you should."

"I'm also a tiny bit afraid."

"You're my sister. I know. But do me a favor and focus on how happy you were a few minutes ago, okay?"

I grinned. "That's not too hard because I'm still *supremely* happy. But that doesn't mean I can't work too, so I'm going back to my desk now."

Emma pouted. "Party pooper."

I went back to my spreadsheet. I could hardly keep my thoughts from wandering, but an hour later, I finished my work and moved on to my inbox.

I groaned. At the top of my inbox was an email from Jared.

"What's wrong?" Emma asked.

"Jared wrote back. I sent him an email semi-threatening legal action if he doesn't deposit my paychecks, and he just gave me the same response, to pick them up myself. The moron. I'm gonna go there as soon as possible and bust his ass. And I'm gonna take pepper spray with me this time."

"You think that's enough?"

"It has to be. I need that money, and I'm gonna get it."

"Why don't you ask Tyler?" she suggested. "You said he offered, right? I bet no one's gonna try robbing you if you've got a mountain of a man next to you."

"I *was* thinking about asking him to come with me," I admitted.

"Whoa."

"It's just... I feel safe when I'm with him, you know? And not necessarily in the sense that he keeps me safe, but *I* feel stronger."

To my astonishment, my sister's eyes filled with tears. "I'm happy you found someone who makes you feel that way. Did you talk to him about it?"

"No, he's got to focus on the upcoming games right now. I'm going to wait a while."

"Don't wait too long, though."

"I know, and it's not like I can afford to anyway. Paying for the damage to the basement ate up all my money. I'm mad at myself for feeling afraid to go there. I mean, I worked there."

She stared at me. "Yes, but last time you were there some guys asked for your wallet. God knows what would have happened if they caught up with you. I'd be more concerned if you weren't scared of going back there."

"Right. Okay. I'll think about it. Let's get back to work."

Around lunchtime, a delivery arrived.

"Did you order lunch?" Emma asked me, carrying two boxes of pizza from my favorite Italian restaurant.

"No. I was just about to ask you what you wanted to have."

At the same time, my phone chimed.

Tyler: Hey, babe. I hope your day is going well. Enjoy your lunch.

"Tyler sent it to us," I exclaimed, feeling like my heart was about to spring out of my chest. I was so happy that I could dance in my chair.

Emma fanned herself with her hand. "My God, this guy is in

a league of his own, and I'm declaring myself his number one fan."

"No you're not. That's me," I exclaimed.

Kendra: Thank you so much!!!

Tyler: My pleasure. Can't let my woman forget about me, can I?

Kendra: Fat chance of that happening.

Tyler: Don't want to take any chances.

Kendra: My sister also says thanks. FYI, you've charmed her.

Tyler: Good. I like having a champion. Call me once you're done.

I was all giggly as Emma opened the boxes on my desk. Mine was with a lot of cheese, and hers was with pepperoni. We devoured them within minutes.

Once we were finished, I stood up. It was time to head out to meet Luke and Declan.

Emma sent me an air kiss before sitting at her desk and putting on noise-canceling headphones. She had an important call, so I tiptoed out of the office and into the entrance hall. The whole office was empty today. It was a sunny day, but the end of November was tricky, and I knew better than to leave without a scarf. I also put a sweater over my shirt.

Just as I was about to leave the office, my phone lit up with an incoming call from Tyler. I answered right away.

"Hey, beautiful," he said. "How was your lunch?"

"Delicious. A certain sexy and thoughtful goalie spoiled me."

"You deserve it."

"Are you still with the team?"

"Yeah. We're probably going to be here until late this evening." They were at a hotel outside the city for a team-building day.

"How was your day?" I asked.

"Same craziness as usual."

I heard the smile in his voice. "Good crazy?"

"Fuck yes. I can't believe I'm back in the middle of things. What are you doing in the afternoon?"

I could just tell him I was meeting his brothers, or I could tease him a bit.

"I'm having a double date with two gorgeous hunks."

"What?"

Oh sweet Lord, that was Tyler to a tee.

Hot? Check.

Sexy? Double-check.

Delicious? Triple-check.

I burst out laughing. "I'm meeting your brothers."

"My brothers. Very funny. I'll get my payback once I'm in Chicago."

I shivered, checking my appearance in the mirror. I was fairly certain it was going to be a delicious payback. "I can't believe your brothers are doing this," I said.

"You're one of us, Kendra. Of course they're doing it." His words moved me deeply, but I still didn't fully believe it. Every once in a while, though, I hoped this could be forever.

"Go get 'em, Mr. Superstar Goalie. I need to go."

I was smiling from ear to ear again as the call disconnected.

I MET Luke and Declan at a small coffee shop near the Field Museum. Even though the weather was terrible, there was still a line to get inside. I loved this building, with the marble steps leading up onto the splendid terrace and the neoclassical architectural style of the museum itself. The coffee shop was five minutes away from the museum, and Declan and Luke were already sitting down at a table when I arrived.

"Hello, gentlemen." I waved at them.

Sitting up straighter, Declan blinked. "Gentlemen?"

Luke smiled. "Who tricked you into believing that?"

"Maybe you meant *gentleman*, as in singular? It could apply to me but certainly not to this one," Declan said.

"I'd give you shit, but you're right," Luke said.

"You're taking time out of your busy day to help. That makes you gentlemen in my book. Emphasis on the plural."

Luke grinned. "You haven't been around us for too long, then."

Declan cocked a brow. "I stand by what I said. *I* am a gentleman."

Luke grasped his shoulder. "Declan, real gentlemen don't say that."

"Okay, while you're debating the pros and cons on this, why don't I get us drinks? It's my treat," I said before either of them could offer.

"She thinks she can boss us into this," Luke said.

Declan placed both hands on the table. "One thing you should learn about us Maxwell guys is that, gentlemen or not, we're for sure not going to let you pay."

"Why don't we order the drinks, and we'll revisit this later?" I suggested.

Luke nodded. "You're good. I'll give you that."

"I know."

We all ordered coffee, and as soon as the waitress left, Declan rolled his shoulders.

"Okay, so I got the report from the inspection. They'd installed a faulty sump pump with no backup system, so there's no argument. They have to pay for the damage. Here's what I suggest as the next steps."

He laid out a detailed roadmap for getting the money back from the previous owners for the water damage.

Luke took over next, taking out his laptop and showing me the timeline for payments if I decided to work with the contractor he suggested after all.

"Wow. I honestly didn't think contractors accepted being paid in installments," I told him.

"They usually don't, but I used my charm to convince them," he said.

"Thanks," I exclaimed.

"Besides, they're only doing one portion at a time, and you're paying that, so they're not at risk. If everyone keeps to the timeline, you'll be ready to move in January. And I *will* make sure they deliver on time."

They worked together as a team, and their energy even energized me.

"You think I'll have a chance of getting the money back?" I asked Declan.

"Definitely. I'm very good at what I do," he said.

"And he's humble too," Luke put in, "but I have to be fair. He's one of the best lawyers in Chicago. And I can vouch for all these handymen. They're working at Declan's place too."

"You're moving?" I asked.

He nodded. "Yeah, as soon as my place is done."

Luke lifted the corners of his mouth.

"Don't start again," Declan warned.

"Don't start what?" I asked. "I want to have insider knowledge."

"He bought a property that has a guest house on it, which is rented out, and he can't get rid of the renter for some time."

Declan tapped his fingers on the table, leaning lower in the chair. "So what? I still don't get the problem. You amuse yourself every time."

"Brother, I don't know if anyone's told you this before, but you're not compatible with anyone."

"We're sharing a yard. That's it."

"Yeah, I'm giving you one week before you go crazy. You're just not good at sharing. You like things a certain way."

"Doesn't everyone?" I chimed in.

"Thank you, Kendra," Declan said.

"But Declan is in a league of his own," Luke countered.

"Don't start again."

"Fine. I'm not starting, but don't say I didn't warn you when you're going batshit crazy about your neighbor doing stuff you don't like."

"We'll have rules about cohabiting," Declan said calmly.

I was slowly starting to understand Luke's point of view. Rules were good, but they didn't always work out.

"If I were you, I'd just wait until the renter moves out," Luke said.

"I want my space. I'll move, and we'll have rules."

I grinned at their banter. They were hilarious.

Declan focused on me. "But back to our conversation. Do you have any questions?"

"Yes. How long do you think it will take until I'm reimbursed?"

"Hard to say. Probably a couple of months."

I grimaced. "Okay, that means I have to see Jared," I murmured, more to myself.

"Jared?" Declan asked.

"My ex-boss. He owes me a few paychecks and is being a jackass about giving them to me. Says I have to go pick them up myself, but the neighborhood is sketchy. Last time I went there, two men followed me and asked for my wallet, and I had to duck into a store."

Luke frowned. "How can we help?"

"I'm surprised Tyler didn't tell us," Declan added.

"I didn't tell him yet that I have to go there to get my paychecks."

Luke and Declan raised their eyebrows high on their forehead. Their expressions looked comically similar.

"Why?" Luke asked, sounding cautious.

"Well, now that he's back on the team, he's got lots on his mind." *And I don't want to be trouble*, a small voice said.

"He'll want to know," Declan said. Luke just nodded, drinking a swig of coffee. I suspected he was trying to weigh his words, and that was troublesome, because Luke didn't strike me as the type to do that. He usually just spoke his mind. "He doesn't like secrets. Remember when I didn't tell him about when Sam went missing because he had a big game coming up? That was a dark time in the Maxwell brotherhood."

"Your brother went missing?" I asked, stricken.

"It was a false alarm. Sometimes he's located in dangerous areas. Once he was sent to a place that was under attack, and the entire unit lost signal. We all decided not to tell Tyler. He didn't take it lightly."

"This isn't the same, though. I'll tell him once things calm down. I just don't want to distract him before his first game."

"And by the way, if he gets mad that you didn't tell him before, we're on your side."

"Wait, what? Why are you picking sides?"

Declan smiled. "It's all about picking teams and making secret plans. Welcome to the Maxwell family."

"Thanks. Gentlemen, I'm going to the restroom. Be right back."

"There she goes with 'gentlemen' again," Luke said. "I'm kind of getting used to it."

Laughing, I rose from the table, heading to the back of the coffee shop.

When I returned a few minutes later, Luke was looking

particularly smug. Declan also seemed very pleased with himself.

"We paid the bill," Declan announced.

"Wow. Damn it. When?"

"You're good, but we're better," Luke said.

CHAPTER TWENTY-THREE
TYLER

"Aaaaand I give you Tyler *Maxwell*. That's right. Our favorite goalie is playing again," the Blades' longtime announcer screeched over the microphone, and the sound echoed off the arena.

It was my first time back on the ice, and it felt intoxicating—like I was on top of the world. Nothing compared to this. Absolutely nothing.

I was in the best shape of my life because I'd taken good care of my body during training. Our new goalie had made a few mistakes I wouldn't have made this season. But this game, Jett was struggling from the start, and though we were leading, Coach Benjamin decided to put me in during the last period. We only had seven minutes left on the ice, and I planned to make each of them count.

I drew in deep breaths. The ice-cold air pinched my nostrils. I skated to the left of the net and then the right.

Always stay in motion. An agile goalie is faster than a static one.

My first coach told me that in middle school, and it was the best advice I ever got.

My pulse thumped in my ears in the same rhythm as the

cheering crowd. I zeroed in on the puck. When it passed center ice, the rhythm changed. My heartbeat was now in overdrive. It heightened and heightened until it drowned out the sounds of the crowd.

It was 3-2, Blades in the lead. If I saved this, we'd win.

I will save this.

I crouched forward, still moving but now in shorter bursts, only skating enough to keep my ankles in motion, ready to lunge in the right direction. Steve reached McLaren and Donnie—the top scorers from today's opponent, the Giants—but I knew he wouldn't be able to take the puck from them. They were just too fast.

I knew the moment McLaren would send the puck to me instead of Donnie before he even touched it. The stance of his shoulders changed—they were more rigid. He was bracing himself for the shot.

The next second, he swung the stick at the puck, sending it barreling my way.

Here was the tricky part about being a goalie. You had to decide if the puck was going to the left or the right before you could see its course. If you waited long enough to know the direction, it was too late. It would be a goal before you had a chance to block it.

The left.

I based the decision on gut and experience, and I lurched in that direction the next second. Holding my breath, I stretched my hands forward, gripping the stick tightly. I blocked the puck, sending it right to Steve. My body was alive with adrenaline, but I wasn't in celebratory mode yet. It was still 3-2 for us, and we had one minute left. Not a lot of time for our opponents to score, but I'd seen it happen before.

This was not the time to relax or declare victory.

I broke the cardinal rule and stood still, hunched forward. Thirty seconds left.

I kept my eyes on the puck. McLaren took it from Steve and was speeding toward me once again.

Twenty seconds.

I couldn't multitask when I was so full of adrenaline. I needed to focus or else risk taking my eyes off the puck.

Five seconds.

He was twenty feet away. He wouldn't risk scoring from that distance.

Zero seconds.

We won!

My muscles spasmed before I became aware of the burning in my calves. The pounding in my eardrums continued, but it was different now. I could hear the surrounding sounds, not just my heartbeat.

The crowd erupted in cheers. The team, including Jett, surrounded me.

Yeah, this right here, this feeling of victory was what I lived for. My pulse thrummed to the same rhythm the fans were chanting.

"Fucking hell, we did it," I said.

"Welcome back, man," Steve yelled.

I looked at the stands, packed with fans celebrating, waving flags, hats, and other paraphernalia. Their happiness filled me with a particularly strong pride, and usually it was enough to make my evening, but now something was missing.

Some*one* was missing.

Kendra.

I wanted to see her in the stands and share this joy with her. I'd never wanted that with anyone I'd been with, but I craved it with her.

One by one we exited the ice and headed directly to the locker room.

"Man, this was a great game. Way to make a comeback," Steve said.

"Thanks, man. I appreciate it."

Jett smiled as he clapped my shoulder. "You did a great job."

"Thanks," I said.

"Dude, you're going out with us, right?" Steve said.

I nodded. "Of course. I want to celebrate this. It feels fucking amazing to be back on the ice."

"We're happy to have you back, dude," Matthew added. He was our center and a damn genius in face-offs.

The next half hour was the usual madness of showering, changing, and then stopping to sign a few things for fans before we headed out to whatever bar we decided on. This time we went to an Irish pub in the area. We avoided sport bars as a rule.

I WAS on my second beer when my phone vibrated in my pocket. It was a message from Kendra.

Kendra: Hello, Mr. Superstar Goalie. Any clue on when you'll be home?

Tyler: I'm honestly not sure, but I can call you. I'm out with the guys celebrating.

She didn't reply, and I was almost about to call her when a message popped up.

Kendra: Okay. Never mind. Just forget about my question. We can talk tomorrow.

Yeah, right. I didn't like this one bit, so I gestured for the guys to be quiet. All I got instead were catcalls.

"Are you all five years old?" I said before walking away from the group.

I stepped outside and called Kendra back.

She answered after the third ring in a high-pitched voice. "Hey."

"Babe, what's up?"

"Nothing. Just go have fun with the guys, and don't worry about me."

"It's me. I can tell you're nervous. What is it? Where are you?"

"Nooooo. Why did you ask me that? I didn't want to lie to you."

Alarm bells rang in my mind. "Babe?"

"I'm at your condo, and I blanked out on the fact that you'd go celebrate."

"You're at my place now?" I asked.

"Yeah."

"Put the doorman on the phone."

"Why?"

"So I can tell him to let you in."

"Oh, okay. Here he is."

"Mr. Maxwell," he said in his usual no-nonsense tone.

"Hi. Kendra's my girlfriend, and you can let her in upstairs."

"Of course. I'll do that right away."

"Put her back on, please."

"Yes, sir. And if I might say so, excellent game."

"Thanks."

Interesting. He was so serious all the time that I wouldn't have pegged him for someone who watched hockey.

"I'm back," Kendra said.

"Okay. He'll take you upstairs. And I'll be home in however long it takes me to get from here to the condo."

"What? No, just stay there with your teammates. I'll be here when you come home."

"Babe, I've been dying to be with you ever since the game finished. I'm going to be home real fast."

"Okay. Then I can't wait to spoil you... help all those muscles decompress."

I laughed because she was throwing my words back at me. "I can't wait. I'll go say goodbye to the guys."

"Okay."

Pocketing my phone, I headed inside, straight to our table. Only half the team was sitting down. The other half was at the bar.

"Guys, it's been a real treat being out here with you," I said, "but my girl is waiting at home for me, so I'm heading there." That earned me more catcalls.

Steve was the only one who just raised a beer and said, "That right there is a real man. Maybe one of these days, you'll follow in his footsteps. Or mine."

Half the guys shuddered. The others grimaced. Aside from Steve and me, they were all single and enjoying it. And they should. I sure as hell enjoyed it in my time. But now, that held zero appeal to me. I was taken, and I was proud of it, and I couldn't wait to get home to my woman.

Half an hour later, I opened the door to my condo. The place smelled like cinnamon.

"Kendra?"

"Hey." She poked her head out from the kitchen before running toward me and jumping in my arms. I caught her by her ass, and she immediately wrapped her legs around me.

I captured her mouth, kissing her like I hadn't seen her in months, but I needed her more desperately than usual. I'd missed having her out there today, and I wanted her to know it.

The scent of vanilla caught my attention. Pulling back, I realized the whole place smelled like baked goods. "What's smelling so good?"

"I made you apple pie at home."

I blinked, looking at her as I slowly put her down. "You baked for me?"

"Yeah. I wanted to do something nice for you." She smiled sheepishly. "My paycheck didn't deposit yet, so I couldn't splurge the way I'd hoped, but I wanted to do something."

I didn't know why this meant so much to me. This woman literally lived one paycheck to the next, but she wanted to do something for *me*. "I'll have the pie, and then I'll have you."

"What? No, no, no." She twirled once, shimmying her hips. "You're supposed to decompress after games."

I laughed. "They just mean no workouts. Trust me."

She took two plates, putting a slice on each, one for me and one for her, and it dawned on me that my place smelled like home for the first time. I had a flashback to my childhood when Gran's house seemed to perpetually smell of something delicious, and this transported me right back there.

I took a bite, and she looked at me, narrowing her eyes.

"Uh-oh, you're not saying anything."

"It's delicious. Thanks. I was lost in thought."

"About what?"

In a fraction of a second, I pulled her against me. "About you."

My life had always revolved around hockey. During the season, I always had my eyes on the Stanley Cup. Being the best at hockey and making my teammates and parents proud were all I'd cared about.

But now I cared about making this woman happy and making it clear to her just how happy she made me in return.

CHAPTER TWENTY-FOUR
TYLER

"Thanks for coming here tonight," I said.

"Really? Even though I sort of ruined your celebration with the guys?"

"Trust me. You didn't. I'll take you over the guys any day."

She pressed her palms on my chest, rising on her tiptoes to kiss my chin. I tilted my head, claiming her lips instead. She moaned against my mouth as I kissed her long and deep, with deliberate strokes.

She was wearing a simple black sweater dress with a zipper in the middle. I lowered it immediately, pushing it off her shoulders and dragging it down her arms. I skimmed my thumb across her skin the whole time, feeling her getting worked up. Her breath quickened in response. I walked her backward, discarding my sweater when we paused for breath. I got rid of my pants and boxers next. She was wearing red lingerie and looked insanely sexy.

I took a step back, watching her.

"I dressed up for you. And got rid of the tights before you came. Whoops, you weren't supposed to know that."

"You look incredible. You're so damn sexy."

I took off her bra first, deliberately not touching her breasts when it dropped to the floor. Then I pulled her panties down, kissing her thighs when she stepped out of them. Her skin looked so smooth, and it felt even smoother. I ran a hand from the middle of her upper thigh up to her waist before bringing her flush against me, her back to my front. I kissed the right side of her neck, tilting her head to the left, alternating between kissing just with my lips and also pressing the tip of my tongue against her skin. She moaned, and I moved my hand from her waist up to her breasts, flicking her nipples.

"Tyler," she whispered.

I smiled against her skin, cupping her breast in my hand.

"I love their shape. I love everything about you."

I slid my other hand down between her legs. She instantly tensed in my arms in anticipation. The things I was going to do to this woman. Tonight I was going to rock her world.

I only teased her clit with my fingertips, feeling her tense even more. I was paying attention to every reaction of hers, the way she sucked in her breath or squirmed in my arms. A thin sheet of sweat was forming between our bodies already, and my cock was rock hard, pressing between her inner thighs.

I moved two fingers farther down her pussy, and she pressed her ass right against my erection.

"Fuck, Kendra, fuck!" I slid two fingers inside her, curving them and pressing my palm on her clit at the same time. She cried out loud, throwing her head back against my shoulder. I brought my mouth to her ear.

"I want you inside me," she whispered.

"Already?" I teased.

"Yes, already."

"I'm not going to be inside you until you come, Kendra, like this, with my fingers in your pussy. The best foreplay is an orgasm."

She shuddered, clenching her inner muscles around my fingers. Fucking hell, this woman! I felt her get more aroused at my words. I held her like that, one hand on her breast and the other between her legs. I kissed her, moving my tongue in a similar rhythm to my fingers. Then I changed it all up.

I kept kissing her, moving my fingers between her legs. I stroked, then pushed in, and then I stroked her clit again. I felt her whole body tighten, and I rocked my hips back and forth. Feeling the soft skin on her inner thighs was daunting.

"That's it," I murmured. Her body tightened even more. "That's it, baby. Surrender to me. Don't fight it. Don't fight me."

"I'm not fighting it," she whispered. "I just don't think I can take it."

"Trust me, you can."

I slid my fingers halfway in, pressing the heel of my palm against her pubic bone, and she let out a groan. It was a long-drawn-out sound. She clasped my back with her hands as if needing to brace herself and needing as much contact as possible. I held her tight, drinking in every sound she made, the way her body responded to the pleasure.

It took her several minutes to calm down, and then she looked at me sideways with a sated smile. I bit her upper lip and then pulled back so I could look at her.

"The best foreplay is an orgasm, huh? I really like it."

"Ready for the second one?" I asked.

She swallowed hard, and her eyes widened a little. "I didn't feel ready for the first one either. But you seem to know my body better than I do."

"You're so fucking ready, I promise you." I bent her over the arms of the couch, putting on a condom. She looked back at me, licking her lips. Her face was flushed, and she was gripping the edge of the couch tightly as if bracing herself for me.

My own body was pulsing. I pressed my fingers against her

thighs, dragging them up her ass, kissing her back until I reached her ear. I brought my hand between her legs, skimming my fingers over her pussy. "Fuck, you're so wet for me."

She let out a sound between a moan and a groan.

"Can't even talk anymore?" I teased. She gasped, pushing her ass up a bit in the air. I slid in carefully, inch by inch, pausing for her to accommodate me. Fuck, she was so tight. "You're amazing, babe. You're so damn amazing."

Her inner muscles pulsed when I was all the way in, so I kept moving slowly, drawing it out. The pleasure was so intense that my thighs were already burning. My whole body seemed to be on fire as energy pulsed through my erection. Moving at this pace, I felt everything more intensely: the way she clenched around my cock, the way her body felt under mine. I was barely keeping my climax at bay, but I focused on her pleasure again. I stopped for a few seconds and worked her clit with my fingers, feeling her tighten and relax around me.

"Tyler, this is so good. I'm going to... Oh my God, oh my God, this feels so good! You feel so good."

"That's it, babe." I was moving again, slowly. I wanted her to come again before I chased my own orgasm.

I moved just a bit faster, and it pushed her over the edge. She came with a loud groan, gripping the edge of the couch so tight that her knuckles were white.

I didn't fight my climax any longer. I gave in, pushing in and out, riding the wave of pleasure until I gave Kendra everything I had. I almost collapsed on top of her out of relief, but instead, I braced one palm against the back of the couch and pushed myself up. She groaned in protest when I pulled out.

"Nooo, where are you going?"

"You don't want me to collapse over you."

"Hmm, Mr. Superstar Goalie, are you so spent that you

couldn't even hold a position for any longer?" She turned sideways, wiggling her eyebrows.

"You're a bit too sassy after an orgasm."

"I know. Apparently this is what you do to me. You increase my level of sass with every orgasm. And you didn't answer my question."

"Yeah, yeah. I was too spent."

She wiggled her eyebrows again, and I hooked an arm around her waist, pulling her flat against me and capturing her mouth, kissing her the way I wanted to do earlier but couldn't, deep and long until we were both out of breath. Her eyes widened when I pulled back, and she braced her palms on my shoulders.

"That's better. Now, I need some sustenance."

I tilted my head. It was my turn to tease her. "So you need some sustenance too, huh?"

She shrugged. "Maybe."

"Come on, I admitted it."

"That's true. You did." She tapped her fingers against her cheek as if this required intense thought. "Fine, okay, I admit it too. That first orgasm made my knees weak. And that second one just took everything out of me. In a good way, though."

"Good to know."

Both our bodies were covered in a thin sheen of sweat.

"Come on, sexy girl, want a shower?"

"Hmm, no. I like you sweaty," She was looking at me with a shy smile. "I'm going to miss you during away games."

I liked that she was opening up to me. Kendra liked to be careful. Considering her past, it wasn't a surprise, but I was damn proud that she was finally letting her guard down.

"I'm going to miss you too. Today, I looked in the stands, and the fans were there being crazy as usual, and I was happy, but I kept thinking that I want *you* there."

Her eyes widened. "Me?"

"Yeah. You mean a lot to me, Kendra."

"I'd love to come to a game. But right now, I'm still sad that you'll be away for a whole week."

"I'll call every day."

She smiled brilliantly. "Promise?"

"Fuck yeah."

"I'm going to be super busy in the afternoons. Luke's handymen have started working on my house, so I'm going to drop by every day to check on the progress. And Reese scheduled a girly evening after your last game. We're going out to celebrate."

"You're so sure we'll win?"

"Obviously."

I kissed her hard and unapologetically, exploring her mouth until she moaned. Her lips were red when I pulled back.

"You're—" I began, but she interrupted me with a shake of her head.

"No, wait a few seconds. I'm still light-headed from the kiss."

I burst out laughing, drawing my fingers up and down her belly.

"You're fucking adorable," I said. "Thanks for going out with Reese."

"Sure thing. Lexi is coming too. And I've heard her sister is also flying in from Paris."

"Kimberly mentioned it, yes."

"I think Reese needs some time with girlfriends. She might not be ready for a new guy, but she's ready for friends."

I liked how well she got Reese and that she was willing to spend time with my cousin. I'd never had this kind of intimacy in my life before—staying naked on the couch, talking about everything important in our lives.

"Hmm... ready to eat some more of that pie I made?" she suggested after a moment.

"Sure. I forgot about it."

She brought a hand to her chest in a theatric movement. "Oh no. I'd say you're mean, but I forgot too with all our sexy adventures. But now I'm hungry."

We got to our feet. Kendra walked in front of me, and I couldn't resist palming one ass cheek. The next second, I wrapped an arm around her waist from behind, and we walked like that to the kitchen island. She tripped halfway through, but I kept her firmly against me as her whole body shook with guffaws.

"This is solid proof that you're dangerous for me," she said between fits of laughter.

"I could say the same."

When we finally reached the counter, she carefully cut two more slices of the apple pie, putting them on our plates from before.

"This is Mom's recipe. We made it all the time during the cold season. I used sugar replacement. I read it's better for pro athletes."

I stopped in the act of taking a second bite, glancing at her. She'd researched it? "Thanks, babe."

She sighed. "I can't believe you're leaving."

"Hey, even during away games, I can think of a way or two to be close to you. Hint: we've got phones, babe. And they've got cameras."

"Are you going to try to talk me into having phone sex with you? I'm just saying that the chances of convincing me are high. And I want it noted that I've never said those words before. You're changing me. Just thought you should know."

She laughed, and I moved behind her, putting both hands

on her hips. I wanted her here, in my condo, baking pies and walking around naked, tripping over nothing.

Drawing the tip of my nose along the side of her neck, I kissed under her ear.

"So noted."

CHAPTER TWENTY-FIVE
KENDRA

The next couple of weeks moved at an insane pace. Tyler was gone more than he was here, and I was happy for him, but I also missed him a lot.

Luke's contractor started working on my house. I was beyond grateful that he'd accepted to be paid in several installments, but I still needed the money from Jared to make it all work. I still hadn't talked to Tyler about it, but I planned to do so tomorrow after he returned from New York. They'd played the New York Hellions today, and they won!

I was in a celebratory mood and couldn't wait to go out with Reese, Lexi, and Kimberly, who was here for a week. They invited Emma too. It was going to be amazing. Truthfully, it was just an excuse to go out, but I'd been so busy lately that I'd take any excuse I could get.

Right before I left my apartment, I had taken a picture of myself in the mirror, sending it to Tyler, though I had no clue when he was going to see it.

I met the girls at a trendy bar in the West Loop, just a block away from Tyler's condo. Emma came with me, and we were both dressed to impress. I was wearing a short red dress, sheer tights, and black heels with a strap, and Emma was in black pants and a yellow top with a pink hat. Lexi had a tight dress that showed off her curves. Reese wore jeans and a black silk top with spaghetti straps and looked like a million bucks.

"Nice to meet you," Kimberly said, shaking my hand and then Emma's. Her hair was in curls. She was wearing a black skirt and a sweater hanging off one shoulder, kind of a carefree ensemble. She looked fabulous. "Okay, so the motto for tonight is 'The girls are having fun.'"

The bar was in a staylish corner building painted green and black. We chose a round table that was strategically close to the counter.

"Tequila is on the house, ladies," the bartender said.

"Wait, did we just step into heaven?" Kimberly asked. "How is tequila on the house?"

"They just want to get us drunk to order more," Reese replied.

"That makes sense," I said.

We all raised our glasses.

"To everyone being together," Reese added before we clinked our drinks and downed them.

"Woohoo," I exclaimed. I was the first one to plunk down my glass, and Emma finished next.

Lexi came in third, and then she tapped her fingers against the table. "It feels good to be out with the girls."

"We should make it a thing," Reese declared. She glanced at Emma and me. "All of us. You two included."

My sister grinned. "Damn, all I have to do is show up and I'm already invited to all future events. I like this family."

I just smiled, feeling a bit shaky. As usual, I was emotional at being included so effortlessly. And also, as usual, my sister just accepted it all at face value.

"Okay. Let's order something," Kimberly said. "Look, they have a special page with *handcrafted* cocktails."

"What the fuck is that? All cocktails are poured by hand." Reese snickered.

"I'm guessing it's just a fancy way to name them so they can charge more. But damn, they sound sexy," I said, perusing the menu. I ordered a strawberry daiquiri with a secret ingredient. Every cocktail was a well-known one but with a twist.

This would be fun. I was so relaxed with these girls, it was like I'd known them forever.

My sister nudged me. "You know what? We should include drinks in our spill-it sessions."

Kimberly straightened in her seat. "What's that?"

"Oh, my sister and I, we just have regular catch-up times. We call them our spill-it sessions."

"I like that," Kimberly said. "We should do the same." She looked at Reese and then at Lexi.

Lexi shrugged. "I'm up for it."

"So, how does it work?" Kimberly asked. I had the impression she might take out a notepad any second now and write down everything.

"We don't have rules or anything. We just say whatever is weighing on us or on our minds."

"Should we start now? I mean, it seems as good a time as any. We have drinks. They have dodgy ways of getting our money. There's a dance floor for us and more drinks. And oh, a hot bartender." Kimberly looked behind the bar before focusing back on us.

Reese nodded. "I'll go first. I'm seeing a new therapist, and I need to know why I still care enough to be hurt by Malcolm and my ex-best friend getting married. The old therapist couldn't help, so I needed an upgrade." She was saying this in a playful tone, but it was obvious she was suffering.

Kimberly put an arm around her shoulders, pulling her in for a hug. "We're not therapists, but we can listen."

Lexi held up a finger. "We can also throw eggs at his car. I offered it once, and it still stands, especially now when I've got some extra liquid courage from the tequila... or from the cocktail."

"Or we can throw them at hers," Emma suggested.

I felt bolder than usual, so I offered, "Or both of them?"

Kimberly looked at her sister intently. The chatter of the people around us was pretty loud, though, so we all had to lean in whenever we spoke so we could hear anything.

"You could come to Paris for a while. I stand by my offer to introduce you to a Frenchman or two. And they'll take your mind off that asshole."

Reese blushed.

Lexi did a little shimmy in her seat and pointed at Kimberly with both her forefingers, moving her shoulders up and down. "You are a genius. I think that's exactly what Reese needs: a change of scenery."

Reese ran a hand through her hair, straightening up at the table, and we all came a bit closer. "You know what? I might do it, but only if you can take some time off. I don't want to be in Paris on my own."

"I'll try," Kimberly said. "There's a lot going on at the travel agency, but it won't go under without me."

"That must be so fun," Emma said, "to work as a travel agent."

"Oh, it is fun," Kimberly said. Clearing her throat, she looked around the table. "I think Gran's seeing someone." Groaning, she tipped her chin into her chest. "That was not my secret to share. I'm terrible. I just felt like exploding if I didn't tell someone."

Reese jerked her head back. "Wait, what? How?"

Somewhere behind us, the bartender turned the music louder. We had to hover around our table even more.

Kimberly bit her lip. "I saw her drinking coffee with an elderly gentleman at the coffee shop next to The Happy Place."

"I go to The Happy Place every day. How come I didn't see this?" Reese asked indignantly.

"I guess she's careful around you," Lexi said.

"I'm happy for her but also stunned. Well, maybe it was just a coffee anyway, and we can't say anything until she does."

"I agree," Kimberly added. Turning to me, Emma, and Lexi, she said, "Sorry, girls, we hijacked this evening."

"Hey, we're enjoying this, aren't we, sis?" Emma exclaimed.

I nodded. "We are."

Lexi was drumming her fingers on the table. "I wish that for Beatrice. But I don't want to get my hopes up, because you know how much she cares about your granddad."

"Has she been a widow for long?" I asked.

"Oh yeah. I think she's been a widow for longer than she was married. To be honest, I can't do the math after so much alcohol," Reese said.

"We never even met Grandad. He died before we were born when Dad was still in college. But I know what you mean, Lexi. She's still so attached to him. Part of why she keeps The Happy Place is because it was the first thing they built together. And every year around the anniversary of his death, she just goes into this sad place inside her, where we can't reach her," Kimberly explained.

My heart hurt for the poor woman.

"But Paisley can," Lexi said. "I mean, not consciously. They don't talk about it, but she's happy when she's around Paisley."

"That's true," Kimberly said.

I couldn't help but wonder how things might be like if both our parents were still with us. We'd probably have a very similar dynamic to the Maxwells. I smiled despite the bout of sadness settling in my chest, bringing the glass to my lips.

For my entire adult life, I didn't feel like I belonged anywhere. It was just me and Emma against the world. But now, for the first time, I felt like I belonged here with these girls.

"Shall we get another round?" Kimberly asked.

"Sure." I made to reach for the menu when my phone lit up with a message. It was from Tyler.

Tyler: Hey, beautiful girl. Guess who's back early. Declan just picked me up from the airport. Where are you and the girls?

"Oh my God. Tyler's back early," I exclaimed.

"Woohoo. Our champion's back," Lexi chanted.

"He wants to know where we are," I mentioned.

Kimberly burst out laughing. "I can't believe he's crashing girls' night."

"I can," Reese singsonged.

"Oh, I'm going to tease him about this forever," Kimberly announced.

So would I, but I couldn't wait to see my man.

CHAPTER TWENTY-SIX
KENDRA

Tyler and Declan arrived a short while later. I jumped to my feet, excited to see my sexy goalie, and wrapped my arms around his neck as soon as he was in front of me. He sealed his lips over mine the next second, kissing me so wickedly hot that my entire body felt on fire. He didn't hold back at all. He tasted like mint and smelled like shower gel, and he overwhelmed all my senses. We only stopped because I heard distinctive whistling sounds even over the music.

Tyler looked at me with hooded eyes as he pulled back, smiling lazily at the table. "What? I've been away. Can't I kiss my girl?"

"Of course you can," Kimberly said, "the whistles were appreciative."

"You were gone for one week," Reese pointed out, "but I think this proves my theory about the true soul mate."

"What theory is that?" I asked, perking up.

"Never mind," Reese said quickly.

I made a mental note to address it in the future. If the girly evenings were here to stay, I was going to make the spill-it tradition a regular thing.

"Declan, thanks for picking him up from the airport," I said.

"No problem," Declan replied. "Couldn't let the star goalie be ambushed by people. I mean, he sort of was anyway."

Tyler waved his hand. "It's nothing I'm not used to."

"Okay, well, since you two are here to stay and crash our girly evening, how about a shot to celebrate the win?" I suggested.

"I don't want to drink," Tyler said. "Too close to the next game. But I'm happy to treat you all to a round."

He and Declan pulled up two chairs, and we made space at the table. Tyler sat right next to me, and Declan sat between Reese and Kimberly.

"Handcrafted cocktails? What the fuck?" Declan exclaimed.

Kimberly made a loud noise between a guffaw and a snort. "I forgot that you and I are two peas in a pod. I'm still annoyed that they have the nerve to charge extra for that."

I shifted a bit closer to Tyler and whispered somewhat shyly, "Welcome home."

He squeezed my thigh, looking at me with soft, heavy eyes.

"I missed you," he said, "and I know it's just been a week."

"I missed you too," I confessed. "I'm happy you came home earlier. Didn't your teammates give you a hard time?"

"Nah. Well, the ones who are single did. The ones who aren't actually came back too."

When our round of drinks came, we all clinked to Tyler, who put a possessive hand on the middle of my back, pulling me close to him.

"This is for you," I said, turning to him and downing the tequila.

"Kendra, Luke says the workers are making good progress at your house. How did it go with getting the paychecks from your ex-boss?" Declan asked.

Crap. I looked at Tyler. "I didn't go there yet... or have a chance to tell Tyler."

"What? Babe?" Tyler asked, turning to me. I bit my lip, ran my hand through my hair, and sighed. "Tell me what?"

"My ex-boss owes me a few paychecks and insists on me coming to the diner. I went once—the evening those guys wanted to mug me—but he wasn't there. I didn't want to go again alone. But I'm cash strapped, so I have to go before the next payment to the contractor is due."

"Why didn't you tell me until now?" he asked as soon as I finished.

"I wanted you to focus on the games, okay?"

He squared his shoulders, clenching his jaw. "Fuck the games, Kendra. Don't keep stuff like this from me. I need to know what's going on in your life."

Declan leaned closer. "I knew you'd react like this."

"How come you knew?" Tyler asked.

Declan groaned. "Fuck, I need Luke for this. I'm no good at playing devil's advocate."

"Luke knows too?" Tyler looked at me expectantly.

I dipped my head. "I told them when we met for coffee. It was a slip of the tongue. I didn't mean to."

He ran his hand through his hair but didn't say anything else.

"Oookay, the mood just turned sour," Reese said. "Why don't we let the two of you talk it out?"

"No, no, it's your party," I protested.

"Let's go home," Tyler said, looking straight at me. His eyes were full of fire, and his jaw was still clenched so damn tight.

I nodded, wanting to be alone with him too.

As the two of us stood up, so did Emma.

"Hey, play nice with my sister. She only thought about not distracting you."

"Yeah, play nice," Reese said.

Kimberly pointed at Tyler. "I'm going to ask for a report tomorrow, just so you know. We're holding you accountable."

Tyler always had a fun comeback for his family's teasing, but he didn't say anything. I glanced at Declan, who was looking straight at his brother. Maybe he picked up on the vibe too, because he didn't attempt to tease him.

"You want to take your bag from my car?" he asked Tyler instead.

"Yeah, let's go."

Declan came out with us. He'd parked across from the bar. I shivered, and Tyler put an arm around me. Then I shivered even more, fretting about the rest of the evening. I felt guilty for not telling him until now. This was not how I'd hoped he'd find out.

Declan unlocked his trunk, and Tyler took out his bag.

"Want me to drive you two home?" Declan offered. "It's just a block."

Tyler looked at me. "Kendra, you want him to drive us? We can Uber or walk, but you're wearing heels."

I melted a little at the fact that even though he was mad, he was still considerate enough to ask about my shoes. "Let's walk. Some fresh air will do me good."

"Okay, then, I'm going back inside with the group," Declan said. "Actually, wait a second. I'll be the only dude hanging out at a girls' evening. What does that make me?"

Tyler patted his shoulder. "Girls' night crasher? I'll let you work out that conundrum for yourself."

We walked away, hand in hand, and Tyler didn't speak one word. I felt a bit tense. He was silent even after we entered his condo. I was expecting him to say something, but he looked lost in thought, as if he was trying to figure something out.

"Tyler?" I asked tentatively.

He put his bag to one side, squaring his shoulders and

looking me straight in the eye. Coming closer, he cupped my face.

"Kendra, I meant every word, babe. You're important to me. Yes, hockey's been my whole life, but that was before I met you. I don't want you to keep anything from me no matter what is going on in my life. You are a priority. You are *my* priority. Do you understand that?"

I nodded but didn't say anything because I had a huge and heavy knot in my throat.

"You don't think I'll stick around? Is that why you didn't tell me?"

I put my hands over his, shaking my head frantically. "No, that's not it." Then I sighed because it dawned on me that he might be right. "Not consciously. Okay, maybe it was just a little bit."

More silence followed. He was looking straight at me. Was I unconsciously fearing people might bolt because Mom's boyfriends did?

"Kendra, I want the privilege to do that. To come through for you every single time and be by your side, know when you're down and lift you back up, be your man no matter what."

My heart seemed to increase in size with every second. Pushing myself up on my tiptoes, I brought my mouth to his and kissed him. I needed him so much. I needed to feel close to him.

Kissing him gently at first, I feathered my mouth over his upper lip and then the lower one. Then I ran my tongue over the lower one, just with the tip. I felt his arms tense around me.

"I love you," I whispered.

Tyler was the one who kissed me now, claiming my mouth and burying a hand in my hair. "I love you too, babe. Fuck, how I love you."

"It's the first time I've ever said it," I whispered.

"It's the same for me."

I felt my eyes widen.

"I've never felt like this about anyone else. I love you, Kendra. Do you understand me?"

I nodded, completely overwhelmed by his declaration.

"Now, come on," he urged. "Tell me everything in detail, okay? Don't leave anything out."

Taking my hand, he led me deeper inside the condo, and we sat on the couch.

"There isn't much to the story, just what I said before. Up until last year, I worked at a diner as a waitress during weekends, and, well, I wasn't on good terms with the boss when I left there, and then he just kept 'forgetting' to pay my last two paychecks. I didn't ask him for it because I was too proud. But anyway, now with the house payments, I do need it."

"Babe, why didn't you tell me you needed money? I can always help."

"No, please don't do that, okay? Emma keeps offering too. I'm a grown woman, and I can sort out my shit... mostly. Anyway, the diner isn't in a great area. It's in Hegewisch."

"That's where you went the evening you were mugged?"

"Almost mugged," I corrected. "And yes. I honestly don't want to go there by myself again, so I was wondering if you could come with me."

"Of course I can, babe. I can't believe you didn't tell me."

"You had a lot on your mind with the games."

"Kendra, I will always have games. That doesn't mean you can't share everything that goes on in your life."

"I don't want to distract you," I said quietly.

"You're part of my life, not a distraction." He pulled me into his lap, caressing my jaw. "I don't have a game tomorrow, just training. Let's go pick up your checks."

"Okay. That sounds good. So, you love me, huh?" I asked, shimmying in his lap.

He clasped my thigh, moving his hand upward on my waist, pressing his fingers into my sweater possessively. "Yes I fucking do."

I smiled from ear to ear, lacing my hands around his neck. "I love hearing it. Just a hint: you can say it all night long, and I won't tire of it."

"Good. That was my plan."

CHAPTER TWENTY-SEVEN
KENDRA

When I woke up the next morning, Tyler wasn't next to me, so I went in search of him throughout the condo. I was an early riser, but Tyler even more so. He wasn't anywhere.

Going back to the bedroom, I checked my phone, and, indeed, he'd messaged me.

Tyler: Morning, beautiful. I'm at the gym on the top floor. I'll be back at 8:00 with breakfast.

Kendra: Okay. I just woke up.

I showered quickly, dressed, and made a coffee. I didn't have my laptop with me, but I did have my iPad in my purse as usual, so I could work on some emails. I didn't have any phone calls scheduled today, but I did have a hell of a list of to-dos.

I got so lost in answering emails that I didn't even realize when the hour went by, and I was startled when Tyler came in.

"Morning, Kendra," he said with that sexy voice of his, holding up a take-out bag.

"What's in there?"

"Breakfast."

I snatched the bag away from him, taking out donuts and

cinnamon rolls. "Oh, look. You even have my favorite cinnamon roll. How did you manage that?"

"As I said, I have my ways."

He looked gorgeous, and he seemed to have already showered at the gym. He was wearing a black T-shirt with short sleeves, and it molded to his muscles in an absolutely delicious way.

"I don't know what's more tempting, you or breakfast," I said.

He laughed, cocking a brow. "I'm competing with breakfast?"

"Oh yeah."

I took a bite of the donut, not even bothering to put it on a plate, and moaned. "Oh my God. This is delicious. And just so you know, you're losing. I love you, but you're losing this competition."

The next second, I felt him behind me, kissing my neck. "No I'm not," he said, almost in a growl.

Having him so near overwhelmed my senses. His abs were pressing against my back, and his skin was still humid from the shower. The smell of his shower gel filled the air: the forest and a cold winter day. He drew the tip of his nose up my neck. Usually it would turn me on, but right then, it tickled the hell out of me. I tried to fight it, but I broke out in laughter when he reached my jaw.

"Oh my God. I'm so sorry. I couldn't hold it in anymore."

He straightened up, turning me around. "I tickle you now?"

I grinned. "Hey, I can't focus on two things at once if one of those things is a donut. My other senses are kind of confused."

"Right. Okay," he said and, to my astonishment, didn't add anything else.

So, of course, I finished the donut and then ate half the cinnamon roll. He was still watching me, but I didn't question it, at least not until I had my portion of sugar and carbs and I was in seventh heaven.

"Okay. So, what's happening? What are you waiting for?"

"For you to finish," he said.

"I'm done."

He sealed his mouth over mine the next second. *Holy smokes!* It was so damn hot, his tongue pressing against mine, his fingers wrapped in my hair. My sexy goalie kissed me until my knees were completely weak.

"Now that was a kiss," I murmured when we pulled apart.

He was looking at me intently.

I narrowed my eyes. "You want me to tell you if you win the competition against breakfast, don't you?"

"Absolutely," he said with a straight face.

"You're such a guy," I whispered.

He laughed, kissing my forehead. "Are you ready to go to the diner?" he asked.

"Aren't you eating?"

"No, I'm not hungry. I'll probably eat with the guys at training later."

"Okay, then, let's go."

We drove in his car, which absolutely didn't belong in Hegewisch. Since it was so early, we found a parking spot right in front of the diner. It was run-down even when I worked here, but now it seemed even worse. It was a car repair shop that had been converted into a diner, and it looked exactly like that. The smell of fried food was pungent the second we stepped in, mixed with alcohol. Oh goodness, the clientele seemed just as bad as before. It was ten o'clock in the morning, yet there were already people drinking beers.

Tyler put on a cap to shield himself from everyone's view. This was the type of place where no one really cared to look at each other too closely. Steeling myself and rolling my shoulders, I headed straight to the back. I recognized Clarissa at the bar; she'd worked here last year too.

"Hey, babe," she greeted with a genuine smile. Her curly hair was now cropped short.

"Hi, Clarissa. It's good to see you. I'm here to see Jared."

"Are you looking for work again?" she asked.

"No, it's about an old thing."

"Okay, well, come on in. He's in there. And you know how he is."

"Yeah I do," I said.

She glanced at Tyler but didn't say anything, so we just passed her. I knocked three times at the back door before Jared said, "Come in."

I opened the door.

He stood up the second I came in. His eyes zeroed in on Tyler.

"What are you doing here?" he asked me. He had thinning hairline and a huge belly.

"You said I had to pick up my checks, so I came to do that."

He gave me a sly grin I didn't like. "And you brought a bodyguard?"

"I'm her boyfriend," Tyler said, looking straight at him.

Jared's eyes widened. "You're dating Tyler Maxwell? Well, at least you're good at something, I guess."

"Shut up, Jared. You're a piece of shit. You treat your staff like garbage. You don't get to lecture me. You owe me money, and I'm not leaving without my paychecks."

Jared opened his mouth, but Tyler interrupted him. "Give her the checks right now. You know my last name, it seems, so stop being a pain in the ass."

"This hellhole you call a diner wouldn't pass an inspection, and you know that," I said.

"No need to threaten me," Jared said, holding up his hands, looking with his slimy eyes from me to Tyler.

"Paychecks. Now," I said, tapping my foot and holding out my hand.

He opened his checkbook and filled out two sheets.

"Here. That's it."

I took them, looking at the numbers.

"Are they correct?" Tyler asked.

"Yes they are. We're done here."

I rolled my shoulders, looking at Jared. And honestly, I felt pity. He was still trying to make a living from this hole-in-the-wall and being miserable every day.

On the way out, I said bye to Clarissa, but we didn't linger because I knew just how much the smell of fried fish could cling to you.

Once we were outside, we headed straight to the car.

"It's good we came in daylight," I said. "I don't know why I came at night last time. And I didn't find a parking spot in front either."

"He's a moron," Tyler said. He seemed visibly mad.

"Oh, that's just Jared. Don't mind him. I don't."

"Was he always such a douchebag?"

"Yes."

"I was so damn proud of you in there, babe."

"Come on. Let's go, sexy goalie. Your training will start soon."

We drove straight to the arena.

"Are you sure you don't want to take the car back to the city?" he asked when we arrived.

"No, it wouldn't make sense. I'm just going to be cooped up in my office all day. And the parking situation is a bit impossible around there. I'll Uber," I said when we both stepped out of the car. "Now, you focus on practicing and forget about Jared, okay? You've got a huge game tomorrow."

They were playing against the Seattle Bulldogs, and guess who was attending? That's right, me.

He was looking straight at me with those gorgeous eyes of his. Rising on my tiptoes, I kissed him just the way he'd done this morning, tongue and all, needing the contact. I only stopped when a groan reverberated through his body. I felt it deep in every cell and pulled back.

"Oops," I said.

"You kiss me like that and want me to think about training?" he asked in a teasing tone.

"Mmm, that was a blip in my control. But since I'm on a slippery slope anyway... Just one more, and then I'll be on my best behavior for the rest of the day. I won't send you any distracting messages. Not even one," I said with a grin.

CHAPTER TWENTY-EIGHT
KENDRA

On the morning of the game, I woke up super early. I had a plan. I wanted to spoil my sexy guy before he started one of the most important days of the year. My mom always said it was important to start a day right, so I got to work as quietly as possible. I wanted to bake a fresh pecan pie. I'd spoken with his mom, asking about her recipe, and I was adding my own touch to it, so I was confident he'd love it.

I put in earbuds while I worked in the kitchen. This was my happy place. I hummed to the music, careful not to be too loud. After I put it in the oven, I cleaned the kitchen until it looked pristine. Then I peeked at the oven. I'd put tin foil on it, so I couldn't see much, but thirty minutes had passed, so now it was time to remove it, which I did quickly. Now it only had to stay in for another twenty minutes. I went to take a quick shower in the guest bathroom so I could be fresh for my man when he woke up.

I was so happy that I couldn't even believe it. I loved Tyler with my whole heart, and I never thought a love like this was possible. I knew, of course, that once upon a time, my parents had loved each other. But as I grew older and, well, more of a cynic, I'd started to wonder if perhaps I'd idealized their relationship. But even if I did, it didn't matter.

I was smiling widely as I danced under the spray, applying Tyler's shower gel and loving the smell of the ocean and winter fragrance. I was so proud that I'd gotten up early and was sure I had some time until Tyler would wake up. But to my astonishment, he was already in the kitchen when I returned.

"Hey. What are you doing up so early?" I asked.

"I woke up, and you weren't next to me."

"What are you doing?" I sounded alarmed, but he was right in front of the oven.

"Looking at the oven." Grabbing the handle, he made to open it, but I ran toward him.

"No, no, no. Don't do that. Don't let the heat out."

Laughing, he let it go, holding his hands up in defense. "Okay, not touching it." He narrowed his eyes. "I can touch you, though."

Instantly, his hands were on my hips, and he pressed me against him.

"Good morning," he said. His eyes were still a bit hazy with sleep. He wasn't wearing a shirt.

Oh, why are you tempting me like this first thing in the morning?

I placed my hands on his chest, near his shoulders, but within a few seconds, they somehow glided down to his abs.

He laughed, tilting his head toward the oven. "What's with that?"

"Your mom mentioned you like pecan pie when we were at their place, and I thought I'd surprise you with one today. I asked for her recipe but also added some secret ingredients."

He looked at me incredulously before his mouth curled in a huge smile. "You woke up extra early to bake me a pie? Fuck, you're cute."

"I wanted to do something to bring you good luck."

He pressed his palms more firmly on my hips. "*You* bring me good luck, Kendra."

"I can't wait to cheer for you. I'll be your loudest fan."

He brought a hand to my face, touching my jaw with his thumb and forefinger. "You do that, and then I'll bring you home and make you scream in other ways."

I blushed. "You can't keep your mind out of the gutter, even before the game, huh?"

"I can always be shameless," he confirmed.

"Of course you can." I turned around, looking at the oven. "Okay, let me take this out. Don't distract me."

"What counts as a distraction? This?" He put a hand on my right ass cheek.

"It *could*," I said in a teasing tone. "I'm not sure."

"How about this?" He pushed my hair to one side, kissing the back of my neck. The skin on my arms turned to goose bumps.

"Tyler," I whispered, rocking back and forth on my feet.

"Okay, so we have our verdict. That's distracting you for sure."

He kissed the side of my neck as I checked on the pie. It was ready. I took it out, putting it on the granite counter,

"It's supposed to cool for thirty minutes and then stay in the fridge for at least two hours before serving."

"Babe, we can't wait for two hours."

"I know. But let it cool at least for a bit." I turned around, looking him in the eyes. "Are you ready for today?"

"Yes. Completely." He interlaced our fingers, holding my right arm up and raining kisses from my wrist to my elbow and then all the way up to my shoulder. I wiggled my ass, enjoying the feeling of his lips on my skin. "I'm completely ready. I love that you're coming to watch the game."

"I couldn't miss an opportunity to show you how big a fan of yours I am. And right now, it's 'spoiling Tyler' time."

"Then let's eat the pie. I don't care if it's hot."

"Okay."

I put one slice on a plate and two little forks on it, holding it between us. He started eating from one end, and I started at the other. I watched his reaction as he shoved the forkful into his mouth and was pleased with the look of obvious pleasure on his face. I ate a bite and shimmied my hips in happiness because it was delicious.

"I don't want to sing my own praises, but this is good."

"It is, babe. Thanks for doing this. Thanks for just being you, Kendra. You're amazing."

"And you're good with words."

"You're perfect, babe. You're just fucking perfect." He took the plate from my hands, putting it on the counter, even though we'd only had one bite each.

"What are you doing? You just had a taste."

"And now I want one of you."

"Oh. Well, by all means, go ahead." I smiled against his lips as he kissed me. To my surprise, it was gentle. He was exploring me exquisitely, and it turned me on to no end.

I tried not to let it show, though. I didn't even press my thighs together when heat shot through them. Nope, I was going to soldier through my arousal, because I knew for a fact that any sexy activities the day of the game were not the best idea. He could have muscle cramps on the ice, and bottom line, he needed to stay focused. Besides, I planned to give him plenty of sexy time after the game tonight.

"We can't do this right now," I whispered, pushing him away. But would you look at that? I had a hand on the waistband of his pants. I immediately let it drop. "Whoops. I don't know how this happened."

With a grin, he straightened up. "Every time I'm with you, I lose my head, Kendra. It's what you do to me. I'm so wrapped up in everything you make me feel that I can't think straight."

"Hmm. I like the sound of that."

"Why are you so well-behaved?"

"My hand in your pants was well-behaved?"

"It was on the waistband," he pointed out.

I placed both hands on his shoulders, determined to keep them there.

"True. I woke up with this mantra in my mind. 'No jumping Tyler's bones this morning. No jumping his bones.'"

He threw his head back, laughing.

"What? You're hard to resist. You know you are."

"I like hearing it from you."

"And I don't mind repeating it. But you could have more mercy on me. You came into this kitchen half naked, with all those delicious muscles on display. You are not making it easy for me to do the right thing."

"I can't wait for tonight," he said in a low, sexy voice. "When we're back home, the game behind us, it's just you and me and nothing else."

"I can't wait either," I whispered. "Now come on. Let's eat some more of this pie. I didn't wake up early for nothing."

We spent another hour together before he had to go to the arena. I had enough time to go home and do some chores for a couple hours before I had to change to go watch the game.

I was on edge the whole time I dressed. I couldn't explain why, but this felt like such a monumental thing. I was so, so happy that Tyler wanted to include me in his life in every way possible. I loved him so very much.

I arrived at the arena ten minutes before the game was

about to start. I followed Tyler's instructions to a T, sitting in the area where many other friends and family members of teammates were seated.

I grinned when I noticed Reese, Travis, Luke, and Declan.

"I didn't know you all were coming," I exclaimed.

"We didn't know either," Travis said.

"It was a last-minute inspiration," Reese added.

Declan nodded. "We know this is an important game for him."

I grinned. I'd read about the rivalry between the Chicago Blades and the Seattle Bulldogs. Some reporters jokingly called the "Dogs" the archnemesis.

"I'm going to buy some drinks. Does anyone want anything?" Declan continued.

"I'd like a soda," I replied.

"I'm coming with you," Travis said.

"Me too," Luke added.

Reese stood on her toes, looking at something in the distance. "Okay, I think there isn't a line to the restroom. I'm going to go fast."

The four of them left, and I looked around, taking it all in.

A pretty blonde turned to me. "Hey, Kendra, right?" She stood on the row below ours, welcoming me and holding her arms open as if to hug me.

"Hi." I stepped closer, bending at the waist.

She kissed my cheek. "I'm Andrea, Steve's wife. He's the captain."

"Oh, nice to meet you."

"Steve told me to keep an eye on you, but I see that's not necessary. Nice to meet you."

"And you," I said, looking around. "It's so full."

"Of course, it's one of the most important games of the season. And the boys are so on edge."

"They are, right?"

"Yeah. They've been training more than usual. But they kicked ass last year, and I'm sure they'll kick ass this year as well."

"The arena is so intimidating," I said. I was still looking around.

"You haven't been here before?"

"No, it's my first time."

"Wow. I think you'll enjoy it."

"I promised Tyler I'll cheer for him super loudly."

Andrea grinned. "I like you, Kendra. I'm so happy Tyler didn't listen to Daniels's warnings."

I knitted my brows together. " What warnings?"

"Well, the guy basically told Tyler it wasn't smart to mix business and pleasure. But Tyler's always had a mind of his own. It's not easy to sway him."

"True. It's not," I said, frowning as I looked at the ice. The team's manager had warned him against dating me? Why hadn't Tyler said something?

I searched for the management box, and though it was easy to spot, it was too far away to see anyone. And even if I did, I'd only ever spoken to management via email. I wouldn't recognize anyone.

My heart started beating faster. I couldn't help feeling even happier knowing he'd gone ahead and pursued me, even though he'd been warned not to. That was how much he wanted me. That was how much he cared.

The Maxwells returned quickly with the drinks, and I was tempted to ask them if they knew anything about what Andrea had said. But then I decided against it. I didn't want to spoil the mood, and besides, my heart was about to burst with happiness. I didn't think it was possible, but I felt like I loved him even more than before.

CHAPTER TWENTY-NINE
TYLER

My woman was in the stands, watching me, and I felt on top of the world when I skated out on the ice. My name reverberated through the rink as they announced me, and I heard the fans cheering in the background. I searched the crowd for one person and found her in the Blades' suite. I kept her gaze, flashing a smile just for my girl.

Steve skated right next to me, putting a hand on my shoulder. "Dude, keep your head in the game. I need you to focus and be the best. I need you for this game."

"Steve, I'm in top shape."

"I know you are. I mean mentally. Yesterday during training, your mind was more on your girlfriend working in that dingy diner for that sleazy boss. I don't want any of that distracting you."

"You have nothing to worry about," I said, loud enough for the MVP of our opponents, Adrian, to hear. He was close enough to eavesdrop—such a jackass. The whole Most Valuable Player accolade had melted his brain.

"Good. Just keep your head in the game."

"Will do," I said.

Adrian snickered. I removed my glove and flipped him the bird. Asshole did it right back.

Fucker.

The rivalry was normal in hockey. If I was honest, it was useful. It pushed each team to play their best. But Adrian and I never saw eye to eye on anything. I didn't like the way he played. It was dirty.

The second the game began, all thoughts of Adrian or anything else evaporated from my mind. It was a blank slate. My eyes were on the puck. I blocked goals left and right, again and again.

I heard the fans roaring as if from a distance. I wasn't able to understand what they said, obviously, but I knew the gist of it. I felt empowered every time they cheered or called my name.

Coach used the first intermission to school us good.

"Men, you were strong, but I know you can do better. Tyler, your game is on point. Leo and Joe, we need more goals. Tyler alone won't be able to win us this game. He can't score any goals. You can, so do it."

"Yes, sir," they both said. They were frowning, and I appreciated that Coach wasn't harder on them because I knew they were being extremely hard on themselves anyway.

I went between the two of them, patting each one's shoulder. "Come on, guys, we can do it. Let's get back on the ice and show them why we won the Stanley Cup."

That made Joe light up. He gave me a thumbs-up. "Yeah. Let's do that, man. Down with the Dogs."

I went back to the crease, moving from left to right, staying as limber as possible. I was blocking everything in sight, and I knew I had to build my mental strength. When a goalie managed to stop every puck that got in his way, there was only one thing to do: distract him, attack him, shift his focus. You couldn't beat a team if you couldn't score.

During the next TV timeout, I skated close to my bench. Steve was there drinking a swig of water.

"Good game, man," he said. "Not sure we'll win this one, but it won't be for your lack of trying."

"We'll win," I assured him.

"Really? Are you sure of that, Maxwell?"

I turned around. Adrian stopped in front of us.

"We don't need your commentary," Steve said, rising from the bench.

"Why not? I can congratulate you on your game."

"No you can't. You're being a jackass, so what's your angle today?" I asked.

"That pretty girlfriend of yours."

"Leave her out of it," I said, not intending to say any more. Kendra was none of his fucking business.

"Maybe I won't. What kind of work did she do in that *dingy diner* with the *sleazy boss*? By the looks of her, a stripper. Or something more? She seems willing enough, jumping up and down like a fucking puck bunny. Maybe she's tired of you and wants to give one of us a spin."

Now that pissed me off. I thought Adrian appeared to have been eavesdropping on me and Steve before the game started, and apparently he'd listened to every word.

"Shut your mouth," I said through gritted teeth.

"Maybe I'll take your wife for a spin too, *Captain*." He said "Captain" like it was a curse word. "She's been looking so sad lately that I think she needs a good fucking, and you aren't up for the job."

The next few minutes were a blur. I wasn't even sure who started the fight. It was probably me or Steve. But within seconds, it escalated the way it usually did in hockey. Our whole team came to stand behind us, and that's when the Dogs' team lined up too.

And then it turned into a shit-show.

~

FIVE MINUTES LATER, we were headed to the locker rooms during another intermission. Coach was furious at what happened, though none of us felt great about what went down. Most of us needed to find our gloves, and change ripped jerseys—it was a brawl, all right. I took off my helmet, holding it in the same hand as my stick. We went through the tunnel to the locker room. The press with special passes were there launching question after question at us.

"We'll talk to you after the game," Steve told them.

"Give us something," one reporter said.

We kept going and hurried to the changing room. Steve and I were the last ones in, and I did a double take when I noticed Daniels.

Oh, for fuck's sake. We already had Coach giving us an earful.

I exchanged a glance with Steve, and both of us nodded. We were going to stay back. Coach didn't want anyone except the team in the locker room at intermission, not even our manager.

"What the hell happened out there?" Daniels said to Steve and me.

Neither of us responded.

"What the hell happened out there?" he asked again, his anger radiating off his skin.

"Adrian was running his mouth," I said.

He narrowed his eyes. "You're not a rookie. You know the deal. That stuff happens. It's not the first time he's done it. You've always been good at ignoring this shit."

Before now, it never affected me. Some players always

played dirty, even verbally attacking family to get under the opponent's skin. But I'd never had anyone else to care about—not until Kendra. That was why it had been so easy to let it all slide by me.

My family, we were strong. Maxwells don't take shit; we hold our own ground. But no one gets a pass at my woman.

"I won't stand by when someone talks shit about my girlfriend."

"He'll try any weak points to distract you. You know that."

"Adrian was an ass. Basically called Kendra a stripper and said he'd take her for a spin. He spewed some shit about my wife too," Steve said. He was a good captain, always standing up for the guys, and we all appreciated it.

"He's just generally trying to provoke everyone," I added.

"You're the captain. Deal with it. Get your shit together, both of you," he said before walking back up the tunnel. The team was already in the changing room.

I did a double take. Kendra and Declan were standing a few feet away from us. My eyes bulged. My girl was crying. I hurried over to both of them.

"Babe, how did you get back here?"

"Declan convinced a security guard to let us back here. I had to see that you were okay," she said, tearing up, checking my face and patting my torso with her palms. She couldn't feel that much, considering all the padding. "Oh my God, that looked so rough. I was so afraid something happened to your shoulder or that you were hurt."

"I'm fine," I assured her, cupping her face with both hands. Fucking hell, her eyes were glassy. *This worried her that much?* "I swear, I'm not hurt. My ego maybe, but otherwise no."

Steve came up to us. "We need to hurry and get in the locker room. Coach is already fuming."

"You go. I need a minute."

As he went inside, Declan took a step back, giving us privacy. The press was far enough away that they couldn't see us. Even they knew not to approach the changing room.

I focused on Kendra. Her eyes were wide. "I listened to what you said to the manager. You got into a fight, and it was because of me?" she asked.

"No, it was because Adrian is a jackass."

She bit her lip. "Andrea said Daniels warned you about not getting involved with me. Why didn't you tell me?"

Smiling, I got closer. "What did I tell you about me barely following rules, let alone instructions, babe?"

She swallowed hard and kept my gaze, but I felt her tense up.

"Talk to me, babe," I said.

"Not now. You have to focus on the game," she said. "I don't want you to get into trouble because of me, that's all."

"I'm not. And even if I did, it wouldn't matter. I told you, you're number one. Don't pull away from me." I accented every word, looking her straight in the eyes so she knew I meant it.

"I'm not. I mean... Why are you saying that?"

"Babe, I can feel you tensing up. Your shoulders, your whole body."

She was silent for a moment, and then she shook her head, biting her lower lip. "I'm not. Come on, Mr. Superstar Goalie. Go get 'em," she said, but her voice was uneven.

The door to the changing room cracked open. Steve looked out at us.

"Tyler, get in here now."

"Okay, fuck. I'll be right there."

All I wanted to do was stay here and finish this conversation with Kendra.

I looked at Declan. "Take care of my girl while I'm out there."

He nodded before I stepped into the locker room.

Coach gave us the shit we deserved, but I'd expected that. A few minutes later, I followed my teammates out on the ice, but I didn't feel the rush of adrenaline that skating to the net usually gave me. My mind was spinning. I was angry at everything that took place tonight. I loved hockey, but for the first time in my career, I couldn't wait for the game to be over. I wanted to be with my woman.

But first I had to defend her honor.

Adrian better watch the fuck out.

CHAPTER THIRTY
KENDRA

Declan and I hustled back to the suite. Biting my lip, I lowered myself onto my seat, gripping the edge of it. I was looking at the ice, but I wasn't really seeing the game. I was a bit lost in my mind.

My whole body was tense. Tyler was right, and I just realized a very important thing. Before meeting him, I would feel insecure right now, possibly even trying to run away, fearing that if Tyler had to choose between me and hockey, he'd choose the latter.

I had no idea when that fear was formed. Maybe when we lost Dad, or when Mom's second boyfriend bailed after her diagnosis. It was how I protected myself.

But over the past few months, loving Tyler changed something inside me. It also changed the way I looked at everything. I was proud of our love, and I believed in us, and I couldn't wait for the game to end to tell him.

"Oh shit. This isn't going well," Travis exclaimed as two players from the opposing team skated toward Tyler with the puck between them.

I swear to God, everyone around me was holding their breath, myself included.

"Fuck, no, no, no," Declan exclaimed, and then the whole stand booed. The Seattle Dogs had just scored a goal.

Shit. My hot goalie wasn't in top shape right now.

I fidgeted in my spot, a plan forming in my mind. I didn't want to wait until the end of the game anymore. I turned to the Maxwells, leaning in so they could hear me. The fans were so loud that my ears were ringing. The stands seemed to vibrate along with their chatter.

"Anyone have any ideas how to go the extra mile to show Tyler my support right now without being super over the top?"

"Hell yes. Let me think," Travis said.

"There are always blank pages and markers at the promo table at the entrance doors. They're for kids mostly," Declan said. "You can make a poster."

"Hey, that's a good idea. How come I didn't come up with it? I'm the one with ideas," Luke said, looking genuinely baffled.

Declan burst out laughing before pointing at him, then at Reese, then at Travis, and finally at me. "Whenever you tell stories about today, make sure you emphasize that I came up with this."

"Oh, you two, give it a rest," Reese said. "I'm going to get a marker and the posters."

"Okay," I said, feeling so enthusiastic that my face exploded in a huge smile. *Now, what should I write on it?*

Looking at the ice, I watched Tyler move between the pipes like a lion in a cage. The last thing I wanted was for him to lose focus.

Reese returned with the paper and a marker a few short minutes later. I had a blank moment just looking at the paper, unsure what to even write on it. It wouldn't make sense to just write something like "Go get it." The fans could do that. I wanted to write something personal, something I knew he'd like.

With a smile, I decided to keep things simple. I wrote "TYLER" in huge letters on the first row and a comma, and then on the lower one, "I LOVE YOU."

"I like it," Travis shouted. "Sweet and to the point."

I realized he'd been looking over my shoulder, standing between me and Reese. Reese was also looking at me and making no secret of it.

"Should we go too?" Declan asked loudly.

Luke raised a brow. "Dude, let her go. Don't be a—"

I didn't hear the next word, but I had a hunch it was "cockblocker." I quickly averted my gaze to Reese, whose eyes were so wide that it was obvious I'd heard right.

With a nervous laugh, I got up from my seat. I went all the way down to the first row off the ice, not caring who was looking at me or what they were going to think. I just held the poster up above my head. I turned slightly so the fans could see it, and they all cheered at once, like a chorus, calling Tyler's name.

He cocked his head toward us, and I was probably imagining it, but I thought that even from here, I could see his grin. The goalie's mask hid everything, but when he nodded at me, I knew for sure he saw it.

My heart was about to burst. I might not know a lot about hockey, but I felt a shift in energy the next second. Something about the way Tyler moved was different. The pacing wasn't angry anymore. It was just agile and energetic.

I was rocking back and forth on my heels and tiptoes, too full of energy to stand still. But I was holding my arms up in place. They were starting to get tired, and I could barely feel my left hand, but I was determined to keep it up as long as I needed to.

My breath caught when the Dogs came with the puck near our goal again, and I almost looked away when they shot it. But I didn't.

"Yes, yes, yes," I chanted along with everyone else when Tyler blocked it. Then Steve got the puck, and the Blades passed between them, all the way to the Dogs' side of the rink.

And *scored*.

"Yes, yes, yes," we all chanted again. The energy was infectious.

Everyone seemed to talk and shout at the same time, and I was happy I'd come down here to the ice because everyone was up on their feet. I probably wouldn't have seen anything from my own seat anyway.

Both my arms were now numb, and I lowered them just for a bit, putting the poster under my arm and rubbing my palms together before stretching them back up.

Two minutes later, time ran out, and the Blades won, 2-1. Our section of the arena seemed to be out of control. I finally brought the poster down because Tyler was being hugged by his teammates, and he wasn't going to see it anyway.

I saw the Maxwells come down to where I was.

"Okay, I need ideas," I said. "I want to get to Tyler. Is there any shortcut around here?"

"I'm afraid not," Reese said.

"A distraction technique would be great about now," Luke said, rubbing his jaw, "but I have no idea."

Declan patted his shoulder. "Mark the calendar, okay? The day I had more ideas than Luke."

"One idea," Reese said. "One."

"Yeah, we won't let it get to your head any time soon," Travis said.

The team went to the locker room, and I knew it would take a while for them to shower and maybe even discuss the game.

We left the arena, heading to the lot where all the players parked, waiting there along with everyone's families. They let a few superfans in as well—apparently they bought special tickets that included meeting the team. Five security guys patrolled the area, and there was a roped section that kept the fans confined to a certain perimeter.

When the team appeared, the fans started cheering. Travis chuckled.

"Tyler's elbowing his way to us. Literally. Look at him."

I followed Travis's gaze and realized he was right. Tyler came inside the parking lot first, but instead of greeting the fans and signing autographs, he just kept pushing forward. His teammates trailed behind him, taking pictures and signing everything in sight. Not Tyler, though. He was making a beeline for us.

I held my poster above my head as he came closer. He was smiling brilliantly. Without a single word, he cupped my face with both hands, sealing his mouth over mine.

His kiss electrified me. I dropped the poster the next second, needing my hands free so I could touch him and hug him. I put my hands on his shoulders, but I wanted to feel *him*, so I moved my arms to his neck and put both hands around it.

He was breathing life into me with this kiss. I was so aware of his body and his connection between us, and it filled me with joy in every cell of my body.

"Okay, I was joking. Obviously he was elbowing his way to Kendra. I mean, Maxwell who?" Travis said.

I felt myself flush as we tore apart to draw a breath.

Tyler was totally oblivious to what Travis said, and when he pinned me with his gaze, I became oblivious to everything else too. Only Tyler mattered.

He still had his hands on my cheeks, and the skin-on-skin

contact was addictive, as was the luminous, happy look in his eyes.

"Babe, let's get out of here," he said.

"But what about celebrating with the team?"

"I can do that another time. Right now, I just want to be with you."

"And the fans—"

"Kendra, babe." His voice was strong, filled with that dominant streak I loved so much. Part of me wanted to stall on purpose, just to see what he'd do. But I wanted to be alone with him too much.

He just wanted me. He didn't care about anything else.

"He's not even aware we're here, is he?" I heard Travis ask, and I burst out laughing.

Tyler snapped his head up, glancing straight at his brother. "Sure I am. I was actually thinking you four can probably help us make a quick escape."

"Sure we can. But first, I got a question: Anyone feeling used?" Luke asked.

Travis shrugged. "I don't mind being used. As long as it's for a good cause."

Declan cocked a brow at Luke. "So, master of ideas, can you come up with an actual idea today?"

"Bro, it's still not a competition. You had one idea today. I've had a million of them."

Tyler took my hand, kissing it before interlacing our fingers. "It's one of those times when the Maxwells are too busy bickering to actually be of any use."

I grinned from ear to ear. "That's okay. They more than make up for that in entertainment value."

CHAPTER THIRTY-ONE
KENDRA

I will never be totally certain how we got home that evening. To his credit, Luke tried to distract the fans, but it seemed to have the opposite effect. They ambushed Tyler, who spent about half an hour chatting with them and signing autographs. After that, it was all a bit of a blur. But now we were in his condo, just the two of us.

The second we stepped into the living room, Tyler put one hand at the side of my waist, the other on my face.

"Babe, tonight was crazy."

"I know."

"But you were amazing."

I laughed softly. "Me? You're the star goalie, remember?"

"You had me at that poster. It means a lot to me."

"I love you, Tyler. And I know I'm not the best at expressing it, but—"

"You were amazing." He kissed my mouth hungrily, making me hum. But then he stopped, looking at me intently. "During the break, I felt you pull away. It scared me."

I swallowed hard, searching for the right words. "I think the old me would have done exactly that."

"The old you?"

"The pre-Tyler Kendra. My fight-or-flight instinct kicked in, thinking I was in trouble. Or maybe it was self-preservation, I don't know." Squaring my shoulders, I made myself taller. "But you've changed me so fundamentally, Tyler. With you, I'm not afraid to feel anymore."

With him, I felt like my heart was finally in the right place, as though the shift inside me was physical.

"Babe, I love you so damn much." He kissed me again, deep and fast and wet. From the desperate strokes of his tongue, I knew he wasn't going to stop at just exploring my mouth.

My knees weakened as he deepened the kiss, pushing one hand under my sweater, circling my navel with his thumb. I moaned against his mouth, greedy for him.

Stepping back, he took off my sweater. I immediately undid my bra, wanting it out of the way. Groaning, he stepped closer.

"I'm going to take off everything else." His voice was strong, sexy, and brooked no argument. And my knees weakened even more.

Taking my hand, he led me into the master bedroom. His eyes were hooded as he pulled me closer. Feeling the back of his hand press against my skin as he undid the button of my jeans was like an intimate touch. It sent sparks of heat through my body.

He pushed them down to my knees and yanked my panties down too. I lost my balance for a second and steadied myself by clasping his shoulders. Then he sat me down on the edge of the bed and tugged my jeans, panties, and socks out of the way. As soon as I was free to move, I stood up. He cocked a brow, but I just flashed him a smile in response.

The plan was to take his clothes off exquisitely slowly. What happened was that I got him naked so fast, I was surprised I didn't tear something.

Tyler skimmed his hands from my waist up to my shoulders, pushing me down on the bed before kneeling in front of me. Moving my legs apart, he kissed up my right ankle. Midthigh, he parted them even wider. He took his time, placing hot, wet kisses on my right inner thigh. I fisted my hands in anticipation, sucking in a breath, then groaned when he moved to the other thigh, totally ignoring my pulsing center. He was teasing me again, but I loved everything he did to me. He started with the left thigh, moving up and up and up until he reached that apex again. But this time, he didn't ignore my pussy. Instead, he planted his lips on my bundle of nerves. I thought I would break out of my skin.

He brought a hand up, touching my breasts while his mouth was between my legs. He kept his eyes trained on me, and I melted from the sheer intensity in them. Not a split second later, I squeezed mine shut. He darted his tongue inside me, pressing his nose on my clit, and a shot of pleasure coiled through me. I momentarily forgot where I was and what was happening. It made my world completely spin on its axis. My back arched, and I bent my legs at the knees, shuddering. I rolled my hips back and forth into him, loving the feel of him between my legs.

Then he gripped my hips tightly, lifting my ass off the bed just a few inches. He was taking control, and I wanted nothing more than to surrender to whatever he had in mind. His mouth was relentless. I felt the orgasm forming deep in my body, tugging at my center, starting from my bundle of nerves. But even though it started slowly, it spread like wildfire, and my climax slammed into me, knocking the breath out of me. I squeezed my eyes shut again, seeing stars behind my eyelids.

"Tyler," I cried out, thrashing on the bed, tugging at the pillow and everything in my reach.

I felt him move up my body, kissing me and running the tip of his nose on the side of my torso. He reached my breast, circling the nipple before looking up at me, staring me straight in the eyes. He was resting on both forearms and knees. Our limbs were intertwined on the bed. His erection pressed against the side of my body. I could barely breathe. The moment wasn't just sexual tension. It was more. It had always been more with him. He made me feel so alive and so loved when we were together.

He reached for the nightstand, but I interrupted him, catching his arm and putting it back on my chest. I cleared my throat.

"It's been a month since I started birth control."

"No more condoms?" His voice was almost a growl.

I nodded, and his gaze turned feral. And just like that, I knew he was close to losing control again.

He lifted his hips slightly off me, and we both looked between us. I reached down, gripping his erection, and then I looked up at him playfully before pushing him onto his back. I only managed it because I took him by surprise, since he was much bigger and stronger than me.

He propped himself on his elbows. "What are you doing?"

The next second, I settled between his legs, forming an O with my mouth and pressing my lips around the tip of his erection.

"Kendra, fuck," he exclaimed before a groan tore from him.

I took a page from the *Tyler Pleasuring Book* and lowered my mouth slowly. He was so huge that I needed a few seconds to accommodate him. I couldn't go all the way down, so I fisted my hand around the base where I couldn't reach. Then I moved my mouth up and down.

"Kendra!" His voice was low and rich and so damn sexy.

I tried to watch him, but I couldn't really, so I just focused on giving him pleasure. When I felt him pulse in my mouth, I pulled back, kissing up his body, stopping first at every ridge on his abdomen before reaching his chest.

He gripped the back of my head and my waist, regaining control, then kissed me hard while he rolled me on my back, settling straight between my legs. I felt him slide in only halfway before he groaned against my mouth. He'd never made such a sound before. I was sure of it. It was long and drawn out, like this couldn't possibly feel so good. And I was right there with him. The skin-on-skin contact, knowing this barrier between us was gone, was almost too much.

"Fuck, babe, this feels so good. Fuck. Fuck." He stopped moving, interlacing our fingers. He pressed his forehead against mine, his hot breath landing on my upper lip. "I want to do this every day with you. Be with you, love you, have you. I can't get enough of you."

He moved again, and I rolled my hips, meeting him halfway. To my astonishment, he pulled out, kissing down my body.

"No, come back." My voice was pleading. I wasn't even going to pretend that I didn't need him badly. There was no pretending with him. It was an open book, and I liked that.

"I need to pace myself, babe. You feel too damn amazing," he said, kissing down my body.

Far from relaxing me, it just increased the tension. Feeling the tip of his nose draw a straight line between my breasts and then to my navel only heightened my senses. I was aware of wherever he touched and kissed and even of his breath against my skin.

I couldn't take it anymore. I wanted him.

And I was going to have him.

I nudged his shoulder, pulling him back up, inching my legs around him. He smiled cockily right before he thrust into me.

His smile instantly turned into a frown, his mouth open and his eyes pinched closed like pleasure was already overwhelming him. We were both desperate and frantic.

I pressed my feet on the mattress, moving my hips as hard and as quickly as I could. My left leg skidded off the edge of the bed. He held my thigh, stabilizing me, bringing it back on the bed. He gripped my right ass cheek, lifting it a bit until the angle was so perfect that every time our lower bodies collided, his pelvis pushed against my clit. Little shocks of pleasure erupted inside me each time. I ran my hands down his arms and then gripped his ass, pushing him farther inside me with every thrust.

My orgasm slammed into me with such an intensity that I gasped, shoving the back of my head against the pillow, lifting my upper back. I didn't let go of his ass, just kept pushing him inside me, wanting every drop of pleasure. He thrust harder in one long push, and then he exploded.

We both collapsed and lay side by side, drawing in our breaths in short pants.

Tyler pushed a strand of hair behind my ear, looking me straight in the eyes.

"You're amazing, Kendra. You're my woman, my partner."

I smiled, inching closer to him. "I'm so happy we got home early."

"Why?"

"I planned this whole thing to help you relax. The list was so long that I could only fit in a few things. But now we have time for so much more."

"Like what?"

I grinned. "You'll see. We'll start with a shower, of course. And then you're all mine. The whole night."

He rolled on top of me the next second, pinning me to the

mattress. Tipping his head, he drew his nose up the side of my neck. "The way I see things, *you* are *mine*."

"Semantics," I teased, tugging at his hair until he moved back a bit. "But either way, tonight will be epic."

"Babe, it already is."

CHAPTER THIRTY-TWO
TYLER
TWO WEEKS LATER

Several things were true in the Maxwell family.

One: birthday parties were huge events.

Two: Gran's birthday party was not. She always insisted we keep it in the family. She chose a different way to celebrate every time. Sometimes we went somewhere outside the city, or we went to a restaurant. This year, she wanted a cookout in my parents' yard. It was cold, two weeks before Christmas, but what Gran wanted, she got.

I arrived alone, later than all my brothers. Sam was here too, and he was staying over Christmas. Reese wasn't here. She'd gone to Paris to visit Kimberly and was supposed to fly in this morning, but her flight was canceled, so she was returning tomorrow instead.

Kendra texted me that she was running late because of traffic.

My brothers were at the huge bar in the living room as usual. Travis was behind it, mixing drinks. Declan, Luke, and Tate were standing in front of it.

Gran, my parents, Sam, Lexi, and Paisley were sitting around the dining room table. I went to greet them first.

"Happy birthday, Gran."

"Thank you, my boy."

I turned to Sam. "Welcome back, brother."

"Thanks." He shook my hand, patting my shoulder. I took a good look at him. He had dark circles under his eyes. The first few days when he was back, he always looked exhausted, and I knew it wasn't just because of jet lag. His work abroad wasn't easy.

"Are we starting the cookout now?" I asked.

Mom shook her head. "We'll wait for Kendra."

"Okay." I headed to the bar with Sam, inspecting the bottles when I came closer.

"Man, what's wrong with you?" Travis asked. "You look like you might need whiskey."

"You know what, why not? Might be good for inspiration."

Declan cocked a brow. "And you need that why?"

"To propose." I said the words loudly and with full confidence, taking advantage of the fact that Kendra wasn't here.

My brothers all started to talk at the same time.

"Holy shit. I go away for a few months and another Maxwell plans to get married?" Sam asked, stunned. Unlike Kimberly, he didn't want to be part of the family WhatsApp group. He said it distracted him from work.

"You have a lot to catch up on, brother," I said.

Travis whistled loudly. "I'll make it a double."

"Anyone have any advice?" I asked. Creativity was not my forte.

Travis put a double whiskey on the bar. "Just go with the flow, man."

Luke shook his head. "Dude, what flow? He's out of ideas."

"Surprise her with a trip," Declan suggested.

Luke groaned. "I think he can figure the trip for himself."

I stared at Luke. "Dude, do you have any constructive

advice, or are you planning to just shoot down everyone else's ideas?"

Luke held up his hands in defense. "No I don't, and unlike some in our family, I don't like to talk just to talk."

"I have no advice, but this is fun," Sam said. "Man, I've missed this."

"Hey, the idea with the trip isn't that bad," Tate said. "You could ask the rest of the family to get involved in getting her where you want. Like me. Make it a surprise."

He'd done well. I was the one helping, but that wasn't what I wanted to do. I rubbed my chin, taking a sip of the whiskey.

"I don't want to do the same trick," I admitted.

"Dude, it's not the idea that matters. It's the execution," Travis said.

"Who's saying that?" asked Declan.

Travis rolled his shoulders, puffing out his chest in a ridiculous way. "I am."

I chuckled. "That sounds like Travis wisdom. No offense, man."

"Right, people only say 'no offense' before or after saying something offensive, and that's *universally* known wisdom. But today, I'm cool as a cucumber."

I laughed and mentally admitted that this wasn't the right bunch to ask for advice on this topic. Aside from Tate, they had zero experience.

A few minutes later, Paisley, Lexi, Mom, Dad, and Gran joined us at the bar, sitting in the armchairs in front of it. It took Gran exactly five seconds to narrow her eyes and point at my brothers.

"What's going on? You lot look like you're giving Tyler here a hard time."

Damn. One of these days, I was going to find out how Gran could pick up on exactly what we were doing *every time.*

I shook my head. "They're not giving me a hard time. I asked for help, and they're just being obnoxious. Business as usual."

"Then why don't you ask Gran for advice, you ungrateful little brother?" Luke asked.

He had a point. Gran also had a sixth sense when it came to stuff like this. But first, I needed to give Luke some shit.

"You're the only one who didn't even give me advice," I reminded him.

"No, I'm doing my job of playing devil's advocate. That's the most efficient way to rile up the others, and they have the best ideas when they're riled up. And you don't appreciate it one bit."

That was Luke to a T.

I looked at Gran and also at my parents. While I liked asking my brothers for their opinions, I usually didn't just broadcast whatever was happening to the entire family over dinner. Then again, I was in search of ideas, and I was never proud of asking others.

"I want to propose to Kendra, and I'm still in the early stages of planning it. Ideas are welcome. I need it to be perfect."

Sam chuckled. "You always do. It's 'go big or go home' for you, no matter what you do."

My mother clasped her hands together, smiling from ear to ear. "Darling, that's great news. Oh, I'd lost hope that you boys would ever find partners, and now you *and* Tate are getting married."

"Did she just call us hopeless?" Travis asked no one in particular.

"She did," Declan answered with a laugh.

"Congratulations, son," Dad said. "I'm not the creative mind of the family, so I've got no input."

"You can take her out to a fancy restaurant," Mom said.

Gran pointed at me. "Tyler, out of all your brothers, you're the one who has the best intuition. So my advice is just to trust your gut feeling, and it will lead you the best way."

"Just putting it out there, but what if the gut instinct sucks?" Travis asked.

"Language, young man," Gran said, and Travis quickly glanced at Paisley, flashing her a grin. Paisley was looking at us with wide eyes. My poor niece.

"I think your gran's idea is excellent," Mom said. "I think most of her advice is on point, isn't it, darling?" she said with an uncharacteristic smile, turning to Dad, who nodded stoically.

A few seconds later, I realized he was darting his gaze around. I didn't call him out on it, though I would keep it in mind for later.

Paisley straightened in her seat. "I have an idea. I wrote a letter for Lexi on my birthday, where I asked her if she wanted to be my mom." Glancing at Lexi, she asked, "You liked that, didn't you?"

Lexi smiled. Her eyes became glassy. "Very much."

I still stood by my principle of not doing the same trick, but Paisley's story sparked an idea.

"Thanks, Paisley." With a wink, I added, "You're the most useful Maxwell in the room tonight."

She beamed from ear to ear. "You can thank me by making me your flower girl at your wedding too."

Damn, she had some serious Maxwell negotiation skills.

"Deal." Turning to Gran, I said, "I don't want to hijack your birthday."

She waved her hand. "I don't mind."

The doorbell rang, interrupting Gran.

"That's Kendra. Not one word to her about the proposal."

"Obviously, dude," Travis said as I headed to the front door.

"Yeah, we're not amateurs," Declan called after me.

"Yes you are," Sam said. "You just can't tell."

As I opened the door, Kendra took off her beanie. She was holding a huge box in one hand.

"What's this?" I asked.

"Sweets. I don't like to come empty-handed."

This woman! It was like she couldn't help herself from sharing.

She stepped inside, and I took the box, putting it on one of the small tables in the entrance hall.

"Why did you do that?" she asked. "I can multitask, hold a box and take off my coat."

"Yeah, but I want to kiss you first, and I don't want any barriers between us."

"Oh, okay. Go ahead, then. I like how seriously you take kissing."

"Always," I said before sealing my mouth over hers.

I brought a hand to the back of her neck and the other to her hips, pressing her against me. Her coat only reached to her ass, so I parted her legs with my knees, needing to get even closer. Fucking hell, I could never *just* kiss this woman—I needed to devour her.

She sighed against my mouth, leaning into me. She fit so perfectly in my life, and I belonged with her.

When we pulled apart, she smiled shyly, covering her mouth. "Are my lips red? You'll give us away."

"You're beautiful," I said.

"That's not what I asked. You're naughty today," she went on. "And I can't wait to see you behind the grill."

"You don't like the cold," I said, and she laughed.

"I'll brave it to see you in front of the fire. It just speaks to me on a primal level."

I burst out laughing, taking her hand and leading her to the rest of the group.

"Shouldn't I take off my coat?" she asked.

"Now that you're here, we're all going to go outside to the grill."

"Okay, then. Just let me take the box." She carried it in one hand.

"Sam's here too," I informed her, pointing to my brother, who walked up to us.

"Kendra, great to meet you!" he exclaimed.

"Sam, hi. Wow, you flew in for your Gran's birthday?"

"I'm staying for Christmas too. Gives me time to catch up with this lot. There's so much going on." He winked at me. I cocked a brow.

As we all reached the group, Kendra said, "Hi, everyone. I brought some goodies from my favorite cupcake shop."

"Oh, you shouldn't have, Kendra," Mom said, "but that's very sweet of you. I'll put it in the fridge for now. We took out the grill supplies before, so I think we can just grab our coats and go."

"Okay, everyone, let's go," Dad said.

I looked warningly at my brothers, especially Travis, because he had this shit-eating grin that would give us away. Luke elbowed Travis, which just made everything more suspicious.

Kendra was looking away, at least, so there was that. There was no way she caught any of it.

A few minutes later, I changed my mind.

As we all went out in the backyard, carrying paper plates, vegetables, and meat, she leaned in to me. "Why do I feel like you've had one of those silent conversations with your brothers back there?"

I pulled her closer with my free hand. "That's between them and me."

"Riiiiight, okay. You know I'm like a bull with a red flag, right?"

"I promise you one thing," I said. "You'll find out soon enough what it's about."

"How soon? Just so I know if I should employ any persuasion tactics or not?"

"Very soon, babe. Very, very soon."

I walked half a step behind her, keeping a hand on her back. She took out her phone just before we got out of the house, reading a text from Reese.

The words "Gran" and "coffee shop guy" popped out. Kendra turned the screen away, looking at me over her shoulder.

"Were you peeking?"

"Yes," I admitted. "But I only caught a few words. What's all that about?"

"Wouldn't you like to know?"

"Babe..."

"Nope. Not telling you. You have your secrets, we have ours," she said, shrugging one shoulder and flashing me a sassy smile.

CHAPTER THIRTY-THREE

KENDRA

THREE WEEKS LATER

"Wow, we should do this again," Emma exclaimed.

"I know, right? I feel so fancy," I said.

Emma had talked me into spending a sister afternoon at a spa in the city. I protested at first because I didn't want her to spend a fortune on me, but then she used her younger sister look—eyes wide, pouty lower lip—and I gave in. I'd gotten a mani, a pedi, and a massage. I felt utterly relaxed. It was a brand-new salon on the Magnificent Mile. This was their first day in business, so they offered everything at half price. I didn't need much relaxation, to be honest, because I'd taken time off during Christmas and New Year's and spent it with my sexy man. But I was glad I got to spend today with Emma.

As we dressed up, my sister asked, "Do you want help with your makeup? Or I can do your hair. You can even borrow my scarf."

I stared at my sister. "I'm going to an ice cream parlor, not a fashion show." The kids Tyler coached at the beginning of the season were celebrating the fact that they were at the top of the ranking in the interschool hockey championship. And they'd invited both me and Tyler. Of course, he was the guest of honor.

We were celebrating at the ice cream parlor right next to the center.

Emma frowned. "I know, but maybe you'll take pics, or... I don't know..."

"Pics?"

She opened her mouth, then closed it again and shrugged.

"Thanks a lot for today," I said.

Emma winked. "My pleasure. Wait, let me do your hair, okay? I have my curler with me."

She took it out of her purse, along with a million hair products.

My eyes bulged. "Why did you bring your hair curler and so many products?"

She loved to doll up on a daily basis, but I was certain she didn't always carry those around.

"Umm." She avoided my gaze. "I'm going on a date later, and I'm going to fancy up. I can style your hair quick too."

I'd washed and blow-dried it after the massage, and I had to admit, it didn't look great.

"Okay. Thanks."

She squealed in delight, plugging in the curler. I liked having her do my hair. It was soothing.

Once she was done, I looked like a million bucks. I blinked rapidly as she sprayed the third product in my hair, feeling like I might go blind soon, or at the very least not be able to see in front of me. My eyes were a bit watery, but the effect was fantastic. I was wearing a blue sweater dress and black wool tights with boots. I'd dressed casually, and my curls went with it perfectly.

"You look great." Biting her lip, she added, "Let me add a bit of makeup."

"Let me check the time—oh my God. I'm already late."

"Shit, you're right. Okay, then. Go. I'll stay here and pack my stuff."

"I thought you needed to get ready for your date."

She laughed nervously. "Yeah, I meant... I'll get ready first, then pack everything. Now come on, go. Don't be late."

I kissed her cheek, slinging on my coat before heading out of the spa. When I stepped outside, a blast of cold wind made my teeth chatter, but I couldn't put my beanie on because that would ruin my hair completely.

There was no time to take the subway, so I jumped into an Uber, checking the estimated arrival time every few minutes. I was going to come in so late, and the boys didn't have a lot of time. Their tae kwon do class was starting in forty minutes. I had fifteen minutes max with them.

When I arrived, Tyler, the kids, and Mr. Dawson were already there, of course, at the huge round table at the back of the room. Early January was far too cold for ice cream, so the parlor now also served cakes and donuts.

"Hey, sorry I'm late," I exclaimed.

Tyler kissed my hand as I sat down. There was already a plate in front of me.

I grinned at him. "You ordered me a donut!"

Tyler winked. "Thought that would make you happy."

"You know me so well."

I bit into the delicious treat immediately, sighing before looking around the table. The kids looked utterly happy, and it warmed my heart. They kept sharing details about their past couple of games.

"I'm so proud of you guys," Tyler said.

His own team was at the top of the rankings too, and I was super happy for him.

"Thank you for coaching us," Tim replied. Next to him, Rupert nodded vigorously.

"Boys, hurry up. Your tae kwon do class starts soon," Mr. Dawson said only a few minutes later. I pouted, truly sorry that I only got to spend a few minutes with them.

They all dressed up quickly, chattering about tae kwon do. Tyler and I waved goodbye, and after they left, I savored my last bite of the donut.

"Want to take a walk?" Tyler asked.

"Sure. Let's ask for the bill."

"I already took care of it a while ago." There was an edge to his voice I hadn't noticed before. There was something different about his eyes too.

Hmmm...

I'd made a small catalog of all my man's looks.

The sexy glint.

The super sexy glint.

The smoldering one.

And the swoonworthy one.

This one was like a mix of them all, and it was truly overpowering.

Stepping outside, we strolled along the street, past the center, until we reached a huge, old pine tree. It looked even more majestic now in winter because it was one of the few trees still green. There were even a few snowflakes falling from the sky. They'd totally ruin my hair, but I didn't care because I loved snow.

"Tyler? There's something different about you, and I can't make out what," I said.

He cupped one side of my face, pressing his thumb at the base of my ear and splaying his fingers on the side of my neck.

"Kendra, you're important to me. I can't imagine not being with you every day. I love you. I've been luckier than most, but even I know life isn't easy. It will always have ups and downs. I want to experience all that with you."

"So do I," I assured him.

He took away his hand, bending, and at first, I thought he'd dropped something. Then I realized he was lowering himself on one knee.

"Oh my God," I whispered, taking a step back so I could see him better. I clasped one hand on my chest because suddenly my heart was beating so fast I seriously felt like it might leap out of my chest.

Smiling, he took something out of his pocket—a ring box. "Kendra, we met right here, in front of the center."

"Oh my goodness. That's true. We did."

"And that day, I told you I don't ever follow rules, let alone instructions, and you told me you were up for the challenge. I wanted to kiss you right then, and not only were you up for it, but with you, I discovered a side of life I didn't know existed. You're my soul mate."

Oh my God. My heart fluttered in my chest. "I thought you didn't believe in soul mates," I whispered.

"Because I hadn't met you. I didn't know what loving you would do to me, but now I do. Marry me, Kendra."

My eyes filled with tears, and I didn't bother holding them back. "Yes, of course."

Putting the ring on my finger, he clasped my hands tightly. It had four stones, one pink, one blue, one green, and one white.

"I love it," I whispered. "It's gorgeous. This is why my sister took me to the beauty salon, isn't it?"

Tyler laughed. "I bet she did. When I told her what I planned, she immediately started making plans of her own and wanted to know exactly where it was taking place and at what time."

"Sounds like Emma," I murmured.

He looked me straight in the eyes, curling a strand of my

hair between his fingers. "I want to build a life with you, Kendra."

"I want it too," I admitted. And then I acknowledged something else. "I've been having these vivid dreams lately. You're always in them." I shook my head. "That sounded dirty. It's not how I meant it."

"What kind of dreams?" he asked.

"About the future. And I never used to have them before." There were *a lot* of snowflakes now, and some were getting on my tongue every time I spoke. The wind intensified too. I looked up at the sky, then back at Tyler. "I think we're in for a storm."

"Looks like it."

"So... does the rest of your plan to make me swoon today include being outdoors?"

"Actually, yes, but I'm adaptable." He touched my jaw again, looking at me intently. "And I can think of a thing or two to do indoors too."

I grinned. "So can I."

EPILOGUE
KENDRA

Three months later

I woke up with a yawn and then immediately smiled. I was lying on one side in Tyler's huge bed. He was spooning me, holding an arm around my waist. I felt utterly happy and blissful and safe in a way I never thought was possible.

I tried not to move my body as I lifted my head, looking for the digital clock that was near the dresser. *Oh crap*. It was already nine o'clock. We were supposed to be at Declan's new house in forty minutes to help him unpack.

I turned around, deciding on the best way to wake up my man. To my astonishment, his eyes were already open but hazy with sleep.

"Morning," I whispered.

He blinked lazily, and I leaned in, kissing his shoulder and his biceps.

"Morning," he said.

"How did you sleep?" I asked him. I liked doing that every morning.

"Like a rock, but you woke me up at some point. You were talking in your sleep."

"Oh? What did I say?"

"Sang my praises. Said I was absolutely amazing."

I laughed but didn't contradict him because I could totally see that happening. "Sounds plausible."

"Damn, I'm good. I was bluffing."

I shimmied against him, flashing him a smile. He asked me how I slept every morning when we woke up together. We spent almost every evening together, sometimes at his condo, but mostly in my brand-new house. I'd moved in two months ago at the end of January, and I absolutely loved every corner of it.

"So, what *did* you dream about?"

I lay back on the pillow, looking at him and feeling suddenly shy. "I dreamed that we had a little girl."

Tyler brought a hand to the side of my neck, brushing his thumb along my jawline. "I'd love that. I hope she'll be just like you."

I shimmied against the cotton sheets, feeling warm all over. "It was just a dream, though."

"Kendra, we can make it a reality whenever you're ready."

"Wait... so *you* feel ready?"

"Yes I am. It's crazy, but I feel like we can do anything we want together."

Tilting closer, he kissed my neck, moving his hand lower on my shoulder. "I love you."

"You're making me melt. Just thought you should know."

He kissed my shoulder again. This time I also felt the tip of his tongue. I shuddered all over.

Tyler groaned. "Why do we have to go out today?"

"Because we promised to help Declan unpack," I pointed out. "Remember the family motto? 'Don't outsource anything you can do well and that can count as a family activity.'"

"We need to rethink it. How about this? 'Don't outsource anything unless it buys you time to spend in bed with the woman you love.'"

My stomach cartwheeled. How could he be so swoonworthy without even trying?

I tipped my head to the side in mock thought. "Hmmm... but then we'd duck out of basically every activity."

"That's the plan."

"No, I like your motto as it is."

"I'll talk to Tate. He's got as good a reason as I do to adapt it."

I giggled. "Come on. Let's get out of bed, or we'll be late."

He pressed his fingers deeper into my skin. I knew what that possessive grip meant. He wasn't ready to let go without a fight, but I knew just how to disarm him. I went straight to his Adam's apple, kissing it lightly, moving up and down his neck. It was his sweet spot.

He instantly relaxed his grip on me, groaning, and I saw my chance to escape. I practically leaped out of bed.

He burst out laughing, pushing himself up on an elbow. "You're tricky this morning."

"Hey, I'm resourceful, and I knew if I didn't get us out, we'd just stay in bed for half the morning."

"That's completely true."

I walked to the bathroom, and he was right behind me. We brushed our teeth at the two sinks. I loved the ease and familiarity between us.

The second I was done, I reached for the shower, but Tyler pulled me toward him.

"I demand a morning kiss before the shower as payback for

tricking me."

"Oh, I deserve that very, *very* cruel punishment."

Grinning, he leaned in to me, speaking against my lips. "Not gonna fight me on it? Say we'll be late?"

"I can make time for a kiss. But only one." I used a teasing tone, knowing he wouldn't resist the challenge.

"We'll see about that."

Despite my best intentions, we arrived late at Declan's house in the Gold Coast neighborhood. I'd seen it in pictures and also been here a couple times while it was under renovation. It was honestly breathtaking. Originally built in the early 1900s, Declan had renovated a lot, but it was worth it. The walnut entry staircase led up to a balcony slash porch made entirely of walnut as well. The windows on either side of the door had stained glass so one couldn't see inside from the street.

The inside was even more impressive. There was a huge open space encompassing the entrance, living room, dining room, and kitchen. I especially loved the mahogany staircase leading to the upper level.

Everyone else was already here. Tate and Lexi were on the right side of the gorgeous living room, next to the gray couch. Tate was taking out books from a box, and Lexi was arranging them on floor-to-ceiling built-in shelves that had a ladder attached to them.

"Where's Paisley?" Tyler asked.

"She decided to spend the day with our parents. Mom bribed her with pancakes," Tate explained.

Travis and Luke were setting up the TV on the wall opposite the couch. Declan himself was sorting cutlery at the granite counter. The kitchen was amazing, like the rest of the furniture. The cabinets were black and looked incredibly sleek.

"What should we do?" I asked him.

"Tyler can start setting up the lamps. You can put the glasses in the red box in the cabinets."

"Right away." I moved carefully because the hardwood floor was littered with boxes and bubble wrap.

"Remind me again, is this supposed to be a housewarming party?" Travis asked while he and Luke seemed to be on a break.

Declan nodded. "Housewarming slash unpacking party. First comes unpacking, and then I'll order food and drinks for everyone."

Luke burst out laughing. "So typical of you. Work first, fun later."

"Hey, we volunteered, remember?" Tyler asked.

"Actually, no, I don't. But it could be that I just heard the part with drinks and completely ignored the part where we had to work," Luke said.

"Thanks for showing up," Declan said.

"No problem."

Travis came to the kitchen island, taking a screwdriver out of the toolbox. Glancing out the window above the sink, he pointed at the guest house. It was obviously a much later addition, because it looked nothing like the original house.

"How long is your neighbor's contract?" Travis asked.

"One year left to go," Declan replied in a clipped tone.

"How is he?" Travis asked.

"She," he practically growled.

I glanced at Tyler, who bit back a smile. "How is she?"

"A damn nightmare. I've been sleeping here the past three nights. She listens to music late in the night, and—" He stopped abruptly without even finishing his sentence.

I put the last glass in the cabinet, turning around.

"And what?" I nudged, feeling like he wasn't being entirely truthful.

"And nothing."

Travis patted his shoulder. "I bet she'll move out in three months. You're a terrible roommate. You know how we know? We grew up with you," he said.

Declan cocked a brow. "She's not my roommate. Just lives in the guest house on my property."

"I feel sorry for her." Travis feigned a shudder, glancing out the window again. "Is that her? She's smoking hot. And she's coming this way."

"Behave!" Declan said with a meaningful glance at all his brothers.

Travis held his hands up. "Sure, don't worry on my behalf."

Luke looked up from the box he was unpacking. "You can worry for me. I don't plan to behave at all. Where's the fun in that?"

"Stay here," Declan said, heading to the front door. He opened it one second before the doorbell rang.

"Wow, she's beautiful," Lexi exclaimed.

A gorgeous blonde stood in front of the door. She looked like a supermodel, wearing dark blue jeans and heels that made her legs look endless below a thick black sweater with a V-cut that fit her perfectly. She was shivering too, but that was to be expected. It was a sunny spring day, but it was still cold.

She was holding a piece of paper in her right hand, dangling it in front of Declan.

"Declan Maxwell, are you serious?"

"I told you to turn down the music."

"It's how I unwind, okay? You should try it sometime. Might take that stick out of your ass."

At my side, Tyler made a strange choking sound. He was trying to repress laughter. I elbowed him lightly.

Luke grinned. Travis looked like he was about to explode with guffaws.

"Boys, behave," I whispered.

Luke rubbed his palms together. "No chance. This is gold. *Gold*."

I was the only one who made an effort to pretend like I was minding my own business as Declan headed back to us, dusting off a cabinet before putting in plates. I hopped on the counter, propping my knees wide apart as I reached into the upper shelf. Seconds later, Tyler was by my side, planting his hands firmly on my outer thighs.

"Babe, are you trying to give me a heart attack?" he asked.

"Not at all. I want to be useful." In a lower octave, I added, "And pretend I didn't eavesdrop on the entire conversation."

Luke walked up to Declan.

"She's hot. I wouldn't know how to handle a hot neighbor," Luke said.

"Well, I'm going to tell you how you'll handle mine," Declan replied with a growl. "You're not allowed to flirt with my tenant under any circumstances."

"I thought she was a neighbor," Tyler teased.

Declan trained his eyes on him. "Semantics don't matter."

Travis chuckled, looking at Tyler and then at me.

"Careful there, Declan. You sound like you're marking your territory," Travis said.

Declan didn't say anything, which, of course, everyone took as confirmation.

Well, well! This is an interesting turn of events.

Tyler and I exchanged a glance, but we didn't say anything.

Travis shook his head but didn't add anything else as we all went back to work in earnest.

Travis had predicted she'd move out in three months, but I had a hunch things were going to unfold in a completely different way.

ALSO BY LAYLA HAGEN

The Maxwell Brothers

Promise Me Forever

Very Irresistible Bachelors Series

You're The One

Just One Kiss

One Perfect Touch

One Beautiful Promise

My One and Only

The Gallagher's

Say You're Mine

When You're Mine

Because You're Mine

The Connor Family

Anything For You

Wild With You

Meant For You

Only With You

Fighting For You

Always With You

The Bennett Family

Your Irresistible Love

Your Captivating Love

Your Forever Love

Your Inescapable Love

Your Tempting Love

Your Alluring Love

Your Fierce Love

Your One True Love

Your Endless Love

Your Christmas Love

The Lost Series

Lost in Us

Found in Us

Caught in Us

Withering Hope – soon to be made into a Passionflix movie

Printed in Great Britain
by Amazon